THE DEATHDAY CHRONICLES

THE CØUNTDØWN

KASIA LASINSKA

DREAMSCAPE
— P R E S S —

CONTENTS

1. Ten Days   1
2. Nine Days   23
3. Eight Days   38
4. Seven Days   60
5. Six Days   95
6. Five Days   119
7. Four Days   148
8. Three Days   173
9. Two Days   191
10. One Day   232
11. Deathday   273
    Epilogue — Ian   334

    A Note From The Author 343
    About The Author   347

THE COUNTDOWN

A Companion Novel to The Deathday Chronicles Series

Copyright © Kasia Lasinska 2020

First edition: October 2020

Published by Dreamscape Press Ltd.

Cover design by Derek Murphy

www.KasiaLasinska.com

Hey look Mom and Dad, I wrote a book!
This one's for you

THE SECØND CITY

GRAND ALLIANCE OF AMERICAN STATES

YEAR: 2225

POPULATION: 20,537,584

TEN DAYS

"SCAN IT AGAIN, Officer — my deathday *is* in ten days."
I stared, wide-eyed, into the barrels of the Safety Patrols'
guns — four deep, black holes in the otherwise blinding
white Atrium of the White Tower.

"Hands in the air," the Patrol closest to me said in a
low voice. His square jaw was set, his finger hovering over
the trigger. "Where we can see them."

Sweat trickled down my forehead. I had a sudden
urge to push my unruly hair out of my eyes, but I
resisted. Instead, I dragged up the left sleeve of my jacket,
revealing the eight-digit date blazing vivid green on my
wrist, and lifted both hands over my head. "My
deathday—"

"Silence."

I sucked in a breath.

The Patrol didn't take his eyes off me. "Rogers, scan the boy's comp again."

"Right away, Lieutenant Johnson."

The Safety Patrol named Rogers lowered his gun and grabbed my comp — a small, gray rectangular device citizens in the Second City had to carry at all times — from Johnson's outstretched hand. He gave me a sidelong glance. Was that a glint of sympathy in his eye? I shook my head. The adrenaline from being held at gunpoint must have made me lightheaded. Safety Patrols weren't exactly known for their kindness.

A shrill beep sounded, followed by a flashing red light on the Patrol's scanner.

"Negative, sir."

Bile rose to my throat. This had to be a mistake. My Ten Day Ceremony was today. I could certainly count backward from the date on my wrist. I'd memorized those digits from the moment I could count, just like everyone memorized theirs. And I wouldn't forget them in a hurry either, considering that once the date lined up with the calendar, I would be dead.

My deathday occupied most of my headspace these days. The whooshing sound of death speeding toward me wasn't something I took lightly. But in that moment, I had other pressing matters to attend to. Like making sure the Safety Patrols wouldn't blast me ten feet into the air right then and there.

"Officer, it's my Ceremony Day, I swear—"

"The technology says otherwise. And technology doesn't lie. Tell us why you're really here. You have sixty seconds."

"I just told you. My Ceremony—"

The click of the safety on Johnson's gun stopped me short. My heartbeat quickened. I closed my eyes, steadying myself, although it was hard to ignore the creeping dread that something was terribly wrong. "There must be another way to verify my identity." There had to be.

Rogers stepped in front of Johnson and smiled. "As a matter of fact, there is." He pulled a small black gadget out of his pocket and looked to Johnson for confirmation, who, after a moment's hesitation, nodded once. Rogers beckoned me over. "Insert your finger here."

My legs felt as if they were made of jelly, but I did as I was told and approached the device, placing my forefinger inside its narrow opening. After a moment, a sharp twinge of pain shot through my finger. I jerked it away, droplets of crimson staining the pristine floor.

"Blood scan," Rogers said with a slight smile. The scanner emitted a series of beeps and flashed green. "Theo Vanderveen. Male. Sixteen years old."

I let out a small sigh as the tension left my body.

Johnson lowered his gun and checked his records. "Everything seems to be in order."

Finally.

"Our apologies, Citizen," Rogers said. "National security reasons, you understand."

I nodded once, wiping my hands, clammy with sweat, on my taupe pants, leaving a smear of red. Did I really look like I posed a threat to national security? I doubted it, but it was all the same to me, as long as I walked out of here alive. Johnson handed my comp back to me and nodded at Rogers.

"Right this way." Rogers led me through the immaculate Atrium, his tall silhouette prominent among the sea of Patrols and Government officials hurrying through the space.

The whiteness was dizzying. Narrow white pillars twisted upward as far as the eye could see, separated by thin layers of plexiglass that caught the bright light streaming in from the tall windows. A grand staircase leading to the upper floors spiraled overhead.

The Atrium was just as big as I'd remembered. I'd been in the Tower once before, years ago, with Dad. He'd taken me up to his office on the seventeenth floor one cold, overcast day in the winter when Loop Sector School was closed because of electricity shortages and Mom was out running errands. I briefly wondered whether they would take me up to the higher floors for the Ceremony.

We passed a series of doors branching off from the Atrium into endless white corridors. Hordes of Safety Patrols manned the posts on either side. I couldn't help but notice the whites of their uniforms, the glint of black metal hanging from their belts, and the clank of their polished boots on the smooth marble floor. A chill crept up my spine; I wasn't in a hurry to cross them again.

If Dad were here, the mishap at the entrance wouldn't have happened. As a high-ranking official in the Grand Alliance of American States — the GA — he would have vouched for me.

But Dad wasn't here.

Today, I had come alone. Today, I would attend my Ceremony and receive my Ten Day Object from the Grand Alliance. A strange mixture of curiosity and dread flooded through me as I continued after Rogers' lean figure through the infinite white hallways. After today, I would have to face what I'd been denying in my head for months: that my deathday was approaching, and there was nothing I could do about it.

Rogers paused before a set of nondescript white double doors. "This is where I leave you, Citizen Vanderveen. May time be on your side." His bright brown eyes danced in the cool white light. "Good luck."

I thanked Rogers, took a deep breath, and knocked.

"ENTER."

The double doors parted before me and I stepped into a high, circular room, white like the rest of the Tower. In its center, a black eagle — the national emblem — was carved into the floor. The echo of my sneakers on the marble broke the eerie silence.

Banners depicting the same eagle on a dark red background hung from a narrow balcony snaking along the far wall. Six banners. One for each of the Cities of the Grand Alliance of American States. I lived in the Second City — they used to call it Chicago. But the Cities' old names had been obsolete for over a century. No one had used them since the War ended.

The dark crimson behind the eagles was the only hint of color I'd seen in the Tower so far, save for the few drops of my blood splotched on the floor near the entrance. I never liked the color — it reminded me too much of Mom's patients, wounded and lying on their backs on the dinner table in our cramped apartment, as she mixed herbs and applied ointments to ease their torment.

The eagles stared at me with sightless eyes as my gaze

flitted to the wall above them. Square compartments filled with glossy black boxes extended upward. I craned my neck, but couldn't see where the last box ended and the ceiling began.

A lone figure dressed in billowing black robes stood with his back to me at the top of a short flight of marble steps beneath the banners, his hands entwined behind him. My pulse quickened. This was surely the Master of Ceremonies.

I paused in the center of the room, my fingers twiddling with the sleeves of my jacket, unsure of the Ceremony protocol. I opened my mouth to announce my presence as the figure slowly turned on his heel and faced me.

"Ahh, there you are, Theo. So glad you could make it." Something resembling a smile crossed his flat, pug-like face. I recognized him from somewhere… "I am General Horatio."

I had to actively stop my jaw from dropping. Of course — General Horatio was Chancellor Graves' Chief of Staff and Commander of the Patrol Forces. He was Graves' right-hand man and consistently appeared alongside the Chancellor during public speeches, Celebrations, the Victory Day Celebrations, or during pre-recorded announcements sent directly to our comps. Wherever Graves went, Horatio followed. But what was he doing here? He was too high-ranked to be handing out Ten Day Objects to citizens with approaching deathdays.

"To what do I owe this pleasure, General?"

"The Master of Ceremonies is ahh, indisposed, so I volunteered to step in."

Indisposed? Was he unwell? I'd never heard of someone stepping in for the Master, let alone General Horatio himself. But I knew better than to ask. Questions of this kind were not tolerated in the GA. But maybe Dad would know… I made a mental note to bring this up with him later.

Horatio's cold gray eyes bore into mine, so I nodded once, signaling that I understood.

"The Grand Alliance of American States has a particularly special Ten Day Object for you today, Theo."

The Object. The reason I was here. My heartbeat increased from a jerky pattering to an incessant pounding. Despite the dark cloud of my death hanging over me like the plague, a small part of me tugged at the idea of receiving my very own Ten Day Object. Usually the GA gave out practical items or food to thank those with approaching deathdays for their service as citizens. Extra food rations: wheat, grain, or even bread or cheese. Sometimes herbs and medicine, if the family was lucky. I'd even heard of one kid getting access to electricity during the scheduled power outages.

And now it was my turn.

"Are you ready, Citizen Vanderveen?"

"I am, General." I was pleased my voice sounded more confident than I felt. I wiped my sweaty palms on my pants again and stood up a little straighter.

"Excellent. Please, recite your pledge."

Clearing my throat, I took a deep breath and began reciting the verses I'd learned by heart since I was a boy. "I pledge allegiance to the eagle, of the Grand Alliance of American States, and to each of the Cities for which it stands." I paused, glancing up at the eagles on the banners above me. "I give my life to the servitude of this great nation, and I hope to be rewarded as the time of my service wanes from brightness of day into shadow of night."

Horatio's smile widened as he inclined his head in my direction. "The Grand Alliance of American States is grateful to you, Citizen."

At his words, one of the small black boxes in a square compartment on the upper tiers of the room jutted out and began its slow descent toward us, as if by magic. I leaned forward and blinked several times to focus my vision. I didn't want to miss this. Upon closer inspection, I realized the box wasn't traveling of its own accord at all. Inch by inch, it slid down on a thin, white platform.

There it was. My Ten Day Object. It was almost here.

Ten more seconds.

My eyes were glued to the glossy black box as it came ever closer.

Nine seconds.

Liv — my best friend — would want to know immediately what I'd received.

Eight.

I could practically see her message on my comp now: *What is it, Theodore? Is it something useful for your family? I hope so! You better take it to school tomorrow — or else!*

Seven.

I couldn't suppress a small smile at the idea, but it quickly dissipated as I realized that since Liv's deathday was in six months, I wouldn't be here to find out what *her* Object would be... My chest constricted and I pushed the thought away, focusing instead on the box as it traveled downward.

Six.

I secretly hoped to receive additional supplies for Mom's medical kit.

Five.

She was constantly running low from tending to those who couldn't afford to check in to the GA hospitals.

Four.

I would love to see a warm smile light up her features

just one more time — it was so rare these days, with my deathday creeping ever closer…

Three.

Just a little longer…

Two.

I pushed my hair out of my eyes, my heart jumping into my throat.

One.

The platform finally came to a halt between Horatio and me. The General stepped forward, collected the box and offered it to me.

"Thank you for your service, Citizen Vanderveen."

THE POLISHED OPAQUE glass box was smooth beneath my trembling fingers. Horatio gestured to a small elevated stand to my left, which I hadn't noticed before.

I closed my eyes and took several breaths to calm my racing heart. Approaching the stand, I carefully laid the box down and clicked open the latches on its lid. Soft black velvet lined the inside. In its center, a cloth made of the same velvet was wrapped tightly around my Ten Day Object.

This was it.

The moment I'd both been looking forward to and dreading my entire life.

Once I accepted the Object, the reality of my impending deathday would settle over me like a thick fog cloaking the forest beyond the Edge on a gloomy afternoon. It would solidify in my heart like water turning to ice.

But it's not like I had much of a choice. This was the way things were, and nothing I said or did would change that, despite what Ian thought. I wasn't like him, and I never would be.

So instead, I took a deep breath and lifted the Object — still wrapped in the velvet cloth — off its cushion and weighed it in my hand. It was heavy — heavier than I'd expected.

I glanced up at Horatio, who nodded once.

Clenching my hands to prevent them from shaking, I slowly unwrapped the cloth, revealing a small black dome. My heart sank a little. I guess Mom wouldn't be getting herbs after all...

I examined the Object from all angles and held it up to the light streaming in from the high windows. It seemed to be made of glass, with irregular grooves and markings on its underside, but its smooth outer surface didn't give any indication as to its purpose.

I bit my lip. Curiosity was frowned upon in the

Grand Alliance, but I couldn't just walk out of here not knowing what the mysterious little dome did. After a moment's hesitation, I sucked in a breath. "General... could you tell me... what is it, exactly?"

"I'm afraid not, Theo." Horatio smiled, but it didn't quite reach his eyes. "Ten Day Objects are very personal. They are for their owners alone to decipher. The Grand Alliance of American States cannot help you."

My stomach dropped as Horatio's words sunk in. He wouldn't help me. And there was no use asking for an audience with the Board that distributed Ten Day Objects. Citizens did not question the decisions of the Board. I shuddered at the thought of the repercussions for even voicing this kind of request.

I was on my own.

"Now, if that will be all..."

Nodding, I pocketed the dome. I didn't want to overstay my welcome.

Horatio clapped his bony hands twice, and the door to the circular room opened. Two Safety Patrols entered and bowed low before the General. I spun around, searching their eyes for a sign of recognition. But it wasn't there — their faces were unfamiliar. The twinge of hope that had ignited in my stomach had just been extinguished — Rogers wasn't escorting me back outside; I wouldn't get a chance to ask him if he knew anything about the dome.

I followed the Patrols back through the Tower's busy Atrium. Johnson, the Patrol who had agreed to let Rogers scan my blood, insisted on repeating the procedure as I departed the Tower. I thought about asking him how exactly I would have had a complete blood transfusion during my Ceremony, but decided against it. It was best not to argue with the Safety Patrols.

I took the few short steps leading down from the Tower's grand double doors two at a time. The sky, which had been clear this morning, was now suffused with swirling hints of gray and black.

My comp dinged as a message from Liv came through. I navigated away from the pop-up video communication from the Deathday Research Fund asking for donations and smiled — of course she'd be the first to ask about the Object. I stroked the cool, smooth surface of the dome in my pocket. But I couldn't go home. Not yet. Not before I figured out the purpose of the mysterious gift.

A light easterly breeze ruffled my hair. I spun around on my heel and faced the wind. And just like that, I knew where I had to go.

"DID YOU TELL HER, THEO?"

I jumped, nearly dropping the glass dome into the icy lake beneath my feet.

Ian plopped down on the Pier beside me. His breaths came in sharp gasps and his light brown skin was flushed despite the bite of Autumn air.

Classic Ian, appearing out of nowhere. But he knew he could always find me here, on the Pier. My feet dangled over the edge of the jagged concrete, but I was careful not to touch the water. They say the nuclear fallout particles never fully dissolved in the lake, and that it was still irradiated, even today, over one hundred years after the War ended.

I raised an eyebrow. "My Mom knows perfectly well what's going to happen in ten days." The date on my left wrist tingled. Those digits were very much a part of me: always have been, always would be. And now that I'd officially accepted my Object, the ten days that separated me from the date emblazoned on my skin felt more real than ever before. The inevitability of what was coming gripped me in its clutches like a vise and refused to let go.

Ian nudged me with his elbow. "Not your Mom. And not that."

I gripped the dome tighter in my hand. I knew Ian wasn't talking about my deathday... but that was all I seemed to think about. During the last few months, on most days I had tried to fold it into the dark confines of my mind, tried to live a normal life.

But nothing about this was normal anymore. I was going to die in ten days, and there was nothing I could do to slow or stop the impact when the time came. That was the worst part. I was helpless, flailing like an exposed duck in the middle of hunting season. What wouldn't I give to live just a bit longer…

"Earth to Theo, are you there?" Ian waved his hand in front of my eyes, snapping me out of my reverie. "Have you told her, then?"

I shook my head. "I haven't told my dog either, no."

"Theo!" Another nudge from Ian.

"No. Not yet."

"You need to step on it." He paused. "Where is Laika, anyway?"

"Laika!" I whipped around, scanning the horizon for the familiar bob of her tail. I craned my neck to see around the Ferris wheel, or what was left of it. Once bright and full of light, it was now rusted, ancient and dead. Its metal rods creaked in the breeze. Looming in its wake, past the derelict auditorium, was the White Tower, casting its vast shadow on adjacent, much smaller buildings.

A pair of black, beady eyes met mine. Laika bounded toward me, tongue out, her black and white coat gleaming in the sparse sunlight peeking through the clouds.

"Easy there, girl." I scratched her pointed ears. She was so little when I found her, she could almost fit in the palm of my hand. A pink, slippery tongue brushed over my cheek, covering my face in slobber, and a loud bark sounded in my ear. Ian laughed, as Laika's fluffy, sickle-shaped tail wagged with life and energy. Laika, for one, didn't have to deal with counting down to her death…

Ian peered at me from behind the collar of his jacket and pointed to his wrist. His deathday peeked out underneath his sweatshirt. The numbers were gray and faded, in stark contrast with my own, which glowed green against my pale skin.

"You're thinking about it, aren't you?"

I didn't reply. A gentle breeze ruffled my hair. I pushed it back absentmindedly, taking in the vastness of the lake that extended before us in nearly every direction. To our left, a concrete peninsula jutted out from the mainland. The water purification plant that used to be there closed down decades ago. Now it was just an abandoned ruin, much like the majority of the old downtown.

Ian followed my gaze to the lake. "I can't blame you. It all comes down to one thing." Ian tapped his wrist several times. "Time."

The wind picked up and the waves swelled, crashing

into one another with increasing force. The tide was changing.

"Time? What about it?"

Ian's eyes darkened. He brushed a hand through his dark, curly hair, lost in thought. "Everything. That's just it. Everything revolves around time. There's not enough of it, for people like you and me."

"For people like me, you mean." I kept my gaze trained on the steely waters.

Ian squeezed my arm. "What happened to me wasn't my fault. You know that."

"Doesn't change a damn thing." Out of the corner of my eye, I registered the hurt in Ian's expression.

"You know it's not worth hoping for an anomaly." I could barely hear him over the whistling and whipping of the wind and the waves smashing against the Pier.

I said nothing, but Ian had a point. What happened to him came with its own set of complications…

And as for time… he was right on that count too. There wasn't enough of it. From the moment we took our first breaths, the clock started ticking. Our deathdays were sealed. It was just the way things were. I glanced down at the numbers on my wrist again. They stared back at me, solid and unforgiving. Deathdays, just like birthdays, were part of life. And the Grand Alliance did what it could to help us live with them and prepare for them.

It didn't make them any less terrifying, but it was comforting to know the GA was there to assist its citizens and protect them from the Outside, beyond the Edge, and whatever radiation-filled creatures lurked there. In exchange, we swore to abide by their rules, carry our comps at all times, do our assigned jobs, respect curfew, and not ask questions. Then, the GA even gave us Objects to thank us for our service…

I shifted my attention back to the mysterious dome in my hand, its black exterior smooth under my fingertips. I rotated it between my fingers. Its surface reflected a distorted image of my face, complete with chestnut hair falling into my blue eyes and the cloudy sky behind me.

But what did it do? I'd spent the rest of the morning tinkering with it, but couldn't figure it out. My knuckles had turned white from my iron grip on the device. Did I think it would magically reveal its purpose if I squeezed it hard enough? And what use did I have for a small glass dome? It was probably just a glass trinket, meant to be deposited on a shelf and admired. A packet of herbs for Mom's medicine cabinet would have been so much better. I pursed my lips and stuck it in my jacket pocket.

Then, thinking better of it, I slowly pulled it out again and handed it to Ian. "That's what they gave me today. What do you reckon?"

Ian's brow furrowed as he turned it over in his hands.

"Cool gadget." He planted it on a nearby rock as the waves crashed ceaselessly on the breakwater.

Nothing happened.

Scowling, he examined it again and set it on the concrete beside him. At once, its surface lit up with red and orange markings that danced like shadows by candlelight.

"How did you do that?" I stared from the dome to Ian, my mouth open. I'd been trying to decipher it all morning, and it hadn't so much as flickered.

"Beats me."

I looked quizzically at my friend. "You didn't ask about my Object earlier. How come? Liv messaged me the second I got out of the Tower…"

Ian shrugged. "I figured making sure you tell Liv how you feel about her is a more pressing matter than some silly Object the Government *so graciously* bestowed on you."

I snorted. Ian never cared much for the GA or its gifts. He had his reasons, after all…

"It's given me an idea though… I'll try to figure out what it does. Can I borrow it?"

I picked the device up again, staring at the markings that continued to sway to and fro, as if propelled by a gentle breeze. I hesitated, unsure if I should part with it.

"Sure." I sighed and handed it to my friend, who

squeezed my hand as I did. After a beat, I squeezed back. I smiled and met his gaze, which shone with warmth. If anyone could figure it out, it was Ian. I knew I could count on him.

"Thanks. Meet me at the Hideout tomorrow?"

"I was going to hang out with Liv after school…"

"You're still going to school?"

I shrugged. "Liv still does."

"You know that Liv would go to school even on her deathday."

I chuckled. Liv *would* do that.

Ian stood up. "Right. Maybe you'll finally tell her." A toothy grin crossed his lips and he winked. "The day after, then."

He scratched Laika behind the ears, and he was off, leaving me on the Pier, my mind swirling with thoughts of the curious gadget like the water in the lake.

I didn't have a clue what the dome did, but the slight twist in my stomach suggested the GA gifted it to me for a reason. I just had to find out what that reason was. Maybe, together with Ian, we could it figure out before my time was up.

Pulling my jacket tightly around myself against the wind, I watched Ian's receding silhouette fade into the distance. With every step he took, the weight in my chest lifted a little, leaving it lighter than it had been in weeks.

I glanced at Laika's furry form curled up next to me and patted her head. Her ears perked up, and she looked at me, head tilted and tail thumping on the nearest stone.

I smiled, despite myself.

I had ten days left, but who said I couldn't make them count?

I STOOD on the steps outside of Loop Sector School, waiting for Liv and Violet to arrive. The squat, gray building before me housed all twelve years of education.

At sixteen, I was a sophomore. I knew the school inside out, like the back of my hand. After this year, some of the boys, like Anton and Asher, who hurried past me now, raising their hands in greeting, had been assigned to train to join the ranks of Safety Patrols. But I didn't care for their early morning drills in Security Compound 3, their rigid schedules, or their white uniforms. I had no intention of working for the GA like Dad did, and especially not the military. Not that I would even be alive long enough to join the Patrols.

The green numbers on my wrist had plans of their

own. They stared back at me, eternal and unchanged, from under my white, long-sleeved crew neck.

The weight of my deathday hung over me like a dark, ominous cloud, following me wherever I went. Every morning, for that one blissful moment between oblivion and consciousness, I awoke with a smile playing on my lips. I heard Laika's tail thumping against my bed and inhaled the smell of Mom's mint tea wafting in from the kitchen.

But then, all too soon, with a certainty as potent and profound as death itself, the realization of my impending demise came crashing down on me with the force of a tidal wave.

Day in, day out.

It consumed me, overshadowing my every thought, my every move. I tried to distract myself, pushing the pulsing digits out of my mind whenever I could. But ultimately, I knew I was living on borrowed time. And no amount of GA bills or coins would buy it back.

My eyes moved left and right, scanning the front lawn for the girls — if I could even call it a lawn. The grass that once dressed the yard was now concreted over; only the twisted old oak remained from the original lawn in all its majestic stature.

"Theo!"

I turned to see Liv bounding toward me, her wavy

brown hair flying after her, her usually porcelain skin flushed and her green eyes bright. Violet's blonde head bobbed just behind her.

Despite my gloomy thoughts, I couldn't suppress a smile as Liv threw her arms around me. She smelled like a fresh spring meadow, even in the chilly early autumn air.

"Hey, pixie."

Liv raised an eyebrow. "You're still calling me that?"

"I've always called you that. Seeing you run around the forest on our countless excursions when we were kids will do that to a guy."

"So it seems." There was a slight tension in her eyes, but she fought to keep her voice casual. It didn't fool me though. I'd known Liv as long as I could remember, and I knew her better than anyone. We could practically finish each other's sentences. So I knew very well what she was thinking: she was putting on a brave face, acting like it was just another day, pretending that nothing out of the ordinary would happen in nine days. Certainly not my deathday. But I wished she would just say what's on her mind.

"That's right, pix."

"We didn't see you yesterday," Vi squeezed my hand. Her usually pristine braids were slightly disheveled, her eyes puffy.

I stared at my feet, pushing down the guilt that

churned in my stomach. Both Liv and Vi didn't seem like themselves today, and I knew why. I just didn't know how to bring it up. Or if I should bring it up at all.

After a moment, Vi spoke again. "How did it go, with the… Ceremony?"

Liv tucked a long strand of hair behind her ear. "What did you get? Tell us everything." The strain in her voice was palpable, like a tangible object hanging in the air between us. It didn't match her words — a valiant attempt at being light and conversational. "I can't believe you didn't want to tell me what you got over the comp messaging system."

Her usually bubbly smile was warped, and the sadness in her eyes pierced me to my marrow. I let go of the ache consuming me. In that moment, I wanted nothing more than to hug her and tell her that everything would be okay. It *had* to be okay. Or would it? Deep down, I knew I didn't want to answer that question truthfully.

So instead, I took a deep breath and faced my friends. "I don't really know what I got."

The girls stared at me, their eyes wide, expecting me to go on.

"It was a… that's the thing. I don't know what it is," I said.

"You don't know?" Vi asked.

"Where is it? Can we see it?" Liv's curiosity got the

better of her, and my heart skipped a beat as I registered the familiar light in her eyes.

"I don't have it with me."

"What do you mean? Is it at home? We could drop by yours after school. I'm sure Mom wouldn't mind if I was a few minutes late." As if remembering something, Liv nervously took her comp out of her bag, checked it, then replaced it again.

"Not here. Come on." I glanced around and led the girls toward the old oak, making sure we were out of earshot. The last thing I wanted was for the Fleeters — kids with deathdays within the next few years who were known to cause chaos in school — to hear about my encounter in the Tower.

We settled down under the tree's broad canopy. Its thick, twisted trunk was a dull brown, almost gray, and the leaves on its many intertwining branches were beginning to change color.

I recounted what happened at the Ceremony, careful to play down the fact that the Patrols couldn't confirm my identity, but Liv wasn't fooled for a second.

"Your comp didn't verify your identity?"

I shook my head.

"But your blood scan came back okay?"

"Yeah. Any idea what that means?"

Liv bit her lip, lost in thought.

"It could have just been a glitch with your comp," Vi offered.

"That's what I thought. Maybe Dad will know."

I tucked these thoughts away for another time and told the girls about Horatio and the mysterious glass dome.

"Why was General Horatio at your Ceremony in the first place? And you asked him *what*?" Liv looked horror-struck. "What your Object *does*?"

I opened my mouth to reply, but no words came out, so I just smiled sheepishly.

Liv shook her head and put an easy arm around my shoulder. "Honestly Theo, did you even pay attention in prep class? You know the protocols, right? No questions!"

"As a matter of fact, I did. I recited my pledge perfectly, pix."

"But you broke the cardinal rule of the Grand Alliance. It's nothing short of a miracle Horatio didn't punish you further than just a slight reprimand."

"He didn't have to." I looked down at my feet. A small insect crawled up one of my untied, muddy laces. "Soon I'll be worm food, anyway."

"Oh, Theo!" Liv's eyes filled with tears and she threw her arms around me. Vi joined us in a silent hug. I closed my eyes, memorizing this moment.

"Hey, Timothy. *Hey*." A snicker sailed through the air

in my direction, making me cringe. "Oh wait, or was it his deathday last week already?"

Releasing the girls, I set my jaw and ignored the jibe, although my hands itched to clench into fists. Emerson Fraser, Jessica Liu and Shane Parker.

"Liv, Vi, come on. Let's get out of here," I muttered under my breath. I preferred to avoid this trio if I could help it. They were the most notorious of the Fleeters — truanting, setting fire to the dumpsters behind the school, and this, their favorite pastime: tormenting the likes of me, with deathdays approaching so soon you could count the days on your fingers. Literally.

"What's the matter, Vanderveen, cat got your tongue?" Jessica said, narrowing her dark eyes and crossing her arms next to Emerson.

I took a few deep breaths to steady myself. There was no dodging them now.

"What's your Ten Day Object? Some dog food?" Shane casually patted my backpack, resting underneath the oak.

Liv stepped between us. "Don't you have somewhere to be? Class, maybe?" She snapped.

My mouth dropped open as I stared at Liv. Was that a note of acid in her voice?

"Careful, Madden," Emerson said, a smirk curling his lips.

"Look! I was right — Vanderveen's got some dog food from the Grand Alliance." Shane had unzipped my backpack and waved around a burlap sack of treats I'd saved for Laika — mainly old chicken bones.

"Give that back," I said.

"Or what? Your family won't eat tonight?"

White hot anger surged through me but I tried to keep my cool. Shane wasn't worth it.

"Maybe we'll just throw this in the Lake. What do you say, Jess?" Shane gestured to the bag.

Something snapped in me. I lunged forward, going for the sack, but Shane was ready for me. He delivered a crushing blow to my face, causing stars to erupt in the corners of my eyes. I ignored them as best I could, tackling Shane to the ground. His eyes widened in shock just before my fist connected with his jaw. His head flew backward, but before I could react, a mixture of blood and saliva obscured my vision. I heard a disturbing crunching sound and a vicious pain erupted on my nose. A girl's scream came from somewhere to my left.

I tumbled off Shane and put a tentative hand up to my face. It came back red. Shane jumped back to his feet, motioned to Emerson and came at me again, fire and hatred burning in his brown eyes. I leapt to the right, trying to dodge his attack. But I wasn't quick enough.

Shane lifted me clean off my feet, slamming me flat into the thick trunk of the oak. My head spun from the impact and I fought to regain my focus. As Shane geared up for another blow, I spun around and kicked hard at his stomach, missing him by an inch. Emerson swung a thick arm at me, striking me squarely in the solar plexus. I doubled over, gasping for air, and collapsed to the ground.

"Enough!" Liv stepped between us, her hands outstretched, her nostrils flared. "Enough!"

Jessica emerged behind Shane and Emerson, flipping her straight raven-black hair behind her shoulder. "Careful, now." Her unspoken threat hung in the air between the girls.

Emerson shot his friends a look and turned to walk up the steps to the school. He paused for a moment, his cold eyes boring into Liv's. "It'll be your turn soon, Madden."

Liv rolled her eyes.

Shane kicked the burlap sack toward me. "Here's your dinner, Vanderveen." Heat rose to my cheeks again, but before I could respond, he was gone, rushing after his friends into the low building.

As I stared after the trio's receding silhouettes, the adrenaline had begun to wear off and the full extent of the excruciating pain in my nose caught up with me. It was bleeding. Badly. I wiped at it with my shirt, staining my white sleeve crimson.

I felt a pair of warm green eyes trained on me. "Are you all right, Theo?" Liv asked.

"Yeah." I pushed my hair off my sweaty forehead. "Thanks for that, pix. For getting rid of them."

She nodded, pressing a clean handkerchief to my nose to stem the bleeding.

A small cluster of kids passed us, averting their eyes and increasing their pace. One look at them told me all I needed to know: neat blouses, combed hair, polished shoes — they were the Timeless. Kids with the deathday biomarker far off in the future, twenty years or more. And in the GA, the longer your deathday, the more money and privileges you were afforded by the Government. The injustice of it made my blood boil. There weren't many Timeless kids here in the Sector School, but the ones who did go here instead of the White Tower Elite Academy stuck together.

Liv followed my gaze. "You'd think they'd say something, for once," she said, her eyes burning fiercely as she wiped blood from my jaw. "They have a lot more influence with Principal Caine than they realize."

"You know the almighty Timeless, with their whole lives ahead of them, don't get involved with the Fleeters, pix."

"They can't just spend their whole lives turning a blind eye to this."

I gave Liv a wistful smile. "Life looks different when you know you have a lot of time."

"I guess it does."

I looked at Liv as she held the handkerchief in place, really looked at her. Her quiet strength, and her ability to remain cool and collected under pressure were two of the many things I admired about her. She was a voice of reason in the chaos of my life. My stomach did a somersault as I realized how close she was in that moment. Her warm breath heated my cheek and I fought the blush that threatened to betray me. Was this my chance to finally tell her how I felt about her? How I've always felt about her? The idea of finally putting my feelings for her out in the open sent a thrill through my body. I needed to tell her, and soon, before it was too late.

I winced as a flash of pain shot through my cheek, and the moment passed.

"Hold still, Theodore, that's one nasty gash."

I did as she instructed, closing my eyes and letting Liv tend to my wound. It was eerily quiet in the school courtyard. The usual student chatter had died down, replaced by soft birdsong. A pair of sparrows conversed in the branches high above us. We were alone.

The first bell must have rung several minutes ago, but

I hadn't noticed. By now, even the last stragglers had made it to class. Ms. Holloway wouldn't be too pleased that we'd be so late to history. Liv wouldn't be either — history was her favorite — but she hadn't said anything so far.

"Hang on," I said after a moment, searching for a hint of blonde braids. "Where's Vi?"

"Went to get Ralph. Thought you could use a hand — two on one isn't exactly what you'd call a fair fight."

"Nothing's fair with the Fleeters," I said. "They think they'd been dealt a crappy hand in this game of life, and this is their way of getting even."

"They don't understand."

"They understand perfectly, Liv. The GA is all Celebrations and '*thank you for your service*', but this" — I gestured to my bloodied face — "is what it's really like when your deathday is coming. My countdown makes me a target."

Liv shook her head. "Or it's just Emerson and Shane."

"No. That kid Timothy Sinclair whose deathday it was last week? They've been treating him like this for months." I dabbed at my nose with my sleeve, which was now soaked through. "I've seen the way he looked over his shoulder every day. The way he was always the first one in and out of class to avoid running into anyone at school, especially Emerson and the other Fleeters."

"Was it that bad?" Liv said in a hushed voice.

"He was chased like a rat through a cage."

Liv bit her lip. "Oh, that's awful!"

"They were scared of you though, pix," I teased, playfully punching Liv's arm. "So I gotta keep you close."

"That's because I'm absolutely terrifying." She grinned and rummaged in her bag for her comp. She switched it on, checked her messages, then put it away again. She'd been doing this a lot lately.

"Everything all right?"

Liv's expression darkened. "Mom hasn't messaged this morning yet."

"She needs her rest, you know that."

Liv glanced down at her worn black boots. "She says hi by the way. She was so happy that you came round on Saturday. She's glad she got to say... hi."

My throat constricted. What Liv meant to say was 'goodbye' and I knew it. I'd known Jean Madden almost my entire life — she was like an aunt to me. My earliest memory of her was when I'd forgotten my lunch token at home one chilly winter day. Liv brought me home and Jean cooked us an impromptu meal — she'd made a feast out of boiled potatoes and a watery stew, even though they didn't have much to spare for guests. I was five or six. I'd never forgotten it.

"How's she doing?"

"Hanging in there."

"She'll pull through. I know she will. I'll get Mom to assemble a packet of pain-easing herbs for her."

The corners of Liv's mouth quirked upward. "She'd like that." She squeezed my hand, and it tingled at her touch.

"So, what should we do after school?" I asked. "We could go up to the Pier, the Ferris Wheel is waiting… Or we could tackle some other things left on our list." I smiled. "Whatever we do, we do together."

"Oh no! I can't today." Liv bit her lip. "Besides, you should probably rest and have your Mom check your injuries."

"Oh… why not?" My smile faltered. "I thought we were going to hang out today?" I didn't have that many days left.

"I know, I'm sorry, Theo, I really am. You know how much our list means to me. We'll finish every last item on there — there's no other option." She squeezed my hand again, and I knew she meant every word. "I promised Mom this morning I'd help her out today."

I nodded; I knew how important Jean was to Liv. Except for Jean's sister, she was all the family Liv had left.

"Send her my best, all right? Let's reschedule for tomorrow. I'll get you those herbs, pixie."

"Yes! I'll be there." Liv brightened. "Oh, and Theodore?"

"Mhm?"

"Dress comfortably."

EIGHT DAYS

I HATED TUESDAYS. At first, I couldn't quite put my finger on why I hated them so much, but lately I'd gotten to the bottom of it.

I hated Tuesdays because I didn't have a single class with Liv. No jokes, no playful teasing, no scheming over what to do next on our list or seeing her bent over her comp, taking myriad notes on subjects she already knew inside out. The best I could hope for was stealing covert glimpses of her in the hallway between lessons, or exchanging a quick hug before she inevitably rushed off to snag a front-row seat in her next class.

Today was Tuesday.

Luckily, I didn't have to wait long — I'd see her after school. Although an unease settled in my stomach as I remembered my promise to see Ian today... I pushed the thought away, hoping he'd understand. Liv had some grand plan she wanted to tick off our list today. I vaguely wondered what it could be as the rest of the day went by in a blur. Students passed me — Timeless by the looks of them — laughing loudly or exchanging gossip about Principal Caine, while I tried to ignore the gnawing feeling that I only had eight days till my deathday. Several Fleeters took it upon themselves to remind me of my impending doom at every possible occasion by throwing insults my way. I resisted the temptation to snap back, fighting to stay calm and ignore them. Liv was right. They weren't worth it. And I didn't need another nose-bleed or bruise on my jaw to go with the one I got yesterday.

The double doors of the school gave way as I pushed out of the stuffy, gray tiled hallway onto the school steps, bathed in the afternoon glow of the September sun.

Vi turned and smiled when she noticed me, tugging at Ralph's sleeve. A stout boy with cropped dark hair and full lips from a well-to-do family took one look at my bruised jaw and shook his head. "What happened to you, T?"

"You should have seen the other guy."

"Fleeters?"

I nodded. Although Ralph was a Timeless, he didn't hang out with the other Timeless — he'd declined their offer on the first day of high school, and instead spent his time with Liv, Vi and I, just like he had for years.

"They're just stuck up kids who refuse to see that all they accomplished was to be dealt a lucky hand in life. A long deathday doesn't make them better than anyone else; it's not like the Timeless ooze moral superiority over Fleeters," Ralph had said that day. "Long or short, a deathday doesn't define who you are." In that moment, the bond of our friendship had strengthened considerably. Ralph clearly didn't care for high school cliques, and I was grateful for it. I shook off the memory and touched my jaw gingerly, wincing at the pain.

"You're not the only one with a bruised face today, Theo," Vi said, lowering her voice.

"What do you mean?"

Vi and Ralph exchanged a look. "I saw two Safety Patrols dragging a kid to sewing class this morning. His face was purple and bloody." Vi shuddered.

"What happened?"

Vi shook her head. "They didn't say. Mrs. Kenning just asked him to take a seat, while the Safety Patrols reminded us that breaking curfew and not attending school were direct violations of the City's laws, and offenders would be punished. I can only guess it had something to do with that."

"They were making an example of him," Ralph said thoughtfully. "To deter us from doing the same."

"He's just a kid, though." I clenched my fists, remembering my own treatment at the hands of the Safety Patrols in the White Tower — I wouldn't forget staring straight into the barrels of four guns in a hurry.

Ralph nodded and lowered his voice, checking over his shoulder if there was anyone within earshot. I leaned in closer, straining my ears to tune out the surrounding chatter. "Father says we need to be extra careful nowadays. He's heard they're tightening the laws…"

I said nothing, studying my shoes. Usually a faded black, they were now coated in a thin layer of mud from recent rains and from yesterday's fight. Violet and Ralph weren't the type to break rules. They kept their heads down and did as they were told. I did too… until I met Ian. But I could never tell them about him… it was too dangerous. I didn't think they'd understand. I wondered briefly how Liv would react if I told her about my friend and his secret. Would her eyes widen and she'd tell me to keep my voice down, or would her deep-rooted curiosity get the better of her? I sighed. I probably wouldn't find out — it wasn't my secret to tell.

A light touch on my shoulder brought me back to the present. I looked up and found myself face to face with

Liv. Heat rose in my cheeks, and I fought to keep it at bay.

"Why so pensive, Theodore?" She asked. Liv's appearance was a little more disheveled than usual — her bag was open, flyaways ousted her usually neatly combed hair, and her olive green jacket looked like it had been crumpled in a ball and left that way overnight. Still, my breath caught at the sight of her — she still looked beautiful.

"Just thinking of you, pix," I said, in what I hoped was a casual voice. "And what you got planned for us today." I handed her a small parcel wrapped in burlap. "Herbs for your Mom, as promised."

Liv's hands shook as she took the parcel from me, and her eyes took on a glassy sheen. "Thank you, Theo. She'll be so happy."

"Anything for Jean."

Liv smiled and hugged me. Her familiar scent, which reminded me of a fresh spring meadow, wafted over me. My skin tingled at her touch.

"Shall we?" Liv inclined her head toward the old downtown. "We've got a list to tick off!"

We bid Vi and Ralph goodbye and set off through the city center toward the shoreline that abruptly collided with the City's numerous high-rises. Leaving the safety of Loop Sector, we crossed one of the still functioning bridges that hung, steely and red, over the corrosive river. Its hinges creaked and protested beneath our feet. To our right, a couple of corn-like structures rose up from among the ruins.

I liked River Sector, mostly because it was so deserted. Several squatters took refuge in the abandoned buildings, but with no electricity or functioning sewage systems, living in the other Sectors was preferable.

Liv had taken out her comp and was perusing the list we'd made over a year ago of all the things we wanted to do together before our deathdays. *Whatever we do, we do together.*

"We've done the Riverwalk, that was fun," she said, her brow creasing as she studied the list. "We've done the walk along the avenue in Millennium Sector on an early summer's evening. Those old ruined buildings are really something else, don't you think? They must have been beautiful, once. What are you most looking forward to ticking off?"

"Umm…" I shot Liv a sidelong glance. Her eyes were wide, expectant. Why was Liv so focused on the list all of a sudden? I knew we'd agreed to tick off as many things as possible, but now that I had eight days left, I wasn't so sure it was a priority anymore. Spending quality time together and figuring out a way to tell Liv how I felt while pushing away thoughts of my impending deathday seemed more important than doing everything on that list. Right?

Clearly, Liv didn't think so — she was so absorbed in it that she hardly spoke of anything else the whole way downtown. Then again, ticking items off *was* spending quality time together. "Honestly, I just want to spend time with you," I said. "Whatever we do, we do together. That's why we created the list, right? To spend time together, before, you know…?"

Liv didn't answer, but plowed on. "I'd like to climb up one of the carts on the Ferris Wheel and pretend the Wheel was still working. We'd find ourselves in the midst of the bustle of a summer fair, munching on sweetcorn bought from a stand and feeling the fresh lake breeze in our hair."

Even as she said it, Liv's shoulders drooped. Neither of us had to say what we were both thinking — the scenario that Liv had just described could never happen in the GA. The Ferris Wheel hadn't worked in decades, the Lake was anything but fresh, and summer fairs were as probable as Chancellor Graves permanently taking over Mrs. Kenning's sewing class. Fantasy.

I put my arm around Liv's shoulder and squeezed. "I'd love to do that with you, pixie."

She tilted her head and leaned on my shoulder. I pulled her close. Was this my moment? Would I finally tell her how I felt about her? I glanced down. Liv's sweet smile threatened to unnerve me.

Before I could open my mouth, Liv spoke, and the moment had — once again — passed. "But today, we'll do something better."

We passed the Mart on our way over the bridge — a large, rectangular building on the river that had sat unused for decades, its glassless windows staring out like sightless eyes. It loomed tall against the gray clouds swarming overhead. Despite the drafty conditions that dominated its halls, the Mart was popular among squatters. Every few months, Safety Patrols would storm in and clear the building. It wouldn't stay empty for long though — sooner or later, the squatters would return, their silhouettes cropping up in the vacant windows like mushrooms after the rain.

After another mile, Liv stopped short, just on the edge of Lake Sector. "There it is," she said, her tone hushed.

I followed her gaze and looked straight up into an enormous dark gray skyscraper. Massive metal beams criss-crossed on its facade and two antennae protruded from its roof, giving off the impression of a steel, oversized insect. Broken glass from the windows pooled at our feet.

"Breathtaking, isn't it?" Liv asked. "It's one of the tallest buildings in the City, second to only the White Tower. It used to be called the Hancock Building, back in the 20th century."

"Wow, it's that old?"

"I know, I can't believe it either. Think of the history it holds! I'd love to learn more about 20th century architecture, but Mrs. Holloway would never agree to it." Liv sighed, but I knew she was right. They didn't teach us anything from the pre-War period at school.

"So, should we go around?" I asked. "See what it looks like from the lakeside?"

Liv's eyes glinted in the afternoon light. "We're not going around. We're going up."

"Up?" I eyed the structure wearily. It must have been at least one hundred stories high.

"We don't have 'walk around an abandoned skyscraper' on our list. What we *do* have is—"

"'Watch a sunset with a view,'" I finished.

"Exactly."

"But pix, maybe we could go to the Pier, watch the sunset from there…"

Liv raised her eyebrows. "You do know the Lake is east-facing, right?"

I did know. I rubbed the back of my neck, staring at the colossal mass that loomed overhead. "But we won't stay up there for long, right? I don't want to get caught in a power outage." They've been more and more frequent these days. Power outages meant dark streets. And dark streets were dangerous, especially here in Lake Sector.

"What, are you scared, Theodore?"

In truth, my legs did feel like jelly, but I wasn't sure if it was the prospect of climbing a 250-year-old building, or the idea of being alone with Liv, one hundred floors up. Both sent my head spinning.

Not wanting Liv to see my hesitation, I grabbed her hand and pulled her toward the base of the building. "You wish!"

Liv's laughter filled the air, clear as a bell. I couldn't help recalling our trips to the forest with Liv's Dad all those years ago. Beyond the Edge, and into the wilderness beyond. We were so carefree back then, not burdened by burning green digits or sick parents. Not scarred by the inevitability of impending loss. But we weren't those little kids anymore, and those burdens were ours to bear. They had become a part of us, weighing down on our hearts like anchors on ships at sea. Ships that, until recently, had fought so desperately to shatter the chains that had bound them for so long, craving the fresh ocean breeze and the freedom of the open waves. But now, with each passing day, it became increasingly clear that we didn't have a choice. I didn't have a choice. Deathdays were a part of life, and that was just the way things were in the GA — the way they'd always been. Hadn't they?

Pausing at the base of the tower, Liv assessed the ancient scaffolding with a critical eye. She then broke into a run and hopped up on the scaffolding in two easy leaps. She leaned over the railing and smiled down at me. "Coming?"

Using the railing for support, I clambered onto the scaffolding with much less grace than Liv. We free-climbed the rusted beams, which intertwined and formed a makeshift ladder that creaked and groaned under our weight. After several stories, Liv stopped before a broken window and peeked inside.

"We're in luck," she said, pointing to a crumbling sign hanging on one hinge just inside the building. "The staircase is this way."

After closing another Deathday Research Fund video message, we used our comp screens to light the way in the dark stairwell. Their glow cast long shadows on the walls. We climbed methodically, careful to leave rogue pieces of rubble that had fallen onto our path undisturbed. A trail of dusty footprints in our wake was the only sign of our lingering presence. Liv counted the floors as we went.

"Sixty-three, sixty-four, sixty—"

I turned just in time to see Liv reach for the handrail. But she wasn't quick enough — her foot slid out from beneath her, sending a loose chunk of the wall flying down the stairs behind her. I dodged it and threw myself toward her, trying to break her fall, but instead sending a cloud of dust into the air. I lost my bearings immediately. Coughing, I groped around the floor for my comp and shined its light in Liv's direction. She had lifted herself up, using the railing for support. Her lip was bleeding slightly, but otherwise she looked unharmed.

"Are you all right?" I asked, but my words were drowned out by a high-pitched wailing. I thrust my hands up to cover my ears. "We need to go, now!" I grabbed Liv's hand and we continued our climb, taking the steps two at a time and leaning on each other for support.

After several minutes, we reached the top of the staircase. Liv tried the metal door that stood between us and the roof of the skyscraper. "It's locked," she said, raising her voice above the blaring alarm.

I threw my weight against the door, but it wouldn't budge.

I tried again.

Nothing.

This was it. If we didn't find a way out of here, the Safety Patrols would arrive in a matter of minutes and carry us away to who-knows-where… My final eight days on Earth would be spent in a jail cell instead of with my family and friends.

"Over here!" Liv pointed above our heads, her comp light illuminating a rusted lock and chain fastened to the door.

"We need a key." I paced back and forth along the landing, panic pounding in my chest. Thoughts of dark dungeons clouded my vision. Was this the way I said goodbye to the world?

"No, we don't." Seizing a piece of rubble that seemed to have fallen from the ceiling, Liv flung herself at the lock. A loud *clang* rattled the landing as the stone connected with the lock, clearly audible despite the alarm blaring in my ears. But the lock held fast.

Liv tried again, heaving with exertion. This time, the lock gave way and fell to the floor with a clatter. Liv rushed outside and I followed her into the afternoon light, slamming the door behind me.

The daylight dazzled me; I had to blink several times

to bring my vision back into focus after the din of the stairwell. When my eyes adjusted, I sucked in a breath. The sprawling expanse of the City stretched out before me. The White Tower loomed in the distance: white, daunting, and suspended high above the other abandoned buildings in Millennium Sector. Two enormous ancient antennas hovered overhead.

Liv slid up beside me and grabbed my arm. "This way," she said, pulling me sideways. I followed her around the corner and stopped in my tracks.

A cold blue-gray today beneath a semi-overcast sky, the Lake extended east before us, as far as the eye could see. Although ominous clouds hung low over the horizon, several rays of light peeked through the veil that had settled over the world. The light shimmered and reflected off the small waves that rolled back and forth over the surface of the Lake.

It was a wonder to behold; there wasn't a hint of land on the other side. If I hadn't known the massive body of water before me was a lake, I would be convinced it was the sea. The Pier and the abandoned Ferris Wheel sat empty not far from our vantage point, slightly to the right. I loved the Pier because of its proximity to the Lake, but this... this was something else. It reminded me of the time Dad took me with him to work in the White Tower, where I had my first glimpse of the Lake from his seventeenth floor office on an overcast day much like today.

I'd always fantasized about seeing that view again, except bathed in glowing daylight, with clear skies and boundless shafts of sunlight painting the Lake a dazzling shade of blue… So unlike the uniform gray mass I saw that day. But with the countdown on my wrist looming, this was probably as close as I would get to the vista I'd dreamed of as a boy.

Except this time, we were higher up. Much higher up. I peered straight down over the ledge at the streets below and suppressed a bout of vertigo. Maybe it was best not to lean so far over the edge.

I felt a pair of eyes on me. Liv had been watching me.

"It was worth it, wasn't it?" she asked. "We probably won't get much of a sunset in this weather, but…"

"Yeah, it definitely was." I smiled at her. "It's perfect."

I rested my palm against the cool metal of the railing. Its surface reflected and distorted the green markings on my wrist. There was something captivating about the streaks of green intermingled with the grays and blacks of the top of the skyscraper behind me. An ominous kaleidoscope.

Liv positioned her hand next to mine, our fingers inches apart. I sucked in a breath, not daring to move. She was so close. If I moved my hand slightly to the right,

I'd feel the warmth of her skin under mine. Her deathday, black as night against her alabaster skin, peaked out from beneath the sleeve of her olive coat. My smile faltered.

"Are you thinking about it?" Her voice was strained, a wistful smile dancing on her lips.

I nodded and looked away, unable to meet her gaze. Tearing my palm away from the metal, I forced my sleeve down over my wrist. If my eyes met Liv's, my expression would give me away. I wanted her to know how badly I wanted to live for the next six months, until Liv's own deathday, but I didn't know how to spell it out.

Maybe this was my chance. Maybe I could take a deep breath and tell her everything that I've kept folded away in the dark confines of my heart for years and years. That she was light, and life, and laughter, and I couldn't imagine another day without her.

I chanced half a glance up at Liv. Her eyes, green and piercing, were still trained on me. Heat rushed to my cheeks, but I ignored it and steadied myself.

This was it.

But just as I'd made my decision, Liv's expression hardened. "Do you hear that?"

"Hear what?" But as soon as the words had left my mouth, I knew.

The wind had quieted for an instant, and I heard it. The alarm we'd tripped earlier was still wailing in the stairwell. Barely audible seconds before over the whipping of the wind, it was now clearly discernible, even through the shut metal door.

We still weren't safe.

"We need to move." Liv's eyes darted back to the door.

"I thought it would have shut off by now."

"So did I." Liv bit her lip. "Come on, over here!"

She led me to the far side of the roof, peering behind what looked like old generators, while all I could think of was the imminent arrival of a squadron of Safety Patrols bursting onto the terrace — their white uniforms gleaming in the afternoon light and their guns pointed squarely at our chests.

Liv lowered herself onto a ledge just below one of the generators. It was wide enough for her to sit on comfortably, although her feet dangled precariously above the City far below. My stomach twisted — we were high enough for my taste without also doing a dance with death on an ancient ledge a hundred floors up.

"Are you coming?" Liv patted the ledge expectantly.

I sighed. Safety Patrols on one hand and a thousand-foot drop on the other. What could go wrong? Liv reached for my hand as I clambered onto the ledge next to her, careful not to look down. My head was already spinning as it were.

"We should be safe here. If the Safety Patrols do come, they won't think to check behind these," Liv said, pointing to the generators.

I focused my gaze on the horizon. My heart rate slowed as I took in the magnificent view — the Second City, in all its glory, sprawling before us.

"Not so bad up here, huh, Theodore?"

I bumped my knee against Liv's and shot her a smile. "No, it's not."

I realized all was quiet. The alarm must have stopped. We sat in silence for a few minutes, while the sun peaked out of the dreary clouds and began its western descent. Its rays played and bounced against the antenna overhead and the neighboring buildings, suffusing everything in a warm, pinkish glow.

My mind raced through ideas — maybe I could offer to walk Liv home? She lived on the far side of Loop, but I wouldn't mind the detour. Or maybe I could ask her to stay behind for a moment tonight?

Liv's hair fell in waves down her back and took on a golden sheen in the dying light, while the strands framing her face caught the light and exuded a rich, brown glow. My hand itched to reach out and tuck a loose strand behind her ear, but I held back.

My thoughts were pierced by a sudden shrill, digital chime. A message on Liv's comp.

As Liv shifted her body to retrieve the comp from the bag on her shoulder, part of the ledge supporting her weight crumbled before my eyes, falling into the depths of the City below.

My world slowed.

Liv's eyes widened in shock. Her O-shaped mouth seemed incapable of making a sound. Instinctively, I grabbed her arm with one hand, extending the other behind me, fumbling for something — anything — to hold on to. My hand connected with a pipe attached to the nearest generator. Praying that it would hold, I twisted my arm around it. With a colossal effort, I swung my leg over the railing and heaved Liv up behind me. She clung to me, her fingernails digging into my skin.

"Hold on!" I dragged her up several more inches, my knuckles white around her arm. Liv managed to secure her foot on what was left of the ledge, and suddenly I knew what we had to do.

"On three."

She nodded.

"One, two… three!"

Liv pushed off hard, using the ledge as a spring-board, sending the loose rubble flying downward. With one last heave, I pulled her up and over the railing, crashing into the generator and onto the floor of the roof.

We lay there for several minutes in a tangle, panting. I blinked the sweat out of my eyes and pushed my hair back off my forehead as Liv detached herself from me. Angry red half-moon marks peppered my arm where Liv's nails had been minutes before.

"You saved my life," Liv said, her lower lip trembling.

I slipped my hand into hers and squeezed. "Anything for you, pix." And I meant it.

"I'll never be able to thank you. What was I thinking, sitting on that ledge? Oh, Theo!" I felt her stifle a sob as she threw her arms around me.

"You'd do the same for me," I whispered.

She nodded, her head planted on my chest.

As we sat there, wrapped in each other's arms, the gravity of what had just happened hit me with full force. I could have lost Liv. I could have lost her, right here, on this roof, in an instant. I don't know what I would have done if I'd let go and seen her fall. Her light pink lips, frozen in shock. Her green eyes wide and marred with fear. Her hair and scarf whipped up above her like a flag in the breeze. I would never have been able to get that image out of my mind. Ever.

Liv looked up and locked her eyes on mine, her face

pale. "If I'd have fallen, at least I wouldn't have had to wait for you to…"

My chest tightened. Even on the brink of death, Liv was still thinking about me. I shook my head. "But I would have watched you die," I said quietly. "And I couldn't live with myself after that."

"But that's what I'll have to do — in just over a week." Liv's lower lip trembled again.

"We'll figure something out." I squeezed her shoulder. "We always do."

Liv cast her gaze downwards. "But not with this. Not with deathdays. They're just so… absolute, somehow."

"Are they, though?" I thought about Ian.

But before Liv had a chance to reply, a series of digital chimes cut through the air. The sound emanated from Liv's bag, which lay discarded by the generator. An incoming call this time.

Liv released me and fished the comp out of her bag. She bit her lip and furrowed her brow as she listened intently to the person on the other end. After a long moment, she clicked off her comp and stood up. "I need to go."

I scrambled to my feet. "Are you all right?"

"Yes." She hesitated. "No. It's Mom."

"Hey — she'll get her herbs today. She'll be okay. You've still got them, right?"

"Yes, they're here." She gestured to her bag. "Thanks, Theo."

"I'll walk you—" I began.

Liv shook her head. "I'll be quicker on my own."

"I'll at least come down the stairs with you."

"All right." She secured her comp in her bag and we began the arduous climb back down the dust-filled staircase in silence, my terror at what could have happened catching up with me. I held Liv's hand the whole way down, not taking my eyes off her.

At the base of the building, Liv gave me a long hug and disappeared into the long shadows cast by the setting sun, leaving me staring after her, a dry hollowness settling in the pit of my stomach.

SEVEN DAYS

I SKIPPED SCHOOL TODAY.

Seeing Ian was more important — I didn't see him yesterday like I'd promised. My stomach twisted at the thought. I didn't want to let him down.

I trekked south through the City, crossing the bridge in River Sector. Safety Patrols were unlikely to be prowling around this part of the City so early in the day — minimizing my chances of getting caught truanting and hauled back to school.

The sky, a miserable gray, hung low over the buildings, mimicking the thoughts enveloping my mind.

For one, I had a week left. The reality of the countdown weighed down on my chest, like a burden I could neither bear nor shake off.

And then, I hadn't told Liv how I felt about her yet. I

was hoping for an opening yesterday, but with everything that happened on the roof of that skyscraper, and with Liv's mom being unwell, it just didn't happen. And today I was kicking myself for it. I wasn't looking forward to Ian's expression when he found out I had chickened out yet again.

As I turned the corner, a large oblong metallic structure emerged before me. Its surface was rusted, but parts of it still reflected the abandoned city around me. They called it the Bean.

As I looked at it now, its surface dull in the pale light, my thoughts drifted back to when I was here last, with Liv, ticking off yet another item on our list — 'laugh at our reflections in the Bean'. It would have been the perfect spot to tell her too — for some inexplicable reason, she loved the old Bean. I grit my teeth, vowing to finally break my silence the next time I saw Liv. No matter how much effort it took to cajole it out of me, or what her reaction might be.

I walked under the Bean, brushing my hand lightly on its curved underbelly. My distorted reflection stared back at me. I was tall for my age, taller than Ralph even. My chestnut brown hair fell in waves over my eyes — I pushed it back absentmindedly. My eyes, which usually shone bright blue in the morning light, were darkened by the shadow cast by the structure I stood under.

With a jolt, I was reminded of my reflection in the mysterious glass dome at the Pier the other day. Had Ian figured out its purpose by now? Was he waiting for me at the Hideout at this very moment? I'd see him soon enough.

I took a step to emerge from under the Bean, but stopped short.

A dull, even thumping noise sounded from the other side.

I held my breath, my muscles tense.

"…the squatters from the Mart, I'm telling you, Johnson…"

My mouth went dry. Safety Patrols.

I crouched underneath the Bean, conscious of the numerous reflections it was casting. One look from the Safety Patrols in my direction would give me away.

I inched backwards, away from their voices.

Peeking out from my hiding place, I scanned the horizon. On my left stood the Pavilion — a huge metallic structure, built from a number of large, flat plates. Long steel arches protruded from it at strange angles. It looked like an abandoned spaceship that had crashed on one of its missions.

On my right, up ahead, two large stone rectangles faced each other — an ancient pair of statues. The top corner of the nearest one had crumbled, breaking their symmetry.

But the Safety Patrols were nowhere to be seen.

A small sigh escaped my lips.

"…raid the Mart this week."

I froze. The Patrols were still here.

Peering out around the Bean, I finally saw them. The eerie, metallic white of their uniforms shined like armor. The sleek, polished black exterior of their boots was as reflective as the Bean itself. From their belts hung gas masks and gleaming white guns.

I swallowed, but my mouth was still as dry as sandpaper. A few days ago, I thought the worst the Patrols could do was drag me back to school and make sure I got detention, but my run-in with the Patrols before my Ten Day Ceremony in the White Tower, Vi's hushed whispers of what happened to the boy in her sewing class yesterday, and the way the Patrol named Johnson was polishing his gun made me shudder and reassess.

I squinted and took a better look at him. I recognized him from somewhere… and then it hit me. It was the Patrol from the Ceremony, who was seconds away from giving the order to shoot me in the Atrium.

I withdrew into the center of the structure, my heart suddenly pounding. Johnson didn't seem like the type to be crossed. I couldn't get caught, especially today, when I was making my way to the Edge. It was dangerous, not to mention illegal, to go beyond the City's limits. And as much as I didn't want to be dismembered by the radiation-filled creatures from the Outside, I had to see Ian. What would the Patrols do if they found out where I was going? What would happen if they found out about the Hideout, about Ian? A sudden chill ran down my spine at the thought.

No. I wouldn't get caught.

I heard the Patrol's boots before I saw them. Several even thuds filled the morning air as they collided with the concrete, growing louder with each passing second.

The Patrols were headed straight toward the center of the Bean. Straight toward me.

HOLDING MY BREATH, I tiptoed as quietly as I could around the Bean, my back pressed into its cool exterior, and emerged into the open, assessing my options. Bits of debris and large pieces of rubble, most likely fallen from neighboring buildings, littered the concrete space around me.

My best bet was to get to the Pavilion and hide under one of the metallic planks while the Patrols were still prowling the area. The pounding of their boots beat in time with my heart.

I knew this territory well; I'd spent countless hours making my way to the Hideout and back, so I knew exactly which piece of rubble offered the most effective cover, when to pause, and when to run. I just had to time it well.

A loud thunk against metal, followed by a mirthless laugh, rang out. The Patrols were beneath the Bean. This was my chance.

I ran toward a large slab of concrete, jumping lightly over fallen debris. I crouched on all fours on its far side, dodging snapped wires and protruding pieces of pipe, rusted and broken. A remnant of one of the deserted skyscrapers towering above me.

With bated breath, I chanced a glance above the concrete stone — the Patrols were still nowhere to be seen. I was maybe thirty feet away from the Pavilion. I could probably cover it in one go — if I was lucky.

It was now or never.

Leaping out from behind the concrete, I sprinted toward the planks, not daring to look back, not daring to breathe, my heart hammering in my chest so loudly that it drowned out the thud of my shoes against the pavement.

Locking my gaze on a tiny opening in the planks,

measuring two feet in height at most, I dove in, skidding to a halt on my forearms.

I held my breath and lay completely still, unwilling to move a muscle or risk peering outside should one of the Patrols spot movement and decide to investigate. I strained my ears for a sound coming from the outside, but I couldn't hear anything over the ringing in my ears.

After several minutes, the adrenaline left my system, replaced by a painful sting under my right elbow. Twisting around a fraction, I smelled blood. I must have scraped the skin off on the way in.

I pushed myself to my feet with a considerable effort and took a few shaky steps forward, advancing deeper into the deserted, caved-in structure. As my eyes grew accustomed to the dim light, I saw nothing but a maze of fallen metal sheets, each one rusted and covered in a rectangular grid. Liv said there used to be a stage underneath, but the metallic plates had collapsed on all sides after decades of non-use and rusted over, making it impossible to tell where the stage used to be. The gaps leading back outside shrank with every step I took, and the pockets of air filling the tunnels were warm and stale, making it gradually harder to breathe. My breaths came in quick, shallow bursts and bile rose up in my throat as I glanced around the confined space.

I had to get out of here.

Beads of sweat formed on the nape of my neck. The walls seemed to be closing in on me, shrinking with every step, weighing down on me like a block of cinder. What wouldn't I give for a breath of fresh air, or the flutter of a gentle breeze on my face…

But I pushed onward.

Willing my heartbeat to slow, I stumbled through the maze, my hands pressing against the metal walls, desperately trying to find a way out. When I reached what I thought would be the final fallen plank, I gasped.

I hadn't arrived at the mouth of the tunnel at all. Somehow, I'd ended up in the heart of the complex.

Just as Liv had said, remnants of an ancient stage stretched against the opposite wall. Bits of old lighting structures were still strewn across the floor, and overturned chairs littered the space before me. The nearest one was missing a leg.

I took in the sight, my eyes wide.

Relics from the War. The GA must not have wanted to spend time, money or precious resources on clearing it up, especially as River Sector, which was so close to the Edge, usually sat neglected and empty.

I took a tentative step toward the stage. Glass crunched beneath my boots. No one must have been here in years…

A low hissing sound slashed through the silence. I

jumped, twisting around to face the source of the noise. But there was nothing there. I waited in silence, pushing my hair out of my eyes and straining my ears.

The Pavilion was eerily quiet again. Apart from my footstep's echoes still reverberating around the metal planks, all was still.

Then the sound came again, from the corner this time. *Don't be ridiculous, Theo. It's probably just a rat.* Still, I reached a hand into my jacket pocket, feeling for something I could use as a weapon. My face fell when I only pulled out my comp and a few of Mom's spare dried mint leaves.

Maybe I could throw some mint at the Patrols. That would make a good fight.

Another of those strange hissing sounds pierced the air. I whirled around, stuffing the leaves back into my pocket, my eyes darting to the Pavilion's shadowy corners. Still nothing.

I had to get out of here. Rat or Patrol, I wasn't taking any chances. My pace quickened.

To my right, a gap the size of a small bush materialized as I turned the corner. Rays of dim early afternoon light shone through, illuminating the grimy floor in bright streaks. It might just be big enough for me to crawl through. Holding my breath, I pushed through the narrow gap, my muscles straining and my jacket snagging against the jagged metal edges.

After a tense moment, the metal gave way, and I was sprawled out on the concrete outside in a heap of exhaustion and blood from my scrapes. I gulped down the outside air as if I'd never breathe again, panting. My hair clung to my forehead in sticky chunks, and drips of sweat rolled down my temples. Natural light hit my eyes and I blinked several times. It was extraordinarily bright after the dark din of the tunnels.

I peered back toward the Bean and studied the horizon for the pair of Patrols with narrowed eyes. There was no sign of them.

I scrambled to my feet. There was no time to lose — I had to get to Ian.

CONTINUING SOUTH, I looked behind me every few feet to make sure the coast was clear.

Wrapping my jacket tighter around me, I passed the remnants of a long-defunct fountain. I hurried onwards, finally approaching the Edge after several minutes. A few one-story, run-down houses peppered the outer border of the City like a patchwork quilt made of concrete and stone. Wires stuck out at odd angles from the nearest one. Most of these dwellings were empty — nobody wanted to live that close to the Edge.

A large concrete field stood between me and the Edge. Several derelict signs punctuated the otherwise empty space: 'Keep out', 'Danger', and of course, the trefoil that was commonly associated with high levels of radiation. I ignored the signs, as usual. The Patrols were said to protect us from whatever roamed the forest and the wastelands beyond the Edge — exposed to radiation, once benign animals had morphed into monstrous beasts that were just waiting to tear off human limbs. I'd heard the stories. I'd even seen a man without an arm once, who claimed it was bitten off by a creature with two heads and two sets of teeth. But I'd never really believed his tales — he must have had too much hallucinogenic herb tea. Besides, I'd been going beyond the Edge for years and I'd never seen anything out of the ordinary. Still, I shuddered and focused back on the crossing.

The tree line rose ahead, the forest's branches beckoning.

As I steeled myself for the crossing, an even clang of boots on concrete rang out in the otherwise still air. I froze. I now knew that this could only mean one thing.

Safety Patrols.

I sank back into the shadows of the nearest house, careful to avoid the low-hanging wires.

Straining my ears for the slightest sound, I waited with bated breath. I wiped my clammy palms on my pants, but it was no good. The stickiness permeated them and refused to give way.

I couldn't be caught now… not so close to the Edge. So close to Ian.

Lately, it had become increasingly dangerous to go into the woods, even without the threat of irradiated creatures lurking beyond the City's limits. Even a short year ago, seeing a Patrol in these parts was as rare as running into Chancellor Graves himself. It just didn't happen.

But now, I had to dodge Patrols every time I ventured into the forest. It was nothing short of a miracle that I hadn't been caught yet. I set my jaw. Today wouldn't be the first time.

I focused on the sounds of the concrete field. A light breeze ruffled several overgrown patches of weeds that had broken through the concrete — a reminder of their incessant resilience to the human hand. Bones were strewn among them. I'd always hoped they weren't human bones, but today, I wasn't so sure.

The ominous marching seemed to have ceased. I took a tentative step out of my hiding spot and peered around the corner, through a small crevice in the dilapidated building.

"Roger that. We're on our way."

An icy sensation spread through my body like a wave. The Patrols were still here. I held my breath, backtracked and pressed my body further back against the house, the stone cold beneath my thin blue-green jacket. The digits on my left wrist prickled.

"…at the Mart. Let's go."

The dull thud of their boots receded, but I stood motionless, not daring to move.

After a long moment, I braced myself and squinted through the crevice again, spotting the silhouettes of the Patrols receding in the distance. I let out a low sigh.

I was safe. For now.

When the Patrols had disappeared from view, I glanced left and right and steeled myself to make the perilous crossing toward the tree line. For those couple hundred yards, I would be completely exposed, with nowhere to hide.

Taking a deep breath, I pushed off against the ground and raced across the field, dodging the warning signs. Finally, I jumped through the bushes forming the forest frontline and took cover in the safety of the trees.

Panting, I wiped the sweat off my forehead, pushed my hair out of my eyes, and took in my surroundings.

The leaves above me were beginning to turn. Red, orange, and even purple melded with the vestiges of summer green. My lips quirked upward. Early Autumn was my favorite. It was still warm enough for a light jacket, but the air was crisp and clear in the early hours and the evenings. Small, misty clouds formed after a sharp exhale of breath.

I began my trek through the forest. Its thick branches offered comfort as they wrapped their protective arms around me, shielding me from whatever lay in wait beyond their perimeter.

It was on a day much like today when I first found it.

Laika and I had been strolling through the woods on one of our long walks, back when it was still safe enough to take her past the Edge. It had been a brilliant summer's day, with rays of sunlight streaming in through the gaps in the vivid green canopy. Birds sang in the branches and insects buzzed with life in the undergrowth.

Laika had just found an excellent stick and was trotting happily by my side, along the familiar path next to the fishing stream where Liv's dad used to take us as children before he died. It's been a while since I was last in the forest with either of them.

All of a sudden, Laika had frozen, her ears flat against her head, her tail pointed.

"What is it, girl?"

Laika had crouched down, her belly level with the

forest floor, her eyes trained on something I couldn't see between the thickets ahead.

Without warning, she had taken off, leaving me no choice but to sprint after her through the woods, in and out of patches of sunlight, my boots slipping and sliding in the sticky mud intermingled with twigs and fallen leaves. It was muddy here today too — my boots squelched with mud and the added crunch of old leaves as I hiked onwards.

Panting, I had finally caught up with Laika. She was sitting, tail wagging, in front of a thick, fallen tree trunk that must have yielded to the winds of the most recent storm. In her mouth, still wriggling, was a gray rabbit.

"Oh, Laika."

I hadn't realized that she was a hunting dog, or at least had the instincts of one.

As gently as I could, I had lifted the rabbit out of her mouth, and when she wasn't looking, set it free behind the fallen tree. The poor thing was terrified, but not hurt.

Then, I had glanced around at the unfamiliar trees surrounding me. The little fishing stream was nowhere to be seen. I'd swallowed hard, my heart beating a little faster than usual. But I had willed myself to stay calm. The stories about the irradiated beasts were just that — stories meant to deter kids from wandering in here and getting lost, or worse — accidentally finding their way into the precarious and empty badlands that lay beyond the forest.

I'd fastened Laika to her red leash to prevent her from running off again, and we'd trudged through the strange trees, searching for a way back into the City. An unease had gnawed at my chest — the sun had already been heading west. I had to get home before nightfall. Before the curfew.

After several minutes, the trees had thinned out and I'd stumbled upon an unfamiliar clearing. Pushing a stray branch with thickets of greenery out of the way, I found myself facing one of the most magnificent buildings I'd ever seen. Made up of hundreds of stones, it had stood, solid and ancient, in the center of a clearing. Vines and green trails of ivy twisted around the building's partially crumbling exterior, virtually obscuring it from view. The structure's rounded dome culminated in a pointed cupola, its tip just reaching the topmost branches of the sprawling canopy. It had been supported on either side by rounded stone archways and crumbling ruins of staircases, which too were overgrown with thickets of vegetation.

The building didn't just look like it was erected in the woods — it had *become* the woods. And I was standing on the precipice of a gated woodland wonderland.

I'd approached it with trepidation and stepped

through the undergrowth that covered what was formerly its front lawn. A mid-sized wall trailed along the building's far side.

My heartbeat quickened. My eyes had darted back to the direction I came from, in case Laika and I had to make a quick exit if someone was inside. I'd kept Laika close as I continued onward, my curiosity getting the better of me. What was an abandoned ruin doing in the middle of the forest so close to the outskirts of the Second City? I'd never seen anything this old in the GA. Ever. Even the dilapidated buildings in River and Loop were decades — if not centuries — younger than the building before me.

I'd reached the building's entrance, my heart thudding in my chest. The ornate iron door before me was adorned with faded gold vines that wound intricate patterns resembling an ancient tree with thick, intertwining branches, roots and leaves. Below the tree, a circular snake that appeared to be biting its own tail decorated the elegant door handles. I'd reached out a hand and traced the design — the metal was cool beneath my palm.

I blinked and smiled at the memory. I stood in exactly the same spot now. At the entrance to the Hideout.

PUSHING THE DOOR OPEN, I stepped inside into a high and hollow space. Through the decades, the woods had reached in and claimed the inside of the Hideout as their own. Overhead, patches of thick green vegetation obscured large chunks of the wall and ceiling. Branches weaved in and out of the topmost windows, their serpentine tendrils winding up through the cupola. Their cool, crisp scent filled my nostrils, triggering the memory of the first time I'd stepped into the forest with Liv and her dad all those years ago.

The dome I spotted from the outside surged upward, cascading down to meet striking floor-to-ceiling windows that spanned the length of the far wall. Tiny shards of multicolored glass were strewn around the makeshift campsite that Ian and I created for him shortly after I found the place. A sagging couch sat next to a thin mattress with a threadbare quilt strewn haphazardly on top. Next to it, a few branches perched against a low, rickety table.

Shutting the iron door behind me with a clang that rattled the spacious interior, I found Ian sitting on the floor, scraping at one of the long pieces of wood. He didn't so much as look up when I came in.

"A spear?"

"Fishing spear," he replied, smiling. "That little creek you showed me is excellent for all my fishing needs."

"You've got Liv's dad to thank for that."

"I would if I could," Ian said quietly. "I still can't believe the corrosion in the Lake and the river had somehow left the stream untouched."

I shrugged. "Maybe it's far enough away from the City that its pollution didn't spoil it."

"Maybe."

I grabbed a stick and a short knife from Ian's rather impressive collection strewn on the floor before him and began the slow process of carving it into something useable.

"What's with all these spears? Isn't one enough?"

"I like to have a few extra on hand, you know — in case one breaks."

I smiled to myself. Ian was thinking ahead, as usual. Thrusting my hand into my jacket pocket, I scooped up the dried mint leaves scattered inside. "Tea?"

Ian grinned and shook his head lightly. "You and your mint tea."

"It *is* good for you."

Ian held up his hands in mock protest. "I know, I know. Let's have some later, then."

We sat in silence for a while. The scraping of our

knives against the wood reverberated around the Hideout like an echo.

My thoughts swirled back to Liv. It had been two days since I'd seen Ian and I'd made exactly zero progress on that front — and saving her life somehow wasn't the same as kissing her. Two days is a big deal when the digits on your wrist never fail to remind you that you've only got seven of them left. My stomach plummeted and I nearly shaved the skin off my fingers with the grubby knife.

Seven days.

Seven.

A week.

I had to come clean to Ian… Maybe he could come up with a foolproof way to tell Liv how I felt. I swallowed hard. Before it was too late.

I took a deep breath and let the words tumble out in a current. "I haven't told—"

"I know."

My eyes widened. I opened my mouth, but no words came out. I closed it quickly again. Then I rearranged my features and tried again. "How did you—"

Ian's expression said it all. His head was cocked to one side and his lips pressed into a thin smile. "I could tell by the look on your face, buddy." He jabbed the hand holding his carving knife at the door. "When you walked in."

I nodded and turned back to the half-carved spear laying in my lap. I had forgotten just how good Ian was at reading people.

"Is that why you didn't show up yesterday?"

"Yeah. I'm sorry, man. I tried to tell her, it was just—"

"Hey, I get it. Girls can be intimidating sometimes." Ian grinned, and I punched his arm lightly.

I took a deep breath and launched into an explanation of what happened on the roof of the skyscraper yesterday.

Ian's eyes widened. "That's one hell of a story. Glad you're both all right. But next time you decide to climb a tall building" — Ian reached behind him and pulled something out from under one of the couch's cushions — "use this." He dropped the object in my lap.

I examined it, turning it around in my hands. It seemed to be a harness attached to a mechanical spool with a metal cord wrapped tightly around it. A grappling hook hung from one end of the cord.

"A spool and wire?"

Ian's eyes lit up mischievously. "A winch, actually. But yeah, something like that."

After a moment, Ian's smile faded. I could feel his

stare burning into me as I focused on my carving. "But really, come on, Theo. It's been months. Promise me you'll tell her tomorrow? Just spit it out, it's not hard. Repeat after me: 'hey — Liv — I — like — you'."

I burst out laughing — a true laugh from within that caused the muscles in my stomach to ache. Ian had this effect on me. A wave of gratitude washed over me as I took in the grinning form of my friend.

"All right. I promise."

"Good." Now it was Ian's turn to give my arm a light nudge. "Which reminds me. I have something of yours." He pulled a small glass object out of his pocket and handed it to me.

I started. I hadn't given the mysterious dome much thought since I entrusted Ian with it — Liv had taken up most of my time.

"What did you find out?"

Ian's smile faltered. "Not much. It lights up with red and orange markings when I'm around, just as it did on the Pier... but I can't seem to crack what it does, exactly." He creased his brow. "I thought it sensed light, but the markings appear at night too."

"Strange. Why would the GA want me to have a device without even telling me what it does? What's the use of that?"

Ian shrugged. "Not sure, buddy." He glanced at me. "Anyway, you need to have it. It's yours, after all."

I opened my mouth to tell him I don't want it, but instead, I held the dome for a few seconds, its weight pressing against my palm. It stared back at me, silent and unforgiving. Shaking my head, I dropped the device in my jacket pocket. I would try to figure out what it does later.

"Now, I need your help." Ian's tone shifted suddenly. It was now brisk, businesslike.

I raised an eyebrow.

"I have a theory about deathdays."

I hesitated. "What theory?"

A grin lit up Ian's face. "First, you help me, then I tell you."

Ian had a tendency of being cryptic like this. He crossed the space in a few brisk strides toward a heavy metal door nestled in the Hideout's wall that neither of us could open and unlocked a rickety cupboard we'd mended a few months ago. He pulled out a graying but sizable piece of cloth, a metal rod, a tiny bottle with a nozzle, and a larger glass bottle filled with clear liquid.

My brow creased as I assessed the objects. "Ian…"

He sighed, then nodded. "All right." Ian pulled up his left sleeve, his forearm bare. The afternoon light pouring in through the high windows bathed his golden-brown skin in a warm glow. His deathday was a pale gray, the numbers faded and only faintly visible.

The date emblazoned on his skin was exactly five years ago today.

"Your deathday? What about it?"

"Yeah. It's… not working anymore, so to speak. Or it never did." His voice was low. "I need to know why I'm alive and everyone else whose deathday has passed is not."

"But it's just a tattoo." I paused. "You don't mean…?"

"That I think the GA knows more than it lets on? Yeah, I do."

My mouth fell open.

"Think about it. No other species in the animal kingdom have these numbers. Why humans?" He looked me straight in the eye. "Why us?"

"I'm sure the GA would tell us if they knew something. They have scientists at the University and the White Tower Elite Academy studying them — surely you remember all those annoying Deathday Research Fund messages on our comps?"

"What if they're not telling us everything?"

I bit my lip, turning Ian's words over in my mind.

"The digits do change color depending on how close you are to your deathday…"

"Or after it." Ian held up his left wrist again.

"A simple tattoo couldn't do that."

"Precisely. So, are you in?"

I pushed my hair out of my eyes and allowed the question to hang in the air for a moment. Was Ian right? Was the GA hiding something?

I sighed.

"You know how important this is to me. To figure out what's going on with deathdays. My family…" Ian hesitated. "And maybe it would even help you save Liv."

I looked up sharply. "Save Liv?"

"Yeah. Her deathday's in a year, isn't it?"

"Half a year."

"That's plenty of time." He squeezed my arm. "Will you help me?"

I hadn't thought of this before. If Ian and I could crack deathdays before the week is done, then maybe I could chronicle it to Liv… and potentially save her from sharing my fate. She could then join Ian here in the Hideout until they figured out how to deactivate death-days — if that would even be possible — on a mass scale. Maybe even get rid of them for good.

And maybe, just maybe, if we were quick enough, I could also bypass my own deathday…

I shook my head. Fantasy.

Ian was the only known citizen of the GA who had survived past his deathday. Why did I think that just because he did, we all could?

But Ian's expectant expression said it all. "Ok, what do you want me to do?"

Ian's eyes lit up as he began rummaging among the items he took out of the cupboard. He handed the cloth and the rod to me. I took the objects from him, still not understanding what he wanted me to do.

"What's in the bottle?" I eyed it suspiciously. It couldn't be water. Water didn't make that distinctive squelching sound as it hit the side of the glass.

Ian unscrewed the top and poured a little of the liquid over his carving knife. Then, as if thinking better of it, he took a swig, his face contorted. "Alcohol." He avoided my gaze.

Alcohol? What did Ian need alcohol for? And how did he even get hold of a whole bottle? It was so rare these days — even illegal in certain sectors.

"Ian, what's going on?"

"You mom's a nurse, right?"

"Yeah…"

"So you know how to make a tourniquet?"

"A what?"

"Better learn fast then."

Ian pushed the spare bit of cloth in his mouth and bit down hard. Gripping the knife tightly in his right hand, he clenched his left one into a fist, his veins purple and bulging.

With one smooth motion, he brought the knife down hard and slashed his wrist open, right along the glimmering outline of his deathday.

Time slowed.

Dark red blood gushed from the wound, spilling onto the floor in an incessant flow, staining it crimson. The shards of glass around us twinkled with Ian's blood, reflecting the light streaming in from the high windows. An image flashed through my mind, making me light-headed: Ian's lifeless body, cold and pale, bathed in a pool of his own blood, his eyes open, but unseeing.

"Ian! What the hell are you doing?"

"Testing — my — theory." Ian let out a soft groan, his words stifled by the cloth in his mouth. Tears gathered in the corners of his eyes, but he blinked them away, his expression stony.

"What? Stop it — you could bleed out." My voice cracked.

"Something — under — the deathday."

And then it hit me. Ian was looking for something. For proof of what? That the GA was hiding something about deathdays? Would he find it in his wrist?

I wanted to tear my eyes away, but I couldn't. My best friend was bleeding to death, and he wanted me to watch.

Ian brought the knife down a second time, carving it into his skin, slicing at the numbers this way and that.

I couldn't see anything under the blood's violent flow. I didn't know exactly what Ian was looking for.

As the seconds passed, the realization dawned on me, my stomach plummeting to my knees, while Ian's knife slashed desperately at his wrist.

Whatever Ian was looking for... it wasn't there.

MY HEART POUNDED in my throat and my eyes searched Ian's for a sign that he was stopping the incessant carving of his own flesh, but he didn't seem to see me. He was still focused on the knife and his wrist, lost in his own world. His face, usually glowing, was eerily pale, even for him, and losing even more color by the minute.

I gripped the cloth and metal rod Ian had handed me so hard my knuckles had turned white. What did he ask me about? A tourniquet? In an instant, I understood. He wanted me to stem the steady stream of blood that had now pooled at our feet. He didn't want to die after all.

"Ian! Enough!" I jumped into action, brandishing the sheet and metal rod like a shield against Ian's demons.

He took one look at his bloodied wrist, his knife arm stained wine red, his boots drowning in a pool of his own blood.

With a deep sigh of resignation, Ian gave me a small nod. His knife tumbled to the floor. His right hand, which had been so active a moment ago, now lay against his side, dull and limp.

I sprang to work, grabbing the spare cloth that Ian had used and instructing him to apply direct pressure to the wound, just like I'd seen Mom do. Then I began securing a makeshift tourniquet — or something resembling one — above Ian's wound, which was now a gaping hole in his wrist. My hands shook so much I had to clench my teeth to stop them.

I inserted the metal rod along the sheet, which was already a deep red, and twisted. I twisted and turned, over and over again, until the muscles in my arms ached, but that just spurred me to twist harder still.

After a while, my arms went numb. But that was better. I could keep twisting. I knew my friend's life depended on me applying this tourniquet correctly.

And then, I was done.

I secured the tourniquet and bent down to pick the bottle filled with alcohol off the ground. Flecks of crimson stained the transparent glass. Without a word, I met Ian's gaze.

He nodded once, removing the cloth from his wrist, his face contorted, his jaw clenched.

Holding my breath, I splashed the contents of the bottle over Ian's wound.

A bloodcurdling, piercing scream that shook me to the core rang out through the Hideout. And with it, a strange sense of relief washed over me. Ian's screams reverberated in my mind. But I knew the alcohol was working — it was cleansing his wound. I doused the laceration with more alcohol. He grabbed the bottle out of my hand and swallowed a mouthful, before handing it back to me.

After several minutes, Ian's screams died down to a soft moan.

A weight lifted from my chest.

We did it. We'd stemmed the seemingly ceaseless river of blood.

I rummaged in the cupboard for a clean sheet, tore it into strips and cleaned off the excess blood, like Mom had taught me when I was younger. Without blood spurting from the laceration, I could see just how deep Ian had sliced into his arm. It made me lightheaded, but I blinked and grounded myself with a few breaths.

I glanced around the Hideout, running through the supplies that we had hidden. What could I use to stitch up Ian's wound? It wouldn't heal by itself — not a cut this deep.

As if reading my mind, Ian jerked his head toward the tiny bottle with the nozzle he'd taken out of the cupboard earlier.

"Use the spray," he gasped.

I did as he said. Immediately, the spray created white foamy bubbles on contact with Ian's gaping wound, fusing his skin together right before my eyes.

"Crystalizing spray. It clots the blood and binds the skin so it can heal without stitches."

I stared at the tiny bottle still in my hand. "Crystalizing spray?"

"High grade." Ian shrugged. "Stole it off an old townie running a black market operation out of his shop in the outer City."

"How did you do that?"

"Easy. During a Safety Patrol inspection."

My mouth dropped open. "During a—"

"Safety Patrol inspection, yeah. How else do you think he would have kept his treasures unguarded in the back?" Ian smirked. "He was too preoccupied with the Patrols to notice."

I shook my head and smiled to myself. Only Ian

could pull something like that off. I got back to work, applying a makeshift bandage to Ian's wrist. It wasn't as neat as Mom would have made it, but it did the job. Then, I slowly removed the tourniquet.

"Can you move your fingers?" I asked, placing my palm on his hand. "And can you feel my touch?"

Ian grunted his assent.

Relief washed over me. "No nerve damage then."

Ian glanced up at me. "You do know a thing or two about medicine."

"Picked it up from Mom." I shrugged. "That's what happens when you grow up with patients on your dining room table who can't afford to go to the GA hospitals."

"Lucky for me, then."

We sat in silence for a few minutes, neither of us daring to break it. Ian's breaths were labored, and he winced when he moved his arm. I wanted to ask Ian what all that was about, what he thought he might find in his wrist, but I could see that the ease with which he told the story of swiping the crystalizing spray was gone. Tears glistened in his eyes, but I knew they were tears of anger. His flared nostrils and his right hand, balled into a fist, said it all.

"Ian?" I placed a gentle hand on his uninjured arm, which still dripped with his blood.

Ian took a deep breath and stared at his wrist.

"Are you all right?"

No answer.

I got up, washed the crimson off my hands with a bit of water from Ian's metal container, and passed it to Ian.

"No, thanks," he grunted.

"You need to drink. Do you think the wound will heal by itself?" I pushed the container into his right palm. "Drink."

Ian's lips were pressed into a thin line, but he accepted the water, sipping it slowly.

"Ian?" I tried again.

After a long moment, Ian finally spoke, his voice no more than a whisper. "I misjudged it. Misjudged everything. And I was so certain… I can't believe it."

I stayed silent, waiting with bated breath for him to continue.

He didn't.

"You misjudged what, exactly?"

Ian glanced up at me and held my gaze for a long moment. His face was still pale, but hints of red had returned to his cheeks as his circulation improved. For the first time, I noticed he had dark circles under his eyes. The corners of his mouth were turned downward.

"There's nothing there." He paused. "I thought that maybe… the GA wasn't telling us everything about deathdays. Maybe their technology was so advanced that they'd been able to find the deathday biomarker and tag it somehow... like through a small computer or a device or something... And that's why we could see the deathdays on our wrists and why they changed color... but..." His voice broke and he let out a long sigh.

I contemplated Ian's theory. It was a good one. Because he was right — why else would humans be the only living species with deathdays actually appearing on our wrists, when all species had the deathday biomarker? That's what we'd been taught at school.

But now, after we'd dug around in Ian's wrist and didn't find anything, we had proof it wasn't true. There was nothing hidden beneath the digits on our wrists. So that means the GA didn't tag the naturally occurring deathday biomarker... because they didn't have to. It was a force of nature after all. Maybe we shouldn't question the way things were.

I squeezed Ian's good arm. "I wish you'd told me this before you sliced your wrist open."

"I knew you wouldn't let me do it if I did."

"And for good reason. I'm not particularly keen on watching my best friend bleed to death."

"Sometimes we need to do what needs to be done."

"And you think this needed to be done?"

"Yeah, I did. But it's not enough."

"Not enough? Ian — you could have died. And I

don't know how I'd be able to live with myself these last few days if you did. It would haunt my every last waking moment." I kept my eyes trained on him. "And now, at least you won't waste any more time digging around in your wrist, and you can continue your hunt for information on deathdays without bleeding to death."

Ian permitted a small smile to pass his lips.

"I guess you're right. I was just so sure there was something there…"

"I know. We'll get there. We just need to keep going, right?" I wasn't sure who I was trying to convince — myself or Ian.

He grunted, staring at the floor. Then, he set his jaw. "But even without proof, I still think the GA is hiding something about deathdays."

We sat side by side and fell back into an uneasy silence. Ian was right — we didn't have any proof. A strange sensation churned in my stomach: relief that Ian was still here with me, intermingled with a darker undertone that coiled my stomach into a tight knot, gnawing at me from within. I couldn't pinpoint its source, but I knew deep down we were back to square one.

SIX DAYS

I DECIDED to go back to school today. I hadn't seen Liv in a whole day, and considering that mine were numbered, that was a lot. I spent the morning envisioning the worst possible scenarios of what could happen once I told her how I felt. She wouldn't like me back. What then? We'd just continue being friends for six days. No big deal.

Would it be awkward? Sure, probably. But the thought of dying without even telling her, without even scraping at the remote possibility that she would like me back? Not to mention my deep, dark, unspoken hope for just one taste of her lips... My throat clenched.

How would I be able to live with myself if I didn't even try? Oh, that's right — I wouldn't have to. I chuckled darkly.

As she approached, Liv pulled me out of my murky thoughts and planted me firmly in the present. She twisted her fingers around the thin, purple scarf that was wrapped around her neck. Her olive-green jacket hung loosely on her shoulders. It was a beautiful Autumn day, and she made it even more so.

It was only when she got closer that I noticed her hair, which usually cascaded in neat waves down her shoulders, was frizzy and slightly disheveled. Dark shadows lined her eyes. Liv gave me a small smile, but it seemed strained.

"Hey pix — you all right?" I asked, trying my best to hide the concern in my voice.

"Fine." She averted her gaze, rummaging in her bag for her comp and checking it nervously, before stuffing it back inside.

I raised my eyebrows; I knew her better than that. As gently as I could, I touched Liv's arm and pulled her closer. "What's up?" I lowered my voice to a whisper.

Liv sighed. "I was up all night helping Mom. She…"

My pulse quickened. I was dreading what I might hear next.

Liv must have seen the alarm on my face, because she shook her head. "No, she's here. She's just… in a lot of pain." Liv bit her lower lip.

"And the herbs?"

"They're helping, but it's not enough, Theo."

"I'll get more."

"No, I don't mean that—"

I pulled Liv into a hug, understanding dawning on me… her mom's illness was serious enough to take her life. "Liv, listen to me. You're one of the strongest people I know. You'd do anything to save your mom, and I admire you for it."

A faint flicker of crimson crept up Liv's neck, but she shrugged it off. "Of course I would. She's my mom."

I nodded, although a knot had formed in my stomach. Deaths outside of deathdays were not unheard of in the GA, but the Government never acknowledged them. Dad told me once they were more common than the GA let on, and the causes varied: illness — I'd seen plenty of that with Mom's patients — or starvation due to food shortages and the ever-diminishing food rations provided by the GA. Dissidents had been known to be found frozen to death in their homes during the unforgiving polar vortexes because the GA had switched off their electricity for weeks at a time. And citizens unlucky enough to cross the wrong Safety Patrols had paid with their life for disobeying orders, not carrying their comps on them, breaking curfew or being seen too close to the Edge. In the GA's eyes, death by deathday was the only honorable death.

I wondered briefly what it would be like to die even *before* my deathday. It could still happen. Someone — or something — could kill me within the next six days. I'd already had a brush with death on the roof of the skyscraper the other day, and so had Liv. Not to mention the Safety Patrols in the White Tower on my Ceremony Day. Gooseflesh rose up on my arms. It was best not to think about it. I didn't want to spiral down this additional deadly rabbit hole.

I squeezed Liv's arm. "Come on, let's get to history. You wouldn't want to miss your favorite lesson, would you?"

Liv pressed her lips together in a thin smile and followed me up the steps into the building. The bell rang just as we entered the classroom, joined by Vi and Ralph.

The plexiscreen fastened to the front wall informed us that in today's lesson we'd be going over what we'd learned about the end of the Great War. Liv took her usual place in the front row, and on a whim, I joined her, ignoring Emerson's, Shane's and Jessica's jeering from the back. Miraculous that they'd even made it to class.

"Well, well, what do we have here? Theodore Vanderveen, the star student?" Liv raised her eyebrows.

I flashed her a smile. "Nah, that's just you, pix."

Ms. Holloway stepped into the classroom, the metal door sliding shut behind her. "Settle down, everyone, settle down." She brushed her black, shoulder-length hair behind her ears. After the buzz of voices dwindled to a hushed murmur, she continued. "Today we'll be talking about the events that led to our city becoming the capital of the Grand Alliance of American States, after the fall of the First City in the Great War."

Ms. Holloway approached the plexiscreen, tapped out a few commands on its interface, and brought out a map of the old United States at the start of the 22nd century. So many cities had been lost to the flooding that followed the War that today's GA was virtually unrecognizable compared to the old U.S.

"Now, we all know that the United States was attacked in 2113. Who was the attacker?" The teacher asked, pacing in front of the plexiscreen.

Crista, a tall girl with an olive complexion and wavy dark hair, raised her hand. "The Asian Superpower."

"That's right. The Asian Superpower claimed their invasion was in line with Protocol VII of the International Peace and Security Covenant, but of course it wasn't." Ms. Holloway stopped her pacing and surveyed the class. "It was not a justified use of force. It was nothing more than meddling in our internal affairs and a threat to our national security."

"And sovereignty," Crista added.

"Precisely. The Asian Superpower wanted to exercise their influence over our great nation, and we had to fight to maintain our independence."

"So then the U.S. retaliated with nuclear missiles?" Ralph asked.

"It wasn't retaliation — it was self-defense. Our country was threatened. We sent the missiles to the Asian Superpower only after the diplomatic talks broke down and the Superpower invaded the First City."

"…who then sent their own nuclear warheads our way," Liv said, jotting down Ms. Holloway's every word on her comp, as usual.

Ms. Holloway nodded. "They sent fighter jets into the First City, which bombed the old Capitol building and the Washington Monument in Washington, D.C., two symbols of freedom and the American way of life. Then, the Asian Superpower blew up several nuclear power plants: including one outside Indianapolis, not too far from here, and one outside Baltimore, just outside D.C. Which meant…?"

"That the First City was completely destroyed in the War," Liv answered, sitting up straighter in her chair. "There's nothing left there today, just rubble and ruin."

"Correct. The First City got the worst of it, but we're still experiencing some side effects from the nuclear fallout in the Second City, even today."

"Like in the Lake," I muttered under my breath.

"What other climate cataclysms did we have to fight through, to get to where we are today?"

"There were the high radiation levels, of course — fallout compounds everywhere. Then there were severe power outages, earthquakes, floods, electrical storms, the lot," Crista recited, checking the e-textbook on her comp.

I shook my head. "Seems a bit excessive for us to effectively start the War and send nuclear missiles to the Asian Superpower. What sort of internal policy did the GA feel so strongly about that they were willing to risk wiping out the human race?" I asked, my head reeling with the idea that the actions of the Government just over a hundred years ago could have spelled the end of Earth as we knew it.

"We didn't start the War — that was the Asian Super-power, as we'd just discussed." The teacher clicked her tongue in disapproval. "The Grand Alliance of American States didn't exist back then — it was the United States. It was only rechristened as the Grand Alliance in the Peace Pact after the conclusion of the War."

"But the policy—" I started.

"Oh, and Theo?"

I looked up at the teacher.

"We don't say the 'GA'."

I pressed my lips into a thin line and nodded once. *The Grand Alliance of American States* was a mouthful, but it was also the official name, and they didn't like us using anything else. Dad made a point of correcting me at home too, but I knew he only did it so I wouldn't get in trouble at school or with the Safety Patrols.

I leaned over toward Liv, cupping my hand around my mouth. "Do you know what that internal policy was?"

Liv bit her lip, checked her notes, then the e-textbook, and shook her head. "There's nothing in here about that. I'm sure it must have been important, though."

My skin prickled. Liv knew everything about our country's history, so if she didn't know the answer, something was up. I narrowed my eyes, following Ms. Holloway as she wandered through the room, meandering between the rows of desks and picking on unsuspecting students to answer her questions.

"Doesn't it bother you that Ms. Holloway won't tell us?"

"It must not be on our curriculum for this year, or something as simple as that. Why are you looking for conspiracy theories where there are none?"

"How can you be sure there aren't any?"

Liv didn't answer, she just shook her head and twisted around in her seat, her eyelashes fluttering as she watched Ms. Holloway with the intensity of a feline stalking its prey.

My thoughts turned to Ian. If there *was* some sort of conspiracy theory surrounding deathdays, he'd beaten it. He survived past his deathday, for five years at that. Whereas I only had six days left.

My throat clenched as I realized I didn't have a choice, conspiracy theory or not. I had to face death, and what came after it. If there was anything after it. A few of the older citizens — and there weren't that many — believed that we would be reunited with our loved ones after death. When I was younger, that had been a comforting thought — that the numbers on our wrists didn't necessarily spell the end. But now, with the end so close, I didn't know what to believe.

Deep down though, I had an inkling that together, Ian and Liv could get to the bottom of this, even when I wouldn't be around to help. I had to convince Ian to meet Liv. She would keep his secret. I knew she would. Then, at least they would have each other... They were both smart, resourceful and could keep a clear head under pressure. Liv could help Ian on his quest to understand deathdays, lending him a helping hand when I no longer could. But Ian would never agree — he wouldn't want Liv to risk her life like I was. We were so young when we met on the streets of the City, we didn't understand the dangers back then…

Still, I had to try.

"And what about Chicago?" Ms. Holloway's voice cut through my thoughts.

"It was rechristened too, as the Second City, and became the Capitol of the Grand Alliance," Ralph said, raising his hand as he did. "The old Willis Tower was destroyed in the bombings, and in its place, the Government constructed the White Tower, the tallest building in the country. It became the seat of the Grand Alliance's Government."

Ms. Holloway smiled. "We take great pride in that, and we thank our country by humbly serving it."

As Ms. Holloway continued her odyssey through the classroom, I glanced at Liv again, her hair falling on her shoulders like a chestnut waterfall. She was once again taking notes on her comp, flipping between the text editor and the e-textbook.

Maybe I should try to take some notes today too… I dug inside my jacket pocket, searching for my own comp. But all I pulled out were the mysterious glass dome and some loose dried mint leaves, leftovers from the tea we'd had with Ian the day before.

A suffocating panic welled in my chest. Where was

my comp? I thought I had it with me just yesterday — or did I? When was the last time I saw it? I definitely had it on my Ceremony Day. But after that? I never left the house without my comp — ever.

My heartbeat thrashed in my ears and my vision blurred at the thought of what could happen to me if I was caught without my comp. The image of Johnson polishing his white gun swam to the forefront of my mind. Now that I knew it wasn't here, I felt naked without it, like an immovable part of me was missing. A shiver ran down my spine, but I forced myself to push the feeling away. I'd take the backstreets home tonight. With a little luck, I'd slink through the City undetected.

I stole another peek at Liv, compelling myself to stop thinking about my missing comp. She was so focused on Ms. Holloway and the lesson that everything else was lost on her. Seeing her like this — so close to me, yet so far — I made my decision. A fierce determination settled in my heart, and nothing would make it waver. I knew what I had to do today.

As the bell rang, I jumped out of my seat and approached Liv. "Listen, pix… can I talk to you for a second?"

She smiled. My knees threatened to buckle beneath me, but I held fast.

"Sure. After school?"

"Yeah. Meet me by the old oak?"

Liv nodded, tucking a loose strand of her long hair behind her ear. "All right. I'll tell Vi and Ralph too."

My stomach sank. I had to think fast.

"Actually..." I paused, unsure how to continue. I wiped my clammy palms on my dark gray pants and sucked in a breath. "Actually, come alone. I've got something to tell you. It's important."

Liv was still smiling, but her expression changed slightly — a spark had lit up her eyes. "All right. Any hints?"

"None." I winked at her and turned to gather my belongings from my desk before leaving the classroom.

I could feel her eyes burning on the back of my head as I retreated. When I turned into the hallway, I chanced a glance back. She was still studying me, her head cocked to one side, wonder and curiosity in her eyes. I strode quickly down the corridor, careful not to let her see the color flushing my cheeks.

AS THE FINAL BELL RANG, I gathered my things and sprinted toward the school's large double doors and joined the crowds of students flooding out onto the front lawn.

The lonely patch of grass underneath the old oak was still empty. I breathed a sigh of relief — I would get there first, which would give me a few minutes to assess the situation and come up with a plan.

I sat down under the oak, fallen leaves crunching beneath me. Spending the remainder of the day's classes thinking about what I would say this afternoon yielded no results. Absolutely nothing came to mind. My words were garbled in my head, and any inkling of what I would finally say to Liv was quickly discarded. I figured that a strategy would come to me now, in what I liked to think of as 'last minute panic.'

A few students passed me under the oak, some of them jeering and hurling insults my way. Emerson, Shane and Jessica — the usual suspects. I ignored them; the last thing I needed now was another fight. Instead, I focused on what I was about to do.

The crowd thinned, and my heart thudded in my chest, blocking out all other sounds.

Finally, the double doors opened again, and there she was.

Liv.

But she wasn't alone. Vi and Ralph were next to her, flanking her like bodyguards.

My stomach sank to my knees. This is what I'd been dreading… How was I going to tell her how I felt about her now? I couldn't do it in front of them... I almost heard the gears turning in my head as I mulled this new development over.

Liv smiled, offered them both a quick hug and started toward me, simultaneously checking her comp and then stuffing it back in her bag. Vi and Ralph waved and hopped down the steps, starting their long walk home to the far side of Loop. Relief washed over me as I realized that I wouldn't, in fact, have an audience for this particular speech.

"Hey." My voice sounded high and breathless. I cleared my throat. "Hey, pix." I tried again, forcing myself to smile even though I was sure it looked more like a grimace. The dull thud of my heart had now graduated into an incessant pounding.

"Hey you." Liv smiled at me again. I couldn't tear my eyes away from her. The dark shadows underneath her eyes didn't detract from the brightness of her eyes, or the curve of her pink lips. Liv came in for a hug, and her sweet scent filled my nostrils. I was mesmerized by the kaleidoscope of color, scent and sound that surrounded her. I held on to her tight, wishing I never had to let go.

Too soon, Liv pulled away, her eyes wide and questioning. "So, what did you want to talk about?"

The corners of my lips tugged upward. Liv was not one to waste time on small talk. "Let's walk?"

We started on the path that wound its way around the school, moving away from the residential area of Loop Sector. The old playground behind the school was now just a flat slab of concrete, its gray surface punctured with cracks and fissures.

I perched on the edge of the small square sandbox — now filled with concrete — and leaned on my arm for support. I tried to be casual, but instead, I stumbled and almost fell backward into the hole. Color rose up in my cheeks. *Smooth, Theo.*

The sound of Liv's laughter filled the air, and I laughed too, feeling the tension ebb away from my body. Like Ian, Liv had this effect on me.

"Just watch, you'll be next, pix." I pulled her arm and gestured for her to join me.

"As if." She faced me, her expression expectant and brimming with curiosity that threatened to spill over at any second. "So. Theodore. What's so secret you can't tell Vi and Ralph?"

I ran my hand through my hair, pushing it out of my eyes. Even though I knew why I asked her out here, there were two immediate answers to that question.

One would be to tell her about Ian. But I couldn't do that, as much as I wanted to. I promised to keep his secret safe. My chest tightened, and I looked away for a moment, so that Liv couldn't see how I bit my cheek to prevent myself from spilling his secret.

The other answer… well. This is what I was here for. I breathed in, steadying myself, and opened my mouth, not sure what would come out.

"Tell me it's about your Ten Day Object," Liv breathed. "Did you finally figure out what it is? Have you got it with you?"

Liv caught me off guard, and I stumbled on my words. "Um, yeah, I do, actually." I stuck my hand in my jacket pocket and pulled out the glass dome, wiping it on my sleeve to get rid of the excess tea leaves. Showing her the dome would buy me some time while I tried to figure out what to say. "What do you reckon?"

Liv took the device from me and spun it around in her dainty hands, her expression thoughtful. "You said it lights up when you're around?"

I nodded and demonstrated how to get the red and orange markings to appear. Liv studied the markings and turned the dome around in her fingers again, applying pressure here and there. "I can't immediately tell what it does — if it does anything at all. I've never seen one before."

My heart sank. "So you think it's just a trinket?"

Biting her lip, Liv cocked her head to the side and

sighed. "Honestly, you said it was a glass dome, but I thought it'd be more than that."

"So did I." There weren't that many pretty trinkets in the Second City. Everything had a purpose. I couldn't shake the feeling that there was more to it than met the eye.

"It's got little grooves on its underside, but that could just be part of the design." Liv pointed to the underside of the dome. I narrowed my eyes and leaned in closer, acutely aware of Liv's presence and the warmth emanating from her. But she was right. The bottom of the object was peppered with small incisions that I hadn't paid much attention to before.

"Maybe you should ask your Dad," Liv suggested. "Devices like these are his bread and butter, no?"

I nodded, putting the dome back in my pocket. She was right, maybe Dad would know.

"Why didn't you want to show Vi and Ralph your Object? Maybe they'd have some other ideas about what it does."

"That's not what I wanted to talk to you about." I regretted the words as soon as they left my mouth.

"Oh? There's more?" Liv's tone was one of mock surprise.

My pulse quickened. I cast my gaze around the playground, looking for something to latch on to, playing for time — again.

"Pix, I…"

"Let me guess, it's about our list!"

My resolve faltered. It wasn't about our list.

Liv's round eyes were still trained on mine, unwavering. The pressure in my chest was unbearable. I was either going to tell her how I felt, or I wasn't.

I cleared my throat and tried again. "Remember when we were little?" I hadn't planned on going down this route, but maybe it would help.

Liv laughed, but made a face. "That's what you wanted to talk about? To reminisce about our childhoods? Why couldn't Vi and Ralph be here? I thought you wanted to tell me about some secret plan or mission or something…" There was a twinkle in her eye.

If you only knew. My thoughts swirled with a thousand possibilities, but I didn't dare break eye contact. It was as if by gazing into Liv's eyes, I could transmit Ian's secret to her telepathically. I imagined the weight that would be taken off my shoulders, the relief it would bring to finally share everything with my best friend.

But I circled back to the present and held my ground. "Yeah, we used to run around here, in this very playground, chasing each other with sticks." I waved my hand in the direction of the playground, toward a dark green set of metal rods that kids would swing on to get from one to the other, now peeling and rusted. "They got rid of the trees when they brought in the concrete, didn't they?"

"Yeah. It's a shame. I loved those trees. I love the forest, the green — all the life in there."

"I know you do. That's why you're the pixie!" I nudged her gently with my elbow.

"What does that make you then?"

"Supreme Forest Overlord, obviously."

Liv's clear laugh rang out across the playground.

"You don't go there anymore, do you? To the forest?" I asked. Maybe I could give her a hint about Ian.

Liv's eyes widened. "You mean past the Edge? No, we're not allowed to go there, you know that."

I shrugged. "Just thought you might want to add it to our list."

"So it *is* about the list! No, Theodore, I'm not going past the Edge with you. You've heard the stories about what's out there."

"What about when we went with your Dad, to that little creek he found in the woods…?"

"Yeah, well — you said it yourself — we were with Dad then. He would have protected us from anything." She paused, the corners of her mouth creasing downward. "I miss him." Her voice was barely a whisper.

Tentatively, I put my arm around her, hoping she

wouldn't notice my shaking hands. "I miss him too, pix. We all do. But you're family now, too."

She nodded, her eyes fixed on a crack in the concrete a few yards away. To my relief, she didn't flinch away from my touch. I took that as a good sign and gave her shoulder a gentle squeeze. "And we'll protect you from anything, too."

She spun around suddenly, her eyes narrowed. "Wait, have you been in the forest past the Edge recently?"

It was my turn to be taken aback. I thought about my promise to Ian, but I settled on telling the truth. I preferred it that way. "Yes, I have, actually."

"You have? Why haven't you told me?" She swatted my arm playfully, but I detected a hint of incredulity in her tone at being excluded from such an adventure.

"With Laika, you know…" My voice trailed off.

"Laika?"

"She needed the exercise, and I figured that she could protect me from… what's out there." If there was anything 'out there' at all. I'd been in the woods countless times with Ian, and neither of us had ever seen anything, especially not irradiated monsters.

Luckily, Liv called my bluff.

"*Laika*? The wondrous protector dog?" She shrieked with laugher, and I conceded, chuckling along with her.

We both knew that Laika would more likely lick one of those creatures to death than attack it.

"Ok, ok. I never believed those stories," I admitted, relief flooding through me that I could at least come clean about this.

"The Grand Alliance told us those stories. That's all they instructed our parents to tell us at bedtime when we were little — '*to steer clear of the baddies that live in the forest and the badlands beyond*', do you remember?"

I laughed, as Liv had perfectly recited a line from one of those tales. "That's precisely why I don't believe them. I don't believe everything authority tells me, you know." I paused, considering her, Ian's image swimming to the forefront of my mind. "Maybe you shouldn't either."

"That is *not* a good idea. The Grand Alliance knows what's best for us."

I shifted slightly on the edge of the sandbox. "Or so they say. You sound like Vi."

"Well, she does have a point."

I didn't reply, but I kept my eyes locked on Liv. We were facing each other now, our faces inches apart. I could clearly see her slender neck, pale in the afternoon light, the curve of her full lips… If I shifted, even very slightly, my mouth would brush against her cheek.

My heart pounded in my chest and blood rushed in

my ears as if someone had turned on a waterfall next to me.

But I took a deep breath, leaned in, and closed the distance between us.

LIV FROZE, her whole body tense.

I didn't know what to do. My lips were still pressed to hers, my heart hammering in my chest. It was as if we were suspended in time. I didn't dare move, didn't dare breathe.

After a few seconds, I felt the gentle push of her hands on my chest, and my stomach dropped several miles as she turned away, her cheeks red.

The Earth had shifted from beneath my feet. I opened my mouth, trying to come up with something to say. But I couldn't think of anything; my head was spinning too much with the implications of Liv's gesture.

Liv spoke first, breaking the terse silence between us. "I — I need a moment to process this — what this means."

All feeling faded from my body. My hands shook slightly and a tightness settled in my chest. It was as if someone had wrapped a rubber band around my heart and gripped it like a vise. I struggled to catch my breath.

My limbs turned numb, and my lips, which seconds ago were tingling with the softness of Liv's, were now dull and cold.

What I had interpreted as Liv being flirty, even earlier today, was just Liv being friendly. I was a fool.

"I— I just thought—"

"You thought what, Theo? That we can be friends for years and then, six days before you'll be gone forever, you can just come in and kiss me like it's the most normal thing in the world?"

I did a double-take, my eyes wide, my throat constricting. I heard the words Liv said, but I couldn't believe my ears, I couldn't believe what I was hearing. It was as if my worst nightmare had come true. Liv, my friend, my best friend, didn't feel the same way about me as I did about her. How had it come to this? I turned away from her, trying, although I was sure it was futile, to hide my hurt.

My mouth had turned dry, but I tried to swallow the lump that had formed in my throat. I stared at a fissure in the concrete, unable to look her in the eye. "I just thought that, well… maybe you liked me too."

"Liked you too? How was I supposed to know? You never told me!" She furrowed her brow, and there was a fiery spark in her voice, but I couldn't tell if it was anger or something else.

Once again, I was at a loss for words, so I just said the first thing that came to mind. "I've told you now."

"No, you haven't. You just kissed me now."

She got to her feet without looking at me. "I have to go."

And she was gone, leaving me on the sandbox edge. I stared after her, the ghost of a half-formed reply lingering on my parted lips.

FIVE DAYS

FOR A BLISSFUL SECOND after awakening from a fitful sleep in the early hours of the morning, I didn't remember neither Liv's rejection nor my impending deathday. But then the realizations cascaded down on me like a hailstorm. One after the other. I couldn't stay in bed. It was pointless — sleep wouldn't come.

Instead, I jumped out of bed and paced around my cramped room, playing back what happened with Liv on the playground. It's only been several hours since I saw her, but it already felt like forever. I skipped dinner tonight, unable to swallow more than a bite. My stomach had shrunk in on itself.

Now, in the middle of the night, I felt like I'd lost more than a chance for a relationship. I'd lost a friend. My best friend. And that grief left me empty, like a hollow space had been carved right into my heart. A void that could be filled by Liv, and Liv alone.

The keen sting of rejection boiled in my heart. Maybe I hadn't given her any indications that I liked her before? Was I that bad at communicating what I felt? Keeping it bottled up inside me and waiting till the last minute to tell her was not a good idea. I should have given her some subtle signs, some indications, so that all this wouldn't come as such a shock to her.

Well, I'd told her now, and there was nothing I could do about it. She didn't like me back. But Liv's words echoed in my mind, cutting through the silence of the night. *'No, you haven't. You just kissed me now.'*

I chewed the inside of my cheek. Liv was right. I didn't *tell* her — I *kissed* her. Is that what she was waiting for? Did she want me to pluck up the courage and actually *tell her* — word by word — how I've felt about her all this time?

Maybe. But it was a little late for that now. She'd pushed me away.

The headache in my temples and sinuses crushed me like a vise and my heart hitched in my chest. This wasn't real, this wasn't real, this wasn't real. Except it *was* real. Like a nightmare I couldn't wake up from, like a bad dream I couldn't shake off.

Everything that I'd been dreading, everything I'd been

terrified of deep down in my heart, everything I hoped would never come to pass... was here. Now. It was real, and I didn't know what to do with myself anymore. What purpose did I have now?

I sighed, pushing my hair out of my eyes. Balancing on the edge of my single bed, I stared at the cracks in the paneled floor. They curled and snaked their way toward the far wall, colliding and separating again, like tiny, dried up rivers on an ancient map. Laika stirred beside me, but didn't wake.

My stomach coiled into a tight knot. It hadn't crossed my mind that by telling Liv I liked her, I risked throwing away years of our easygoing friendship. The castle we had built together was now swaying at the foundations, threatening to collapse and turn to dust. If they hadn't already.

Pushing my hair out of my eyes, I thought back to all the times Liv and I had spent in the forest as kids, or the endless summer evenings where we'd roam through the deserted downtown, pretending there was no one in the world but us. Or the countless times we'd laugh at school, or when we'd tick off all the things from Liv's never-ending list. Despite what had happened yesterday, Liv was still my best friend. Her not having feelings for me didn't change that. It didn't erase the years of friendship we'd built. And if I could, together with Ian, find a way to figure out deathdays and save her… my last few days on Earth wouldn't be in vain.

I had to try.

And I would tell Ian as much.

I grabbed my worn brown boots from where I abandoned them earlier beside my bed. I needed my friend now, more than ever, when I've possibly lost another.

My eyes swept the surface of my flimsy chest of drawers, hunting for my comp to check the time. But it was nowhere to be seen.

And then I remembered.

The realization that I hadn't seen my comp for at least a day and a half took hold of me and refused to relent. A tightness that had nothing to do with Liv settled in my chest, suffocating me. I was about to travel across the City and through the woods to Hideout, to Ian. Without my comp, I'd have to be extra careful, but still there was a gnawing feeling in my stomach that I couldn't quite push away, no matter how hard I tried to ignore it. I took several deep breaths, as I always did when I felt the sudden rush of anxiety threaten to overpower me.

Inhale. Exhale. Inhale. Exhale.

After several moments, my heartbeat slowed, but the knot in my stomach refused to unclench.

I pulled back the curtain that hung limp over my tiny bedroom window. Once vibrant and radiant, especially when it caught the summer sun, it was now the color of faded sapphire. Judging by the pre-dawn light outside, curfew would soon be over.

Crossing the room, I grabbed the clean bandages I had prepared for Ian and thrust them in my jacket pocket. An image of his blood-soaked wrist flashed in my mind with a pang. I hoped it had healed well.

My eyes lingered on the glass dome lying motionless on my bedside table. After a moment's hesitation, I shrugged and tossed it in my pocket alongside the bandages.

I tiptoed toward the door, hoping not to wake Laika. But the sound of her wagging tail hitting the wall told me otherwise. She gazed up at me, her head tilted to one side, her eyes questioning.

It's been a while since I took her out beyond the Edge. I sighed. "All right, girl, come on."

She hopped off the bed in one fluid motion and followed me downstairs, the floorboards creaking beneath us.

I pulled the front door closed with a gentle click, careful not to wake my parents. I wanted them to sleep soundly through the night. Dad already had dark circles under his eyes these days, and Mom spent a lot of her time crying, but she would never let me see. Guilt coursed through my veins at the thought, but it was not up to me when I would die. They knew that. A hollowness rang through me at my helplessness. I wish I could do something to alleviate their pain, but in truth, there was nothing I *could* do.

Laika and I set off down the dark street in the residential area of Loop Sector, the dim, purple light on the eastern horizon turning steadily brighter. Dawn was approaching, and judging by the clarity of the sky and the crispness of the air, I could tell the morning would transition into a beautiful day. A light breeze tickled the back of my neck, but aside from that, all was still.

Walking through the deserted streets, I passed rows upon rows of streetlights. They were defunct, of course; no one had seen a working streetlight in decades. The GA shut off electricity in residential homes every night at 10 pm — and illuminating the street was seen as a waste of valuable resources.

Although curfew officially began at midnight, most citizens didn't venture out after dark, simply because the City was shrouded in a veil of darkness. The Safety Patrols made their usual rounds though, protecting the Sectors from nightly disturbances.

But now, it was bright enough for me to see the silhouettes of the ancient lampposts as I made my way south toward the Edge, Laika by my side, her red leash in my hand. By the time I reached the cover of the forest, the sun will have cleared the horizon and I'd be able to navigate the bramble with relative ease.

As I passed the Pavilion I had hidden in a few days ago, the metallic Bean glistening in the dawn light on my right, my thoughts drifted back to the caved-in stage. What had happened on that platform? Did former Chancellors deliver their speeches there? What else could it have possibly been used for?

But I didn't have time to give it any more thought, because I heard the unmistakable click of a gun's safety right behind me.

I FROZE.

The cool metal of the gun's muzzle pressed firmly against the back of my head. I knew it belonged to a Safety Patrol, but I didn't understand. Curfew was already over — it was too light to be before 5 am.

"Hands in the air and turn around slowly." A harsh voice sounded behind me.

I did as the Patrol ordered, still clutching Laika's leash. Her muscles tensed and her ears folded down onto her head.

As I turned, my gaze locked on the Safety Patrol, and my eyes widened in recognition. It was Johnson — the

Patrol in charge of checking my identity before my Ten Day Ceremony, and who I'd seen polishing his gun next to the Bean the other day. The areas surrounding the Pavilion must be within the remit of his regular duties.

His lips were pressed into a thin line beneath his cropped dark hair. A deep crease separated his eyebrows.

"Your comp." It was more an order than a request.

My muscles tensed and the skin on the back of my neck prickled. I slowly dug my hand into my pocket, but I knew it was futile. I glanced around, playing for time, as I made a show of searching for the comp in my other pocket. My hands shook, but I willed them to still, trying my best to ignore the gun pointed directly at my head.

"I — I — forgot it at home, Officer." The words came out in a harsh whisper. I bit my cheek, hoping that Johnson wouldn't see through my lie.

"That's a violation of the City's law in and of itself." Johnson's lips curved into a leery smile, revealing yellowing teeth.

I fought to keep my expression neutral. "I know. I'm sorry, Officer. I can go get it—"

"No need." He took a step toward me, gun still poised, and grabbed my left hand. Laika whined beside me.

"It's okay, girl."

"Silence."

I swallowed hard, keeping a firm grip on Laika's leash, as the Patrol jabbed my forefinger into a small black device. With a sudden jolt of pain, I realized it was the same scanner the Patrols used to verify my identity on my Ceremony Day. My finger throbbed, raw and red from the Patrols extracting two blood samples within five days. Specks of blood dotted the cracked asphalt as the scanner emitted a series of beeping noises.

"Theo Vanderveen. Correct?" Johnson's eyes lit up, as if in recognition. Did he remember me from the mishap on my Ceremony Day?

I nodded once, my eyes trained on Johnson. On his gun.

"Five days… ah, yes." he muttered under his breath, but his expression was as hard as ever. "Mr. Vanderveen, I'm going to ask you to hand over the stray."

My mouth fell open and a gasp escaped my lips. "What? Laika? She's not a stray." Stepping aside and letting him take Laika was the last thing I would do, but my stomach plummeted all the same.

"All dogs in the Second City are strays, young man. Now hand it over."

"She's not a stray." Warmth rose up in my cheeks. I tightened my grip on Laika, who moved closer to my leg, as if sensing danger.

"Hand it over."

"No. I have a special permit from the Head of the Department of Animal Control himself certifying that Laika isn't a stray."

"Is that so? Where is this permit?"

"I — I don't have it with me."

Johnson's gaze shifted from me to Laika and back again, his sneer ominous. "Just like your comp, eh? A likely story. Now, I'm going to ask you one last time, boy. Hand it over."

"No. And she's not an 'it', she's a she, and *she's* got a name!" I was shouting now, but I didn't care. White hot anger coursed through my body, my hands balled into fists. I didn't care that Johnson had a gun. I knew I was right. He'd lose his rank over this.

Johnson took a step toward me and the butt of his gun connected with my jaw. Spots appeared in the corners of my eyes, and the street swam before me.

"I sentence this stray to execution. Effective immediately. And as for you, you're coming with me." A gruff hand cinched the fabric of my jacket's rumpled collar. "You're under arrest for disobeying orders from the Head Safety Patrol."

Johnson clicked his safety again. But this time, he wasn't pointing it at me. He was pointing at Laika.

Without thinking, I lunged forward, shielding her body with my own.

A crack whipped through the morning air. A piercing pain shot through my upper left arm and ruby red blood spurted from my veins. A scream escaped my lips, and I dropped to my knees as my eyes clouded over. Laika whimpered behind me. A strange sense of relief washed over me — at least I knew she was alive.

"Move aside, boy." Johnson's voice was muffled, as if he was very far away, or underwater.

A boot collided with my chest, knocking the wind out of me. Momentarily disoriented, I recalled Ian's blood gushing in a stream from his wrist. I'd seen an awful lot of blood in the past forty-eight hours.

Suddenly remembering where I was, I looked up at Johnson. His arm held onto mine like a vise.

"No."

To my surprise, it wasn't my voice that uttered the word. It was Dad's.

"Dad…" I croaked.

"Hello, Johnson. Drop your weapon." Dad stepped forward, brandishing his official government ID, shaped like a small comp. "Reg Vanderveen, Head of the Department of Technology and Science."

"I know who you are, Reg," Johnson snarled, but the hand holding his gun didn't waver. "Just following orders."

"I said, drop your weapon." Dad lowered his voice. "We're not in school anymore, Alistair."

Johnson's eyes narrowed, but he stood his ground. "This filthy mutt is a stray. And this boy was protecting it, going directly against the laws of our City, as I'm sure you're well aware, Reg." Johnson bared his yellowing teeth again.

"I'm well aware of the laws of the City, having written a good few myself."

"Always the show off," Johnson spat. "Nothing's changed in twenty years. Lofty Reg, the fierce protector of a stupid boy and his mutt."

"That's my son and his dog you're talking about." Dad's voice was cold and low. His right hand inched to his holster, which I knew held a concealed gun. "If you don't drop your weapon, you will be stripped of your rank. Effective immediately. You've made it to Head Safety Patrol now, haven't you, Alistair?"

This seemed to have the desired effect on Johnson. His features contorted and his eyes flashed dangerously. But after a moment, his gun clattered to the ground with a dull thud as it connected with the asphalt.

"Good." Dad kicked the gun aside. He turned to me, slipping an arm around my back and supporting the majority of my weight. Laika curled around Dad's leg, sensing his protective warmth. "I happen to have the dog permit my son mentioned. But," he faced Johnson again, "I will not show it to a disgrace of a Safety Patrol who threatened my son. If anyone asks, tell them Vanderveen sent you away."

"Like hell I will," Johnson growled, his nostrils flared. "This isn't the end — you'll pay for this. You mark my words." He took one look at his gun but didn't move to pick it up. He then spat on the ground, turned on his heel and retreated into the dawn light.

"Dad…" I gasped, searching for air, unable to coax it into my lungs. My arm felt as if it had torn away from my body, my muscles screaming in protest at the fire that had ignited in my bicep. I vaguely registered the unceasing river of red that flowed from the epicenter of the pain onto the street below. The sight made me light-headed and nauseous.

"Theo, it's okay. Here—" Dad grabbed hold of Laika's leash, prying my fingers open as he did so. My grip on her was so tight that my knuckles had turned white.

With my good arm under Dad's shoulder, we started back home, Laika trotting in our wake.

A million thoughts swirled through my mind, each one racing past the next. Laika, oh Laika, and Dad… Dad had saved Laika… twice… The street swam before me, sprinkled with spots of red. I couldn't think clearly. I was losing a lot of blood.

"What are you doing here?" That was the first thought that came out of my mouth.

"Rescuing you, of course." He chuckled darkly. "Let's not talk here. Save it for when we get home."

I nodded, but Dad was focused on our surroundings. His eyes darted to dark alleyways still shrouded in shadow, despite the rising sun. Together, we trudged on, limping through the deserted streets.

By the time we reached the front door of our apartment building, people were stirring and starting the day. Shopkeepers opened their blinds and beat the dust out of their rugs.

Dad pushed the door open with his free hand and we started the arduous climb up the five stories to our apartment — the elevator hadn't worked in decades. Dad muttered encouraging words to me every few steps. My panting and groans filled the stairwell, sweat beads forming thick and hot on the back of my neck. My legs burned, while my left arm seemed to have lost all feeling. I glanced down at it. I couldn't see anything but a stain of crimson. Bile rose to my throat and refused to come down.

Mom met us at the door and caught me in her arms before I collapsed onto the floor. She took one look at my arm and her face turned ashen. Her eyes, normally bright brown, were gaunt in the morning light.

Inside, Laika whimpered and lay down on the thread-bare rug in our cramped living room.

Dad helped me onto the musty couch as Mom rushed to the cupboards to retrieve her medical kit. She always had the necessities in stock, even if they were meager. A packet of medicinal herbs as my Ten Day Object would have been useful right now…

"What happened, darling?" Mom creased her brow and tore my left sleeve away from the gaping wound, examining it.

I flinched, and stars erupted in my line of vision again. "They tried to kill Laika," I managed to say between gritted teeth, as the pulled-back cloth stung my arm. "Tried… shoot her."

"Oh, Theo." Mom's eyes glistened with tears, but she blinked them away. She turned to Dad. "Luckily, the bullet only grazed Theo's upper arm — the gash is deep, but I should be able to clean and patch it up quickly."

Dad handed Mom a clean set of bandages and filled her in on what happened with Johnson while she worked on my injury. The creases in her brow deepened the longer Dad talked.

"Johnson? That awful kid from school? I can't believe this…" She poured a bit of rubbing alcohol on my injury and cleaned my wound as I grit my teeth and fought back tears of my own.

I thought back to Ian and the pain he must have felt only two short days ago. How was his wound healing? I never got to deliver the clean bandages… Now we would have complementary scars on our arms. This one thought emerged through the haze and solidified in my mind. It comforted me somehow.

My arm was still bleeding, staining the rug crimson. Pain lashed through me in waves, throbbing as if it had a heart of its own. I forced it down, folding it back inside me, but it was no use. It refused to be quelled, bouncing back at once and doubling in strength. I couldn't think straight.

I fought to stay conscious, to be lucid while Mom patched me up. A rush of warmth passed through me as I studied her face, her kind features creased with worry.

"Lie down." Mom pushed my hair, damp with sweat, off my forehead and planted a gentle kiss. "You need to rest."

I did as Mom said. Laika jumped on the couch and curled up next to me, as Mom kissed me on the forehead once more. "You could have died! I wouldn't have been able to bear it, to have these last five days with you taken away from me like that."

"Laika could have died too," I mumbled, as I resisted the oblivion that dragged me under.

"I know. And you care about her more than you care

about yourself." Mom stroked my cheek. "That's very brave."

"She's everything to me."

The last thing I remember before the tendrils of darkness dragged me into their depths was Laika's warm body pressed next to mine. I smiled and gave into sweet nothingness.

I woke up with Laika still beside me, her belly rising and falling in time with her even breathing. Mom had put a patchwork blanket around us both. The sun was already high in the sky, just visible behind the assortment of residential skyscrapers outside the window. I cuddled up to Laika, heat emanating from beneath her black and white coat. She stirred, looking up at me with dark, sleepy eyes.

I pushed myself to sit up on the couch, but my left arm gave way immediately, followed by a tidal wave of pain and nausea as the nerves in my arm exploded. I had nearly forgotten about my gaping injury.

But now it all came crashing back at once.

Johnson's leery grin, the sound of the gun going off in the morning air, Laika's whimpers, the white hot pain…

How could I have let this happen? How could I have been so foolish? My left arm stung, reminding me with each throb of how reckless I'd been today. Liv's rejection must have done me in. It'd taken over my entire existence and consciousness so fully that I wasn't able to think rationally about the dangers of sneaking out of the City, beyond the Edge, without my comp.

Still, deathdays wouldn't wait — neither mine nor Liv's. I was wasting my limited time in bed, sleeping off the agony and drugged up on painkillers, instead of being with Ian and trying to get to the bottom of this.

I moved my arm gingerly, testing the waters. The force of a thousand daggers beat down on my wound — the pain almost blinded me. I let out a heavy sigh and felt my stomach sink. How was I going to save Liv now? It was going to be so much harder for me to try to find anything out about deathdays and ultimately save her with a bullet hole in my arm. Both Ian and I were wounded now… it wasn't looking good.

But as I played back this morning's events in my head… one thing consistently tugged for my attention. Dad. Dad had saved Laika. Saved me.

For the first time since the attack, I let relief wash over my body. Laika was alive, and she was safe. That's all that mattered. I breathed in her fur, so warm and comforting, and scratched her behind the ears, just where she liked it. She snuggled closer and laid her head on my lap.

Brushing her head with gentle strokes of my fingers, images from that fateful day a few years ago swam to the forefront of my mind...

Walking back home from school on a day just like any other, the sound of muffled whining had filled my ears. I had drawn closer — the sound had been coming from the alley next to our building, just behind the trash containers.

Curious, I had walked toward the sound and carefully moved a fallen container aside. There, trapped between it and the cracked brick wall, was a puppy so small that it could fit in the palm of my hand. I'd called her Laika.

The air had been cool and crisp, and she was shivering violently. Her whimpering had nearly broken my heart in two. I'd scooped her up and put her inside my jacket and zipped it up, sharing my body heat.

At home, Mom and I had nursed her back to health. She'd said that if I hadn't found her, she probably wouldn't have made it through the night, either due to starvation or the freezing temperatures. I'm not sure what happened to her mother or her littermates — I'd only ever found Laika. Dad then had a few conversations at work and got a permit for us to keep her.

I blinked, and I was back in our living room. I shivered, despite Laika's warmth emanating from beneath the patchwork blanket. It was cold for a September day.

Laika's head rested comfortably in my lap. I don't know what I would do without her. For all I knew, she was the only dog in the Second City that wasn't marked as a stray and killed on the spot. Johnson obviously saw to that... I'll never be able to thank Dad enough for saving her today.

Laika shifted slightly, and something around her neck caught the light. A silver metallic disk, perfectly round. Her pet tag. I ran my fingers over the smooth engraved lettering: 'Laika. If found, please return to Theo Vanderveen.'

I glanced up as Dad strode into the living room, setting a tray of food on the low table beside me.

"Eat. Drink. You need your strength."

I nodded and took several bites of the bread roll with butter without tasting it, followed by a bite of the red apple.

"Thank you." I swallowed hard. The bread could hardly pass my parched throat, so I washed it down with a swig of water. I let out a soft sigh — the water seemed to cleanse my body like a crisp mountain spring.

"Don't mention it, I only cut the apple." He laughed, but the smile didn't quite reach his eyes.

"For the food too — but I meant, you know... for earlier." I looked him in the eye. "For Laika."

Dad nodded, but said nothing. We sat in silence for a few minutes, broken only by Laika's even breathing.

My mind swirled with a burning question… it was on the tip of my tongue. Finally, unable to hold it in any longer, I blurted it out. "Dad, will you… take care of her, after…?" I couldn't bring myself to finish.

Dad gripped my uninjured arm and lowered himself next to me. Our eyes were level, our faces inches apart. "Of course." He squeezed my arm, offered me a brave smile and pulled me in for a hug, careful not to touch my wound. When he next spoke, his words were soft, whispered like a secret. "Do not fear death, Theo. For in death, our next journey begins."

My vision clouded over, but I blinked furiously to clear the moisture. A heaviness weighed on my chest.

I knew what he was thinking. Because we were both thinking the same thing.

Five days.

AFTER DINNER, Mom changed my bandages. The ceaseless flow of blood from my wound had finally subsided. In between doses of painkillers, I could almost pretend that nothing out of the ordinary had happened that morning.

Dad sat with me at the dinner table, a sudden seriousness in his expression.

"Everything ok, Dad?"

He shifted in his seat, as if weighing his words. Mom passed around mugs of her signature mint tea and joined us at the table. My eyes widened as I stared into my mug. Fresh mint leaves? How on Earth did Mom get *fresh* mint leaves?

"Drink," she instructed, and I did. The warmth of the peppermint liquid filled my throat and traveled down to my stomach, heating me from within.

"Have you had a chance to look at your… Object?" Dad asked, sipping his tea and shifting his weight again.

With everything that had happened with Laika, I nearly forgot about the mysterious glass dome. But now that Dad mentioned it… maybe he could help solve the mystery.

I nodded. "Yeah, but I don't know what it is or what it does." I walked over to the coat hook next to our front door and pulled the dome out of my jacket pocket. I considered what could have happened if Johnson got his hands on the Object. Nothing good, I expect. Tension left my body as I rejoined my parents at the table, Laika's tail wagging next to me.

A sudden thought struck me. "Dad, is it normal for General Horatio to officiate the Ten Day Ceremony?"

Dad froze, his mug suspended halfway between the table and his mouth. "What did you say?" He asked, his voice low.

I recounted what had happened at the entrance to the Tower when the Patrols had failed to verify my identity through the comp, about the blood scan, and finally about how General Horatio was my Ceremony Master.

Dad listened intently, his expression grave. "I see."

"What's it mean?"

Dad offered no response. Instead, he asked, "Where's your Object, then?"

I set the dome in front of my parents. "I've only managed to make red and orange markings, resembling waves, appear on its surface. But that's all." I paused. "Actually, I couldn't even do that. It was my friend who managed it."

"Which friend? Was it Liv?" A small smile played on Mom's lips.

My breath caught. An ache not unlike my bullet wound slashed through my chest. I didn't realize it would be this painful to think about Liv.

"No, not Liv." My voice was so quiet, Mom and Dad had to lean in to hear me. I saw them give each other a knowing look out of the corner of my eye. Did they know how I felt about her? Was it that obvious? Who else knew? Not Liv herself, at least that much I had established… My cheeks reddened, but I cleared my throat. "Ian."

"Ian? I don't think you've told us about him before." Mom put her hand over mine.

"He's one of my best friends."

"Well, tell Ian that he's welcome here anytime, ok?" Mom always knew what to say. I smiled at her, grateful that she didn't ask any more questions.

"May I?" Dad pointed to the dome, lying as still as ever. I nodded once. "You turn this switch and set it on a flat surface. Then you place your palm over it. If you don't turn the switch, the heat sensor will still light up though — a little something extra for the design." He took in his hands, turned it around, pressed a tiny groove on its base that I hadn't noticed before, and set it back down on the table.

At first, nothing happened.

After a moment, red and orange markings appeared on its black surface. But they were different from the ones that Ian had been able to produce. They were brighter, more vivid somehow. And there were far more of them. Upon closer inspection, they were also swaying faster than before.

Dad positioned his open palm directly over the dome. Streaks of white light streamed out, scanning the surface of his hand. It beeped, and as Dad took his hand away, a 3D hologram appeared where his hand had been moments before.

I leaned in closer in my seat, my eyes wide. It was a perfect 3D rendering of some sort of indoor space. I studied it for a moment, taking in the thin lines created by the holo. I've never seen one before.

And then it hit me. It was a rendering of an apartment. But not just any apartment. Our apartment.

My mouth fell open as I stared at the map.

Dad pinched his fingers together near the holo and then moved them outward in one quick motion. The image zoomed in. There, in one of the rooms, were three tiny red and orange specks. I narrowed my eyes, squinting. They almost looked like…

"Us," I breathed.

Dad nodded. "In our apartment, yes." He glanced from Mom to me. "It's a heat sensor."

"How do you know?" How could Dad possibly know ahead of time what my Ten Day Object was? He even knew how to work it too. I knew that Dad was a high-ranking GA official, but… "Hang on…"

Despite his earlier seriousness, Dad was smiling now, too.

"You invented it? At work?"

Dad's smile broadened into a grin. "I worked on it,

yes. I wanted to share it with you, so you could… get a glimpse into what I do every day."

"But that's not allowed, right? You're sworn not to reveal what you're working on to anyone."

"That's true too. But there's nothing that said I couldn't submit the heat sensor to the Board for consideration for your Ten Day Object."

My eyes widened like full moons. "And they agreed?"

"With some persuading from your father, but yes, they did." Mom's eyes burned bright, her chin held high.

"It was the only way I could share it with you." Dad pushed the heat sensor toward me. "And…" He paused. "I thought it may prove useful one of these days."

"One of these days? Dad, I've got" — I swallowed hard — "five left, you know that…"

A chilling silence swept the room. Goosebumps rose up on my arms, despite the flickering candles and the hot steam emanating from the mint tea before me.

I took a deep breath and asked the question that had been on my mind since Ian cut his wrist open the other day.

"Dad… deathdays… where do they come from? Do they have something to do with the deathday biomarker?"

Dad remained silent, a stony expression on his face.

I tried again. "Can you… is it possible… to survive past your deathday?"

Dad glanced at me sharply. "Theo, why are you asking me this? Do you know someone like that?" There was a note of urgency in his voice.

"I — I—" I faltered, unsure whether I should tell Dad about Ian, when I swore to never reveal his secret.

"The Grand Alliance is very… particular on the information it holds on deathdays."

"They're studying them though, right? Trying to understand the deathday biomarker? At the Elite White Tower Academy, and the University?" Those constant video messages popping up on our comps asking for donations to the Deathday Research Fund couldn't be for nothing.

Dad hesitated. "Yes… and no. But there is a governmental department overseeing deathdays. The unit is not far from my office, actually. On the same floor."

My mouth dropped open. "There's a Deathday Department in the White Tower?"

Dad nodded. "Who else do you think oversees the Board awarding Ten Day Objects? Who helps citizens prepare for their deathdays? The Board is part of the Department."

"They don't teach us that at school."

Dad's expression darkened. "There's a lot they don't teach you at school, Theo."

"What else don't they tell us? What else do you know?"

Dad exchanged a surreptitious glance with Mom, who was chewing the inside of her cheek, but I pretended not to notice. He inclined his head toward me. When he spoke next, I had to strain my ears to hear him — his voice was no louder than a whisper.

"Listen, son." He placed a hand on mine, and on my other side, Mom did the same. "Between you and me, there are bigger things at work here. I wish I could tell you more, but it's too dangerous. Even for you." He paused and looked me straight in the eye. "Especially for you."

"But, Dad—"

"No. I can't tell you more about that. But I will tell you this. As with all devices, pay special attention to the grooves and markings on the heat sensor. They're often more than just a design feature." Dad paused. "Take it and… use it well."

"What bigger things? Who's doing them?" My heart pounded in my chest. What did Dad know? There's more to this than Dad was letting on, and I had to find out what it was.

"Theo." There was a note of warning in his voice that took me aback.

I glanced to Mom, a silent plea in my eyes. Hers were wide, but she shook her head imperceptibly.

My stomach clenched, and I steeled myself, fighting the sudden onset of heaviness in my chest. It was no use. I knew my parents and how stubborn they could be.

Instead, I nodded and retreated to my bedroom, my shoulders slumped, Laika trailing behind me.

My mind whirred with a thousand questions. What bigger things were at work? Why couldn't Dad tell me?

And why did it matter, since my deathday was approaching like a freight train, huge and unstoppable?

And what was that Dad said at the end, about the heat sensor — 'use it well'?

Use it well to do *what*?

FOUR DAYS

I HOBBLED to my bed and plopped down on it, Laika at my heel, my mind still reeling.

It was already past midnight. My muscles grew heavy, coaxing me to give into sleep's sweet oblivion, but my mind was alert. I clutched the heat sensor tightly, examining it by the flicker of candlelight.

Laika sniffed the sensor and licked it. The corners of my mouth quirked upward. "What do you reckon, girl?"

She put her head down between her paws and yawned, but I turned my attention back to the device. What had Dad said? To pay attention to the markings. I fiddled with the sensor, its dome-like surface smooth beneath my fingers. Then I flipped it over and, for the first time, inspected its underside in earnest. Its base was uneven, covered with grooves of varying lengths and depths, intersecting like a maze of tiny canyons.

One of the grooves on the side of the base caught my eye — it was small and round, and didn't converge with the others. I pursed my lips, examining it. It seemed out of place. Tentatively, I reached out and pressed down on the groove.

Nothing happened.

Glancing around the room, my eyes landed on a small nail that was only just hanging on to the floorboard in the corner. I grabbed it and thrust it into the groove.

A gasp escaped my lips as the device opened with a click. With trembling hands, I pulled the dome and the base apart. They were held together with a minuscule hinge, invisible from the outside. The inside of the dome was hollow and empty at first glance. But upon closer inspection, I noticed a design embossed directly beneath the crown of the dome. I traced my fingers over the cool metal and held it up to the light. At first, I thought it was a circle. But as the candlelight danced on the wall of the dome, I realized it was a snake, seemingly eating its own tail.

Strange… the GA's emblem was an eagle, not a snake. I shook my head. It didn't make any sense. What would a snake be doing inside my Ten Day Object? I crossed my bedroom and opened the door a crack. Maybe Dad was still awake and I could ask him? But our apartment was still and dark.

As I turned to close the door again, the flicker of a candle in the back of our apartment caught my eye. As quietly as I could, I tiptoed across the hallway and paused at the door of the kitchen, which was left ajar. Mom and Dad were speaking in low voices. I pulled at my collar, knowing that I should go back to my room, but my curiosity got the better of me.

"Horatio? At Theo's Ceremony? Reg, do you think—"

"No. They couldn't possibly know."

"But the—"

"Is safe. Hang on." Dad crossed the narrow kitchen and shut the door as I sank back into the shadows. My heart pounded in my chest. I put my ear to the door but couldn't hear any more.

I shuffled back inside my room, making a mental note to ask Dad what on Earth that was about. What was safe? He wouldn't be happy I overheard their conversation…

I stared at a couple of candles perched on my windowsill, the flames licking the stale air. What had changed since the last time I was here, some twenty hours earlier? Well, I had a hole in my arm, and the conversation with Dad and my discovery of the mysterious snake design had raised more questions than answers. And now this cryptic late-night conversation between my parents had complicated matters further… But Laika was still alive, and Liv still didn't like me.

Right. Liv.

Somehow, even with everything that happened today, my thoughts drifted back to her. Like chunks of wood thrown into the sea, always floating back to the rocky shore. Through the misty haze of painkillers and the throbbing in my arm that now accompanied the ceaseless and familiar pulsing on my wrist — she was always there.

I walked to the dresser, snapped the heat sensor shut and set it down. I'd think about how I was meant to *use it well* in the next five — no, four… how was it already four — days tomorrow, after I'd accomplished the haughty task of putting Liv firmly out of my mind. I'd always admired her from afar, her gentle smile, the bounce in her step, her kind, thoughtful eyes.

Not that any of that mattered anymore.

After a few seconds, I realized I had crossed the room and was staring at my own reflection in the old mirror propped up against the dresser. Thin cracks, much like the ones on the floorboards, carved through the glass. Dirt smudges streaked across its surface. I tried to wipe it clean a few weeks ago, but promptly gave up. The mirror's frame, made of heavy iron, serpentined into intricate patterns. In places, the metal had taken on the copper color of rust.

My blue eyes, now red-rimmed and puffy, stared back at me from under the waves of chestnut hair that fell into them. I pushed it out of my eyes. My narrow nose and square jaw looked gaunt in this light. I had lost a lot of blood today, after all. When I smiled, a dimple formed on my left cheek. But I wasn't smiling now.

Was I really the same Theo I'd always been? When my deathday was only a distant speck on the horizon of my life, I was more carefree, more relaxed. But that's understandable. Every situation is more relaxing if you don't have death rushing toward you like a rock hurled off a cliff, approaching the ground at breakneck speed.

But now, with Ian cutting his wrist open and nearly bleeding to death, me throwing myself in front of a gun and emerging with a gaping hole in my arm, and then the mysteries surrounding Dad's heat sensor, things were different.

And of course, there was Liv. I could never forget about her…

Something tugged at my weary mind, a feeling I couldn't shake.

'There are bigger things at work.' That's what Dad had said. It sounded awfully like… my eyes widened in the mirror. Like what Ian had been saying for months.

Was Ian's theory about the Government hiding something about deathdays right after all? Dad's tight-lipped silence certainly seemed to suggest so.

And my parents… usually so open and upfront, were now walking on eggshells, tiptoeing around the truth. They were keeping silent for a reason. But what reason?

I glanced at the heat sensor, lying perfectly still on the dresser. Dad wanted more than to just share the fruits of his labor as a GA official with me. But what wasn't he telling me?

Mirror Theo's expression changed. His mouth was a thin line, his jaw clenched. His hands balled into fists, and there was a quiet determination etched on his face.

I liked that Theo.

And in that moment, I became him. I would find out what it was Dad wouldn't tell me outright.

The lights were already off in the whole City, so I blew out my candle and clambered into bed. Tomorrow — or today — would be a new day, and I was going to use my new days well, while I still had them.

THE NEXT MORNING, I waited until Dad left for work and Mom went on her daily errands to pick up herbs before pulling on my worn boots. I shouldn't be leaving the house again so soon. My arm still throbbed and sent waves of pain cascading through my body whenever I moved it.

Mom changed the bandages on my wound this morning, and I watched her carefully so that I could help Ian change his later. She urged me to stay in bed today and let it heal. My reckless behavior made it that much harder for me to get to Ian and to find something out about deathdays, but I couldn't just sit around… the clock was ticking, and the green digits of my deathday were as unrelenting as ever.

It was dangerous for me to venture outside during school hours. Johnson could have recounted our little meeting to the other Safety Patrols in his unit. If he did, they would be on the lookout for a truant sixteen-year-old boy and his dog. And I still didn't have my comp… an icy shiver ran through my body at the thought. But they were risks I was willing to take. I had to find Ian and tell him what I knew.

I grabbed the heat sensor off my dresser and stuffed it in my jacket pocket, next to the clean bandages for Ian.

Laika yawned and plodded toward me, her paws beating against the floorboards, tongue out, tail wagging idly. I scratched her behind the ears.

"No Laika, you need to stay here today. Dad will take you out later."

She tilted her head and gazed up at me, but I shook my head. With one last look at her, I eased the door shut behind me. Climbing down the stairs, I paused every few seconds to listen for any sounds coming from the neighbors. The smell of vegetable broth wafted into the stairwell as I passed Mrs. Goodwin's second-floor apartment. A small smile curved my lips. I wondered what she was cooking today. Judging by the smell, it was likely one of her signature soups.

It was a bright, chilly morning; the crisp air sharp in my lungs. Summer was definitely over. I pulled my hood up over my head, shielding my face from the wind and any questioning stares of passerby, grateful for Autumn's biting chill. Despite being out in the open and an easy target for Safety Patrols, I let the air pass into my lungs and inhaled deeply.

If I was certain of one thing, it was that I wouldn't let a Safety Patrol near me today. I was on high alert. As soon as I spotted the white uniform and heard the familiar clank of their boots on the concrete, I slunk into a nearby alley.

There were definitely more Patrols than usual prowling around once I passed the Mart and crossed the red iron bridge into the abandoned part of River. Or was that just my imagination? I slipped through dank alleyways, shielding my nose from the smell of rot wafting out from overflowing garbage cans. I jumped over containers, fallen street lights and loose wires.

My pace quickened as I passed the Pavilion and the Bean, my neck and lower back warm with sweat.

The wound in my arm throbbed with every step I took. So did my wrist, but I'd learned to ignore it by now. The pulsing poison green digits were my constant companion. I dug into my jacket pocket and pulled out a vial of clear liquid, swallowing it in one go. That should take care of the pain, before the imminent onset of nausea. I couldn't afford not to make it to Ian's.

Reaching the concrete field separating me from the Edge, I pulled my hood tighter over my eyes and disappeared in the shadow of a crumbling building — my usual one, the one with the low-hanging wires. Its squat shape shielded me from onlookers, but the chasms in the concrete were large enough for me to peer through to the Edge. The trees loomed in the distance, swaying gently in the crisp breeze.

I held my breath, straining my ears for the familiar, even sound of boots on concrete.

But none came.

The coast was clear. Maybe the Patrols had been called back from the Edge to monitor the downtown Sectors after yesterday's incident with Laika? My stomach dropped. Or maybe they were looking for me... I pushed the thought out of my mind and braced myself for the crossing with a deep breath.

Lunging forward, I sprinted across the concrete. The Edge was just within reach... Jumping across the brambles, I skidded to a halt as my feet collided with the malleable forest floor. Panting, I doubled over, resting my good arm on my knee for support. I willed my heart to slow and my breaths to even.

After a moment, I crouched behind a sizable berry bush and peered through its thick leaves back toward the concrete field and the City beyond. There was no sign of the Patrols: no white uniforms, no thuds of their boots or snatches of conversation muttered into their com-link wrist communicators.

Here, under the cover of trees, the tension in my chest eased a little. I could breathe freely again. I was safe.

Well, relatively safe.

I wound through the woods, ducking under low-hanging branches, while thorny brambles scratched the inside of my palms. Images from the stories we'd been told as kids surfaced in my mind. Creatures — or whatever Liv was so convinced they were — supposedly roamed these woods. *And the badlands beyond.*

A smile tugged at my lips as I recalled Liv reciting those stories perfectly just the other day in the playground. But it vanished just as quickly as it had appeared though, when the memory of Liv walking away from me came crashing down like a tidal wave, impossible to contain. My chest tightened and my breath caught in my throat. It was a good thing I was on my own right now. I sped up, aching to feel the burn in my muscles during the long trek to the Hideout. What a shame it was, that thinking of Liv — one of my best friends — was so painful. But I clenched my jaw and pushed all thought of her aside, instead focusing on putting one foot in front of the other.

Fallen leaves crunched under my boots as I trekked on, my injured arm still throbbing despite the painkillers. The forest stretched south, where I was now, and west of the City — past the fields where the GA grew apples and potatoes. To the north, a wall ran along the border, heavily patrolled. And of course, the lake bubbled in the east, corrosive and deadly. Not many citizens entered the woods, and an even smaller minority had permission to venture outside the City's borders. The few who had traveled outside, to the other GA Cities, could be counted on the fingers of one hand — Chancellor Graves and several high-ranking GA officials. Most of the cities from the old United States had been claimed by floods, nuclear fallout, or desolation. Dad had been outside the Second City once, but he was sworn to secrecy and wouldn't tell me anything, not even after I'd begged him. Maybe I'd try again before my deathday… but after our conversation last night, I didn't count on much. Still, I had nothing to lose now, after all. The digits on my left wrist tingled, eerily on cue.

After another quarter of a mile, I arrived at the clearing and let the air out of my lungs in one long, slow breath. Ian was busy picking berries with one hand off a bush on the outskirts of the Hideout's clearing.

I gingerly brandished my injured arm as I approached. "Look, we're matching."

Ian scowled and eyed me up and down. "What happened to you?" The forgotten berries tumbled back to the ground as he dropped the purple-stained cloth he was using as a makeshift basket.

"Oh, nothing. I just got shot by a Safety Patrol trying to save Laika's life."

Ian's eyes widened. "You *what?*"

"I'm fine, promise. I'll live… for now." I laughed, in spite of myself.

Ian's tense muscles relaxed a fraction and he returned the chuckle. I recounted what happened the previous day with the Safety Patrols, Laika, and Dad rescuing us both. I also told him about Liv and her reaction when I kissed her. Ian just shook his head. I swallowed hard, ignoring the knot in my stomach, and changed the subject.

Ian started gathering the fallen berries, so I crouched

next to him and picked a few up from where they'd landed behind the bush.

"There's one more thing…"

Ian froze and cast me a sidelong glance, his eyebrows raised. "What's that?"

I told him about the heat sensor and the conversation with Dad. As I did, his eyes lit up, bright and round, like a child's. "Do you have it with you?"

"Course I do. That's why I came to see you." I pulled the heat sensor out of my jacket pocket and handed it to Ian. "Because it's time for us to do something. For *me* to do something. I'm tired of just sitting around, waiting for, you know — *it* — to happen."

Ian grinned, but his smile quickly faded, the corners of his mouth turned downward.

I frowned. "What's—"

Ian held up a hand, staring into the trees behind me, his jaw clenched, his eyes on high alert. "Did you hear that?"

"Hear wh—" I stopped short.

The distinct sound of a snapping twig reverberated in the forest air like a gunshot.

MY BREATH CAUGHT in my chest and bile rose to my throat.

Something — or someone — was here.

I willed my heartbeat to slow. It was probably just an animal.

But what if it wasn't? What if a Safety Patrol had followed me here? Had I been so lost in my own gloomy cascading thoughts, so wrapped up in what happened with Liv that I didn't notice I was being tailed? I swallowed hard. Could I have been so reckless?

Everything hinged on keeping the Hideout a secret. If they found Ian, they'd kill him. They'd kill me too, but I wasn't worried about that. I was worried about Ian, my parents… and Liv. What would happen to Dad? Would they think he had something to do with this? Would he lose his job? Would they… I couldn't bear to finish the thought. And Mom… And there was Ian's family too, his younger siblings… My chest tightened. Then there was Liv. Everyone knew she was one of my best friends. If they thought she had something to do with the Hideout… with all *this* — no, I couldn't let that happen.

I exchanged a glance with Ian. His expression mirrored mine: eyes wide, lips a thin line.

"Let's check it out?" I moved closer to Ian, keeping my voice low. It was better to know what we were up against.

He nodded, and circled around me, his footsteps light, taking cover behind a large oak, not unlike the one in front of the school. I hid behind the nearest elm, creeping around its solid trunk and peering into the thicket of trees beyond.

A gentle breeze ruffled the leaves on the branches overhead, and soft birdsong sounded in the distance. But there was no sign of life on the forest floor around us. Still, a lump had formed in my throat and the general sense of unease refused to let up.

Ian waved a silent hand toward me, and I joined him by the oak.

"The coast seems to be clear."

I nodded. "Let's hope it stays that way."

"Come on, let's get inside." Ian's eyes studied the trees again. "Before it — whatever it was — changes its mind."

BACK INSIDE THE HIDEOUT, Ian took care to lock the ornate door behind us.

"When's the last time you did that?"

Ian shook his head. "Not for a while. But from now on, we need to be vigilant when we travel to and from the Hideout. We don't know what — or who — saw us out there."

Or heard us. A thousand thoughts bubbled in my mind, and my stomach clenched at what could happen if someone found out about the Hideout, about Ian's deathday… about us.

When I couldn't hold it in any longer, I turned to Ian, choosing my words carefully.

"Do you think — if someone was out there — they heard what I said about the heat sensor? Or about the conversation with Dad?" I bit my lip. That worried me the most. It pointed straight back to Dad. And coupled with our conviction that the Government was hiding something about deathdays… I swallowed, but my mouth was as dry as sandpaper. It didn't look good. Dread filled every inch of my body in a steady, icy wave, and the tips of my fingers had gone numb.

"For all we know, it was an animal." Ian voiced the one comforting thought I dared to cling to. "A deer, maybe."

"Or one of those — creatures." I thought back to what Liv said again. Why did she keep resurfacing in my mind?

"Those are just stories."

"For once, I hope they're true." A dangerous creature in the woods meant that it wasn't a Safety Patrol in the woods.

Ian raised his eyebrows. "Don't you have a heat sensor? Let's see if there's anyone out there."

The heat sensor. Of course! I demonstrated how the device worked for Ian, who eyed the sensor with wonder and a slow smile budding on his lips. The 3D holo showed two red and orange specks in the Hideout. Thankfully — the area surrounding the building was clear. Whatever it was that had snapped the twig was gone, but the tense knot in my stomach refused to relent.

"I'm just worried, Ian. About what might happen to you if the Patrols found this place. And about my parents." I paused. "About Liv."

Ian crouched next to me by the small campfire in the middle of the Hideout. "I know. But didn't you say you wanted to do something? That you're tired of sitting around waiting for — *it* — to happen?" He jabbed the small stone he was holding toward my wrist, which throbbed steadily, as if in response. "Well, now's your chance."

I glanced at Ian, my jaw set, and my eyes glinting. "That's why I'm here."

My resolve was set in stone. It had been since late last night. I wouldn't let fears for my family and friends get in the way of making a difference before my deathday, saving the people I loved. My time to act was now, and I knew it.

Ian's lips curled upwards as he picked up another stone and struck the first to get a flame going. "So what did you have in mind?" The tips of the branches in the campfire began to smolder, and within moments, a small flame flared up. Ian coaxed it to life, using his hand as a fan.

"Something drastic." I shot Ian a look full of meaning. "I mean, drastic for me. With Liv feeling how she does, I'm the one that has nothing left to lose. But you, your family, my parents, Laika, and of course Liv, Vi, Ralph… You have everything to lose. And I'd die first before I let anything happen to you."

Ian stared at me, his expression unreadable, but his eyes were soft. The flames danced in the afternoon light streaming in from the high windows.

I sucked in a breath and continued. "But as for me… something's changed." I just couldn't put my finger on what 'something' was. All I knew is that I couldn't sit still anymore. I had become part of something bigger than myself. I could feel it in every lungful of air, in every word I uttered. In my every bone. Ian and I were both part of it, whether we liked it or not. And I was ready to dedicate the rest of my life to figuring out exactly what that was. "We have to do what we can with the limited time that was given to us. So here I am. Doing what I can."

"Theo, come on. Just because Liv doesn't like you in that way doesn't mean she doesn't care about you. Don't be stupid, all right? I'm not going to let you jump off the White Tower now or something."

I laughed, but the sound was hollow in my ears. Was Ian right? Was I only feeling so brash because of what happened with Liv? Did I want to prove something to her? But my last conversation with Dad swam to the forefront of my mind. He'd specifically given me the heat sensor and told me to use it well. *There are bigger things at work here.* There was more to this than just me feeling reckless as a side effect of Liv's rejection. Why couldn't Ian see that? "I want to do something for you. Be useful to your cause, while I still can."

"My cause?"

I paused, turning it over in my head. Ian surely understood that what we did — what I did — during the next few days could change everything. I needed him to know that I was on his team, willing to risk it all in pursuit of the truth about those tiny green digits that plagued us since the day we were born.

I looked Ian square in the eye. "I'm going to help you get a step closer to figuring out what deathdays are, how you've survived past yours, and how we can help others survive past theirs." I paused. "Or maybe even get rid of them altogether. Imagine…"

"Others?"

"Your family, and mine... and you know. Others." Liv.

"Liv?"

My cheeks burned. "Yeah. Liv."

Ian leaned over and squeezed my uninjured arm. "As I said, she still cares about you. Remember that."

I nodded, but said nothing, staring, unseeing, into the little flame. Somehow, my thoughts always returned to Liv. I couldn't ask her to like me, and I would never hold that against her. Although, I wasn't being completely honest with her either. She was my best friend, and yet I was holding things back from her... like where I went some afternoons after school. What I knew about death-days. What happened to Ian. I couldn't stand lying to her anymore. But those were not my secrets to tell. They were Ian's.

But maybe I could change that. Secrets were meant to be shared, after all.

After a moment, I spoke again. "Why don't we tell her?"

"What?"

"About you? About surviving after deathdays?" The words spilled out of me before I could stop them. "You could meet her, Liv, you'd like her. You two would be great friends. After, you know…" I swallowed, but didn't finish the sentence.

Ian sighed, and his eyes met mine. The hazel in them glowed golden in the firelight. "It's too dangerous, Theo. You have to understand. There's been a lot of unrest in the City lately. The people are getting restless, and the GA is keeping it quiet. You won't see it on the evening news on your comp."

"It's dangerous for me, too."

"I know, and I worry about you every day. And after what happened yesterday…"

I chewed the inside of my cheek. "Liv's smart. She's the best in the year, by a long shot. Especially at history. If you want someone that I could pass the torch to… keep the momentum going… it's Liv."

"I'd be putting her at risk — no, *you'd* be putting her at risk—"

"She would want to know. Trust me, Ian. I know her." I paused. "Besides, I… I don't want to leave you alone. Either of you, really. You could use some company when…"

Ian's expression softened and he squeezed my arm again. "I'm sorry." His voice was low. "But I'll look out for her, though. From a distance."

I shook my head. "That's not good enough, Ian. We need all the help we can get — all of us. And then my

Dad knows something, so you could always go to him too. Liv knows my family well, she could—"

"Theo. Stop, please." He looked me dead in the eye. "It's too dangerous for me to go to your parents. Especially since no one has ever seen me around there. People would ask questions." He sighed. "You know how they are."

I did know how they are. Neighbors betraying neighbors to the Safety Patrols for a bit of extra GA bills slipped under the table during the regular inspections. People prying on passerby, or even their own family and friends, just to report a bit of gossip in exchange for an extra ration of potatoes. It was hard to know whom to trust.

I trusted Ian, Liv, and my parents. No questions there. But I couldn't prevent Mrs. Goodwin, our neighbor, from going to the Patrols with something she'd seen or heard in our apartment building. Not that she would — Mrs. Goodwin wasn't the type to go running to the Patrols for anything. For all I knew, she hated them as much as I did. But I wasn't sure. No one ever was. And so I couldn't take any chances. Not with Dad's position in the GA…

I sighed, glanced back at Ian and nodded. "You'll look after her, though? Promise?"

"Promise."

We set to work cooking two small fish that Ian had caught with our newly carved spears. The delicate meat was soft on my tongue, and I chewed slowly, savoring every bite.

The heat sensor rested on the floor in front of us, still and quiet. Dad's voice echoed in my head, over and over. *Use it well.*

I still hated the idea of keeping Liv in the dark, but I did see Ian's point. It was dangerous. But idly waiting for my deathday wasn't an option either.

I sighed and glanced up at my friend. "I need to do something. I can't just sit around, waiting for death. I'm tired of waiting, watching the minutes slip by."

"What do you suggest?"

"Any information about deathdays that could save Liv must be kept in a central government building," I reasoned.

"Makes sense. But there's plenty of those in the Second City. At least six Security Compounds, not to mention the GA hospitals, research labs, and countless specialist buildings."

I chewed on a fishbone, replaying the conversation with Dad. Then I shook my head. "You're thinking too much. Sometimes, the answer is right in front of our eyes."

Ian shot me a quizzical look, while I smiled to myself

as the realization sunk in. "Dad mentioned that there's a Deathday Department in the White Tower…" My eyes met Ian's. "And I know where it is."

Ian's mouth dropped open. "What? Where? How do you know?"

"On the seventeenth floor of the White Tower. On the same floor as Dad's office — he told me so himself."

Ian's smile now mirrored my own. "Looks like we're headed to the White Tower, then."

We spent the rest of the day coming up with a detailed plan for our venture into the Tower. We would meet in a cracked building on the riverside just off Eagle Square, straight after the Celebrations in three days' time. There was usually a large turnout, so Ian would be able to blend in and get lost in the crowds more easily. The Safety Patrols also wouldn't be checking everyone as closely, and wouldn't be verifying everyone's identities on their comps. With those numbers, it was simply unfeasible. We would use it to our advantage.

In the meantime, I would try to talk to Dad again and see if I could find anything else out, while Ian would spend his days investigating and mapping the potential entrances into the White Tower. Once inside, we'd travel to the seventeenth floor — I'd been there before, so I'd lead the way.

"Theo?"

"Mmm?"

"On the day of the Celebrations… Come alone."

I bit my lip. "I can't."

"Why not?"

"Minors aren't allowed to attend the Celebrations without a parent or guardian anymore. Not since last year. And although Liv, Vi and Ralph hate the Celebrations, once they hear I'm going, they'll insist on coming too. Same with my parents."

"They're tightening security…" Ian muttered under his breath, poking at the fire with a branch. He glanced up at me. "You'll have to find a way to separate from them. Can you do that?"

The thought of leaving my parents and Liv on the eve of my deathday burned my throat and constricted my chest. It was difficult to catch a breath. But I steeled myself and nodded. The alternative was worse. Much worse. There was no way I'd let Liv risk her life and come with us into the Tower. I had to protect her, no matter the cost.

"Good." Ian threw a branch onto the fire. The flames crackled and spat. "Oh and one more thing." His lips curled into a small smile as he tossed me something.

I caught it with one hand — it was the heat sensor.

"Bring your heat sensor."

THREE DAYS

Sundays were my favorite. The smell of baking bread mixed with coffee wafted in from the kitchen as I lay sprawled out on the threadbare rug in the living room, rain pattering on the windows.

We hardly ever had fresh bread, and coffee was reserved for Sundays only.

This Sunday morning was a special one. Mom brought out her sourdough whole wheat bread recipe and poured us all steaming mugs of the black liquid. Dad had gone to the butcher's and even bought some beef. My mouth watered at the thought of these unthinkable delicacies. I couldn't remember the last time we had any fresh bread or meat.

But this Sunday morning was also my last.

I lay on my usual spot, but this time, instead of

fiddling with my comp, I clutched the heat sensor tightly. The fact that I still hadn't found my comp made my stomach roll. Where *was* it?

Laika snoozed next to me, her breaths even.

Dad peeked out from the kitchen, carrying a platter teetering with plates. "Ladies and gentlemen, I've cooked the beef to perfection. Lunch is served."

"Lunch?" I asked, pushing the hair out of my eyes. "Isn't it too early for lunch? It's only 11 am."

"It's never too early for lunch. If you don't want any Theo, that's all well and good, there'll be more for your mother, Laika and me." Dad shook a fork at me playfully. I couldn't suppress a smile as I joined him and Mom at the table.

The beef *was* cooked to perfection. I bit into it and chewed slowly, allowing the flavors to explode in my mouth. Beef was rare these days, as not many cows were kept in the specially heated indoor fields outside the City. Most were used for milk, and couldn't be spared for meat.

Laika's dog tag jingled as she yawned and rearranged herself on the rug. Surprisingly, Laika wasn't very food-motivated. She preferred toys and exercise, so she never begged at the table. Good thing, too — I wasn't sure how much fresh food we could spare for her these days.

"More coffee, dear?" Mom asked, her tone gentle.

My mouth fell open. "More?" We never got more coffee. It was one mug on Sundays, and that was it.

"You can have an extra one today, if you like."

My lips tugged upward and I nodded, my hand quivering as I handed Mom my empty mug. "Yes, please." Maybe an approaching deathday wasn't so bad, after all.

Mom poured the coffee, still smiling, but I couldn't help but notice that her smile was stilted, and her hand shook slightly as she poured.

A sudden booming knock on the door startled all three of us. Several drops of the coffee intended for my mug splattered on the table, but none of us seemed to notice. I glanced from Mom to Dad, all of us contemplating the same unspoken question. Who could be coming to see us at this hour? And on a Sunday, of all days?

My thoughts drifted back to Johnson, the Safety Patrol. The color drained from my face, and the hairs on the back of my neck stood on end. What if Johnson was back, this time with his Patrol unit? What if they were back for Laika? An icy dread filled every inch of my body, and my eyes instinctively flashed to Laika. I was ready to spring up at a moment's notice to shield her from harm.

As if sensing my unease, Dad stood up and said in a low voice, "I'll get it."

A second knock sounded, more urgent this time. Dad

closed the distance between the table and the front door in three large strides, his muscles tense beneath his gray long-sleeved shirt.

I couldn't see him from my vantage point, but the groan of the metal knob and the creak of protesting hinges cut through the silence like a knife.

Then silence once more.

Total. Absolute silence.

I waited with bated breath, clutching Mom's hand. I didn't even realize I'd grabbed it. My heart pounded in my chest. Who was it? If it was Johnson, if he was here for Laika…

My hands grew cold in Mom's warm ones. I exchanged a glance with her, biting my lip. Her pallor and wide eyes mirrored mine.

"Liv!" Dad's voice rang out across the apartment. "Come right in."

Momentary relief, followed by a new surge of panic, washed over me in quick succession. If it was possible for even more color to drain from my face, and for another biting chill that had nothing to do with Laika's safety to pass through my body, it did.

Liv was here? What did she want? My stomach did a somersault. Or a backflip. I couldn't tell which. My head was spinning and I couldn't think straight over my heart hammering in my ears.

Liv crossed the room and headed straight toward me, raindrops glistening in her hair, her purple scarf hanging loosely around her neck. Her lips tugged upward at the sight of me, but her movements seemed jittery. Or maybe that was just me, trying to stop my hands from shaking. Had I had too much coffee?

Dad followed right behind her. He was probably ushering her in and offering her a seat at the table, but I couldn't hear his words — everything was muffled. It was like being underwater, submerged in the icy depths of an aquarium whose slippery walls I had no chance of scaling.

"Liv dear, would you like something? I have your favorite baked apple rolls." Mom smiled at Liv.

"Baked apple rolls! Yes, thanks, Lisa."

"I knew you'd want some — you always have them."

Liv flashed my Mom a brilliant smile. "Some things never change — and my love for anything involving baked apples is one of them."

I stared at the half-eaten bread on my plate and my hand moved of its own accord to my freshly poured second cup of coffee, which had lain abandoned just seconds before.

Mom stood up from the table to fetch the rolls, but her hand lingered on mine. I lifted my gaze to meet hers. Below her raised eyebrows, Mom's eyes blazed into mine, betraying her thoughts. I knew how this looked to her. Her son was all but ignoring his best friend when she was a guest in his home. The one he had been inseparable from since the days of sandboxes and diaper rashes.

Heat burned my cheeks, so I swallowed a gulp of smoldering coffee and finally lifted my eyes to meet Liv's. My mouth fell open. She was smiling — no — positively beaming at me.

"Hi, Theo." Liv sounded breathless, as if she'd just ran a few miles.

"Hi," I stammered, trying, but ultimately failing, to keep my voice from shaking. *Get a grip, Theo.* I cleared my throat. "Hey, pix."

Liv still hadn't slid into the empty seat next to me. She kept her gaze trained on me, expectant. As inconspicuously as I could, I took a deep breath and forced myself to stand and smile, although I was sure it resembled a grimace more than anything else.

I'd known her for so long. Why was I letting what happened between us get to me like that? It didn't matter much now… And I could use a friend, after the incident with Johnson.

I maneuvered around the table and enveloped Liv into a hug. She hugged me back with a fervor I didn't expect, her fingers wrapping around my neck, pulling me into her. I buried my face in her long, chestnut-colored hair and inhaled deeply. The familiar smell of a spring meadow lingered around her.

She gripped my left arm as she pulled away, and I winced. Liv's eyes traveled downward. She let out a small cry when she noticed my bandaged arm, crimson blood soaking through. The dressing needed to be changed.

"What happened to your arm?" She hesitated a fraction of a second, then lifted her fingers and gently brushed the bandages.

"A Safety Patrol tried to kill Laika, so…"

"They tried to do *what?*" Liv dropped into the seat between Mom and I, still in her olive green jacket and worn brown boots, shaking the rain from her scarf.

Mom returned from the kitchen, carrying the apple-baked rolls. The smell of warm apples wafted through the room and made my mouth water. Mom poured Liv a mug of coffee and offered her a few slices of bread, wrapping some of it in a gray cloth. "For your mom, dear…"

Liv accepted the bread with a brilliant smile and turned back to me, her wide eyes glued to mine.

I took a deep breath and glanced to Dad for support, who nodded. I explained what happened with Laika and Johnson. Dad stepped in when I couldn't go on.

"I can't believe it, you've got a permit, it doesn't make sense…"

A low sigh escaped my lips. "I know it doesn't."

"The Safety Patrols don't always have our best interests at heart." Dad's voice was so quiet that I barely heard him over the incessant splatter of rain on the windows. If it wasn't for his creased brow and stern gaze, he might not have said anything at all. My heart thundered in my chest. I leaned toward him — was he going to add something to our last conversation? Would he finally tell me what bigger things were at work? And how I should use the heat sensor?

Then again, Liv was here, and she'd hear everything — questions and answers. On one hand, I swore to protect her, and to keep Ian's secret. But a stray thought tugged at the quieter, more stubborn part of my brain. Liv deserved to know the truth, no matter what Ian thought.

I took a deep breath, making up my mind. "Dad, you said the other day there are bigger things at work. What bigger things? Does this have something to do with the Safety Patrols not always looking out for us?"

Liv looked up sharply, the baked apple roll frozen in midair halfway to her mouth

"Reg." Mom touched Dad's hand lightly. He caught her eye. I could tell Dad wanted to say more, but was holding back.

"It does." He paused. "Your Dad would have wanted you to know that, Liv."

Liv said nothing. She stared at the slice of bread in front of her, her lips parted slightly.

"He told me so himself. Now, excuse me…"

"But Dad—"

"I stand by what I said before. It's too dangerous for you to know more. Just remember what I told you about the heat sensor."

Use it well.

Dad gathered the remaining bread, baked apple rolls and empty plates from the table and deposited them in the kitchen. Liv's face turned pale, but there was a quiet determination in her eyes. Mom reached over and squeezed her hand. "He loved you so much, dear. We miss him every day."

Liv nodded. "I miss him too."

Mom gave Liv's hand another gentle squeeze and joined Dad in the kitchen.

A tightness settled in my chest. I'll never forget the sense of carefree freedom that went hand in hand with going into the woods beyond the Edge with Liv's dad. The summer sun peeking in through the canopies in midsummer, accompanied by the soft sound of birdsong and Liv's laughter. Back then, we could escape from the City, experience something different, and still feel safe. I wish I could say all this to Liv, and so much more, but in that moment, my words failed me.

Liv spoke first, her voice shaking slightly. "I just remembered something he told me when I was little, five days before he…" She swallowed, and fumbled in her pocket. "And he gave me this."

It was an old pocketknife. I remembered seeing it before, its dark brown facade rusted with age. Liv unfolded it, revealing a set of strange engraved markings on its surface.

"What did he say?"

"He said… he said not all GA officials are good. I didn't understand it then, I was only eleven…"

"But it sounds just like what Dad said." I finished for Liv. She nodded.

Our Dads had been inseparable — best friends at school, and then they both got jobs working for the GA. It was no wonder they thought alike.

I chanced a glance at Liv. Her green eyes snapped up to meet mine, piercing me with an intensity that I hadn't seen before. "What's that your Dad said? Something about a heat sensor?"

I nodded.

"Can we go to your room? We need to talk."

Laika followed us through the apartment, her paws echoing off the cracked, creaking floorboards.

I shut the door behind us. Liv perched on the edge of my bed, while Laika curled up near her legs.

I didn't know what to do with my feet, so I stood awkwardly next to the door. I also didn't know what to do with my hands, so I shoved them in my pockets, feeling the cool glass of the heat sensor against my skin.

Liv's laughter filled the chilly room with warmth, and my stomach did another backflip. It was, without a doubt, my favorite sound in the world.

"Are you just going to stand there?" She patted the bed next to her. "Come here, silly."

I did as she said, my lips tugging upward, despite myself. All it took was one laugh from Liv, one smile, one look, one word, and she could put me at ease better than anyone else ever could. Even if the source of my unease was Liv herself.

"You wanted to talk?" I forced my eyes to meet hers. Her cheeks were still rosy from the crisp morning air, her hair still sprinkled with raindrops.

She nodded wordlessly, twisting the patchwork quilt I threw haphazardly over my bed this morning around her finger. I waited with bated breath, a tight knot squeezing my chest.

My thoughts drifted back to what happened between

us on the playground. My stomach dropped. I was not looking forward to hearing her reject me again. It was best she didn't say anything at all. My eyes searched the cramped room for an excuse to leave, but nothing came to mind.

I avoided her gaze. My eyes darted around the room again, resting first on the ancient mirror, then on the threadbare curtains, and finally on Laika. Maybe I could take her out for a walk? That way I wouldn't have to endure Liv's explanation why she didn't like me. That's surely why she was here — to tell me that she didn't like me in that way, but that we could still be friends. Her running off from the playground was explanation enough. But I quickly discarded the idea — Laika was already snoring loudly on the floorboards. I let out a loud sigh and slumped my shoulders, waiting. I guess I should just hear her out and get it over with. How bad could it be? My heart constricted at the thought.

Liv's voice cut through my thoughts. "What did your Dad mean with the heat sensor? What is that?"

A wave of realization — and relief that Liv didn't want to talk about our encounter at the playground — washed over me. I hadn't had a chance to tell her what my Ten Day Object actually was. I pulled it out of my pocket and demonstrated how it worked. Like Ian's, her eyes shone with curiosity, her pink lips smiling. The knot in my stomach loosened a notch. Despite what had happened between us, Liv was here, spending time with me, just like old times. I allowed myself to relax.

Still, she was so close, and I couldn't help the flashbacks that surfaced in my mind, her words on the playground echoing over and over. *'You just kissed me now.'* I'd kissed her, not told her how I felt. I'd considered this before, but maybe this is what she really wanted. Maybe Liv wanted me to spell it out and tell her how I've felt about her all this time. Now, things felt more at ease between us. Did I really want to risk ruining everything all over again? Then again, did I really want to die without even having tried?

I was alone with the girl I loved, and I really had nothing to lose. It was now or never.

I took a deep breath, steadying myself. The world spun around me, and Liv's dazzling smile didn't make it any easier to focus. I itched to tuck a loose lock of her wavy hair behind her ear, but resisted. *Focus, Theo.*

Glancing up, I locked eyes with Liv. "Listen, pix… I—"

But Liv didn't let me finish. Instead, without a word, she leaned over and touched her lips to mine.

Shockwaves surged throughout my entire body. My stomach dropped several miles and my lips tingled. The pounding of my heart was so deafening I was sure Liv could hear it. I closed my eyes, savoring her taste. Her lips were soft against mine, and the sweet scent of a dewy spring morning filled my nostrils. I dreaded the moment when she would pull her lips away from mine.

But she didn't.

Instead, she wrapped her arms around my neck in a gentle, but firm hold. I wound my own arms around her and pulled her into me, until there was no space left between us. My wounded arm screamed in protest, but I ignored it. I brushed her lips with mine, breathing her in, wishing that this moment would last forever.

But I had to tell her how I felt — the weight of my unspoken words bore down on me like a stone.

I took another deep breath, and whispered, "Liv… I like you. I always have…" I shook my head. That wasn't right. "No, Liv Madden, I… I love you."

Liv's soft lips smiled against my own. "I know," she whispered, and kissed me again. Her kisses were fierce, and I lost all sense of time. When she finally pulled away for a breath, she kept me locked in her embrace, her green eyes fixed on mine. They reflected the dim light pouring in through my small bedroom window. Looking into them felt like getting lost in an enchanted forest in high summer.

"Theo…" She breathed, and kissed me again, gently

this time, sending another electric shock coursing through my body.

"Liv…" I took her face in my hands, our lips only just touching. "So is *this* what you really wanted to talk about?" A smile tugged one corner of my mouth upward.

Liv blushed. "Yes. I wanted to tell you that…" Her voice trailed off. "What happened the other day, with me running off like that… I'm so sorry."

"It's all right."

"No, it's not. I should have been clear. I should have told you that I liked, no, loved you too, instead of just… running away."

"I didn't exactly tell you I liked you though, did I?" I grinned. "You told me so yourself."

Heat colored Liv's cheeks, but she bounced back immediately. "No, you just did this." She put her mouth to mine again. I closed my eyes, savoring the feel of her lips on mine. After a moment, she pulled back, her expression serious. "I am sorry though. It was just… a lot to take in, that's all."

"You don't have to be."

I glanced out the window, suddenly lost in thought. I hadn't really considered the effect my actions could have had on Liv. I was a jerk for not thinking about that, for thinking only of myself. "I just… love you so much that I had to tell you. Before… you know."

"Today's the first time you actually told me!" Liv laughed, but after a moment her eyes filled with tears and she threw herself into my arms.

We stayed like that for a few minutes, motionless and entwined as one, neither of us daring to break the embrace.

"That's just it." Her voice was muffled, her mouth pressed against my shoulder.

"What's it, Liv?"

"I — I can't stand the thought of losing you so quickly. In three days. Three days, Theo." She pulled out of the hug and looked me square in the eye. Her gaze intensified, the green of her irises glinting in the dull Sunday light. "I was hoping for so much more."

Now I felt even more like a jerk. Telling her I liked her just to disappoint her by dying in three days. Great. Just great.

It was in moments like these when I wished, even though I knew it was impossible, to be like Ian, to survive past my deathday and live out the rest of my days in the forest. Maybe Liv would even want to come with me, and we'd make a new life for ourselves outside the City. But, deep down, I knew these were just daydreams. I was going to die in three days, and nothing I did would change that.

Then there were my parents and Laika… and Liv's

mom. No. Liv would never leave her behind, especially not now, when she's been ill for weeks.

I discarded these thoughts, calling them out for what they were. Fantasies.

Liv looked up at me, her eyes glassy, threatening to spill over again. "Why did it take so long… for you to tell me?"

A single tear fell down her cheek. I kissed it and brushed it gently away with the tip of my finger. "I'm so sorry, Liv. I just… didn't know how to."

Liv looked down at the floor, her gaze following the tiny cracked rivers in the floorboards that I so often stared at. After a moment, her eyes snapped back to meet mine again. "I'm worried about you, Theo. And your family… Laika…"

I thought about this too. How would Laika react when I didn't come home one day? No, not 'one day' — in three days. Would she miss me? I read somewhere that back when people used to keep dogs as pets, before it was outlawed after the War, the animals would get attached to their owners. Some were never quite the same after their owners passed. Some waited for days, even years, for them to return. But of course, they never did. My chest tightened. I hoped that Laika would be spared this kind of anguish.

"Mom and Dad will take care of her." I offered her a

weak smile. I knew that my parents would do everything in their power to make sure of it. Dad proved as much the other day. "She's in good hands."

Liv hung her head. "I can't bear the thought of being without you. As a friend or… something more."

I took her into my arms once more. "Hey… you don't have to. I'm here. I'll always be here."

Liv's lower lip trembled. "For the next three days…"

"No." My voice was firm, and I was surprised at the force in it. "Always."

TWO DAYS

Liv skipped school on Monday to spend the day with me.

"Liv Madden, star student, skipping school?" I teased, as we walked through the streets of the City. The dilapidated buildings in this part of town towered over us, their windows empty, gaping like sightless eyes.

"Oh shush, you." She laughed, her voice warm and sweet, like the first sip of mint tea on a chilly winter day.

We crossed our usual red iron bridge, leaving the Mart behind us, the twin corn-like buildings looming to our left.

"You're missing history today, one of your favorites."

"I'll be just fine without one history lesson, Theodore."

"Theodore?" I smiled, nudging her with my elbow. Only Liv ever called me that.

"Yes. Besides, Ralph said he will transfer over his notes."

I shook my head. Of course Liv would make sure she'd get the notes from her classes. "It's not like you need them, though. You know the GA's history inside and out."

We made our way past the Pavilion and the Bean, its oblong shape glinting in the morning sun that peeked through the clouds, and headed farther south.

"There's always more to learn. Like what happened before the War… there are centuries that we hardly touch on in class." Liv gave me a sidelong glance. "Don't you think so?"

I nodded, thinking back to our last history lesson together. "We still don't know what kind of internal policy the GA was so intent on keeping intact that they risked sending nuclear missiles to the Asian Superpower."

"I did a bit of extra research on that point… but nothing came up in the digital library stores."

"It doesn't make sense. Why would the GA leave this out from their history lessons?"

Liv shrugged. "As I said before, whatever this internal policy was, it must have been important."

I said nothing. Instead, I took her hand and squeezed

it gently. To my delight, she didn't protest. But her cheeks did take on a little color.

She squeezed back, and we walked on, hand in hand, side by side, occasionally checking around corners for lingering Safety Patrols. This was how it should be. How I pictured us — Liv and I — in my mind for so long. And this is how it *would* have been, if only I had more time…

Up ahead, the old fountain loomed in the distance. As we got closer, it came into focus: large and beige but blackened by years of neglect. Its three-layered facade, which resembled a wedding cake, had crumbled in places, and the fountain itself was flanked by rusty green mythical creatures. Were they fish, or horses, or dragons? I could never tell. The nearest one's head was missing.

There was no water, of course. The GA would never spend precious resources like clean, non-corrosive water to power something as fanciful and impractical as a fountain. I closed my eyes and tried to imagine what the fountain would look like with water flowing through it on a balmy summer's day. The sunlight reflecting off the green creatures, as if magically bringing them to life, the droplets of mist fresh and cool on my skin, offering a much needed reprieve from the sweltering heat of the concrete, and the smell of nature and life intermingled with soft birdsong in the nearby trees and greenery.

I could just about picture it.

My eyes snapped open again. Now, there was only concrete. "We're here, just like you wanted."

Liv smiled. "Thanks, Theo. I really love this place. The Bean, the fountain… all of it." She paused, gazing up at the fountain. "It must have been beautiful, once."

"Yeah, it must have."

I took Liv in my arms and leaned her against the wiry railing surrounding the fountain. Smiling, I pulled her close, feeling her soft breath on my face. I lowered my lips to hers, taking in every bit of her. She felt strong in my arms, her face flushed despite the chill of the autumn air.

I shifted Liv's purple scarf to protect her from the bite of the breeze and gently pressed my mouth to hers again. She reciprocated, and I left the world behind once more. The electricity that jolted through me yesterday as she kissed me surged with every second. My heart pounded in my chest, and my stomach somersaulted again and again.

Part of me just wanted to stay here, with Liv, wrapped in her arms until the very end. I wanted to savor this moment, while I still could. Liv's sweet kisses made my head spin, and if she asked me to stay with her, I didn't think I'd have it in me to say no…

But an inkling of guilt gnawed and twisted in my stomach. Ian and I had a plan. We were going into the White Tower, after all. All the same, I didn't know how much time I had left to spend with Liv. I had to focus on the plan, and I couldn't allow myself to be swept away by Liv's electric presence… which is exactly what I was doing. Her admission that she liked me too, and the taste of her lips on mine endangered the whole plan and threatened to turn it on its head. I was meant to be finding ways to save Liv from her own deathday, not spending the minutes leading up to mine wrapped in her embrace. The digits on my left wrist tingled, reminding me of the limited time I had.

But at the same time, I couldn't bring myself *not* to spend what was left of my time with her. Finally, after everything, I was here with Liv. And that's all that mattered. I wouldn't cut this time short, not if I could help it.

I didn't know how long we stood pressed against the railing of the old fountain, lost in each other, but I did know that I wanted nothing more than for this one moment to become my eternity. Even forever wasn't long enough.

Liv laid her head on my chest, her fingers twisting around my open jacket. I rested my chin on her head and closed my eyes. I breathed in deeply, savoring the moment and inhaling her sweet scent. As always, it reminded me of a spring meadow.

In that moment, a piercing crack split the silence.

A gunshot, followed by a distant scream.

I BLANCHED and instinctively glanced down at Liv. Her face had also turned white. Her hands clutched my shoulder, her fingernails digging into the skin underneath my jacket. I winced — my wound still burned, but I pushed the pain away. Whipping around, I scanned the horizon, searching for somewhere where Liv would be safe.

"What's going on?" Liv's voice was small, muffled by my jacket.

"It must be more unrest in the City."

"Unrest? What unrest?"

"It's what—" But I stopped short. It's what Ian had mentioned the other day. Unrest in the City. People growing restless. Ian had an inexplicable knack for this kind of intel.

"I didn't know about any unrest, Theo. What's happening? Why are people doing this?"

I lowered my mouth to Liv's ear. "I'm hazy on the details, but I think people aren't happy with the way the GA is running the City."

Liv pulled away, her expression thoughtful. "But I haven't seen anything in the news."

I shook my head. "They're trying to keep it quiet, Liv. They don't want people catching on. They want to snuff out the ember before it flares up into a wildfire that sets the whole City alight."

"Is it the Fleeters? It can't be the Timeless…" Liv bit her lip. "Does it have to do with the food shortages, or the lack of electricity during the freezing sub-zero winter nights? That last polar vortex was awful…"

I shrugged. "Not sure. Could be."

"How did you find out?"

I bit my lower lip. I wanted to tell her, more than anything, about how I knew, about Ian… but I knew I couldn't. Not right now. Not after Ian's warning. "I — I heard from a friend."

Before Liv had a chance to reply, another ripple of gunshots exploded from behind the building to our left. Except this time, it was a lot closer. My stomach sank.

"We need to move." I took Liv's hand and led her back toward the Bean and the Pavilion, my pace brisk. "This way."

She followed without a word. More gunshots rang out, cracking the cool air like a whip. I stopped in my tracks, dazed by the blasts and now unable to tell where they were coming from.

"We need to find another way. Come on!" Liv took the lead, tugging at my hand. She was quick on her feet; we ran side by side, swinging around corners at random. We lurched into a side street and down an alley, stopping short when our way was blocked by a few large, abandoned containers.

We were trapped. I spun around, calculating the time it would take to retrace our steps and take a parallel alley. Liv dropped my hand and assessed the containers before us. I followed her gaze — they were at least ten feet high.

I glanced at her. "What now? We go around?"

She brushed back her disheveled hair and tucked it behind her scarf, letting her breath leave her rosy cheeks in a steady exhale.

"No, Theodore. We're not going around. We're going up."

I couldn't suppress a smile. "Why is it always 'up' with you, pix?"

"Well, it's better than down, isn't it?"

"Can't argue with that."

"How's your wound?"

"Still painful."

Liv gave me a small, pained smile. "I need you to give me a boost. It's the only way."

Glancing back up toward the containers, I realized she was right. I set my position, grit my teeth, and steeled myself for the fire that would surge through my arm in a moment.

Liv kicked off from the ground hard. I pushed her up as high as I could, my upper left arm screaming in protest. I wasn't prepared for the wave of nausea that hit me as Liv's weight left my hands. I crumbled to my knees, my head swimming and my arm burning as if it had been split in two.

"Theo!" Liv's voice ricocheted around the narrow alleyway, intermingling with the steady stream of gunshots. "Theodore! Can you hear me?" Liv's voice cut through the noise, loud and crisp.

I looked up, blinking several times to steady my vision. Liv creased her delicate features, perching on the ledge of the nearest building.

"Go," I croaked. "I won't make it up there."

"Like hell you will." She shimmied out of her jacket, tied one of its sleeves to a crooked lamppost, and tossed it back to me. "Grab this!"

I grunted and caught the sleeve of her jacket with my uninjured hand.

"Now come up."

I nodded and took a deep breath. I gave myself a shaky running start and pushed off from the concrete, gripping the jacket tightly between my fingers. The world swayed dangerously before my eyes.

"Hold on," Liv shouted.

I steadied my breathing and began the slow ascent to the ledge. To Liv.

"Take my hand." Liv's outstretched fingers were inches from my own. Will one last heave, I lunged forward and threw my right arm to meet hers. Our fingers connected, and I felt Liv hauling me up the last couple of feet.

We fell in a heap on the ledge, my breathing labored, the world still spinning. "Why do we always end up on top of precarious ledges, pix?"

Liv grinned. "It's what we do, Theodore." She clambered to her feet, untied her jacket from the lamppost and dusted off bits of debris from her black pants. "But you know what?"

"What?"

"You're an idiot for letting that Safety Patrol shoot you, you know that?"

I did know that. It was foolish, and reckless, and now I'd have to live with a firestorm in my arm when Ian and I ventured into the White Tower.

We hobbled from ledge to ledge, making our way back down toward the street. The sequence of ledges resembled a large, makeshift staircase. It would even have been fun to climb, if it wasn't for the hole in my arm. We jumped the last few feet to the ground, my feet grateful for the stable concrete beneath them.

The gunshots grew louder still, almost as loud as the pounding of my heart in my chest. But we had to keep going — we had to get back to the residential area of the City… back home.

We crossed several more alleyways and took a few turns in the general easterly direction — or so I hoped. I couldn't rely on the sun, as I usually did, as today's heavy overcast clouds had shrouded the whole City in a veil of gray.

"Are you sure we're going the right way?" Liv asked. "I don't recognize these buildings."

"I — I think so," I said, sounding more certain than I'd felt. The gunshots and screams reverberated in my head, louder than ever. I shook my head. Impossible. That climb must have really messed with my head.

We pressed on, clutching each other's hands tightly. After a moment, we emerged onto a wide avenue and came to an abrupt halt.

Somehow, among all the confusion, we'd take a wrong turn. Or several.

The City, usually quiet and abandoned in these parts, save for the occasional squatter lurking in the shadows of a dilapidated building, was now submerged in utter chaos.

People were sprawled on the crimson-stained asphalt. Some were coughing. Others spitting blood. A small fire had started in the tall, crumbling skyscraper across the street, black smoke billowing from inside. The smoke stung my eyes, and I blinked several times to clear my vision.

A man, who looked to be in his thirties, wearing ragged, dirty clothes and sporting a shock of messy brown hair threw something into the air, toward a line of figures advancing from the opposite end of the street.

As my eyes adjusted to the scene, I realized with a jolt they weren't just any figures. They were Safety Patrols, marching toward us, masks down and shields out.

And we'd wandered straight into their line of fire.

AND THEN I SAW HIM.

Johnson. His gas mask was up, his face contorted with rage. Beneath him, a small blond boy, who couldn't be older than twelve, knelt on the broken asphalt, his nose bruised and bloody. Johnson lifted his gun and struck the boy's face with its butt. Liv screamed next to me and clamped her hands over her mouth as the boy fell to the ground, dark red blood pooling around him.

Liv rushed forward toward the boy, but I grabbed her arm and spun her around to face me.

"No, it's too dangerous."

"But the boy…"

"That's Johnson," I said in a low voice. "The Safety Patrol that tried to kill Laika. And kill me."

Liv's eyes widened.

"Come on, we need to get out of here." Grabbing Liv's hand, I pulled her after me, dodging people as their paths criss-crossed with ours. A stone flew next to my left ear. I ducked, and it missed my head by inches. We crossed the avenue, Liv's hand still planted firmly in mine.

In that moment, an explosion rocked the street behind us and I was hurled off my feet. Stumbling, I lost my balance and crashed face first into the cracked asphalt. My knees and elbows scraped the ground as I skidded to a halt, the sudden pain in my foot dulled by the agony of my gunshot wound. If the stitches hadn't come loose during the climb, they certainly had now… I wish I'd asked Ian to borrow some of his crystalizing spray the other day…

"Theo, are you all right?" Liv was kneeling beside me, concern etched on her face.

I nodded once, willing the pain to subside. "Must have tripped over a rock or—"

"A bomb went off — just there." Liv glanced behind me. She blanched and her mouth fell open.

"Theo, we need to go. Now." Her voice was low and urgent. "Can you stand? Here." She gingerly put one of my arms around her shoulder and began hauling me up.

"Well, well, well. If it isn't the young Mr. Vanderveen."

I froze and felt Liv stiffen next to me. An icy chill spread through my body. I knew that voice.

With Liv's help, I twisted myself upward and sprang to my feet, ignoring yet another wave of nausea that accompanied the jolt of pain in my extremities. I looked up and found myself staring straight into Johnson's eyes. Black like the night, they were filled with a terrifying frenzy.

My stomach sank, but I was still lucid enough to thrust Liv behind me.

"And he's got a lady friend," Johnson jeered. "Has she got a filthy mutt too?"

"Don't you dare talk about her like that."

"Or what? Daddy's not around to save you today."

"I don't need saving."

Johnson let out a harsh laugh. "Of course you don't. Your mutt would have been long dead if your daddy hadn't come running. Where's the mutt now?" He looked behind us, his greedy eyes searching for Laika.

I leaped forward, but Liv grabbed my good arm and held me back. "No! He's got a gun."

I glanced back at Johnson. Sure enough, his gun was poised at the ready, pointed directly at us. Liv was right. In this chaos, Johnson could fire and we'd both be dead within seconds, with zero repercussions for him. He'd say he acted in self-defense, and that we breached the peace by participating in… whatever this unrest was.

I hesitated for a split second, just as another explosion went off behind Johnson. He was blasted off his feet; his gun flew out of his hand and landed several yards away.

This was our chance.

I grabbed Liv's hand and we flung ourselves in the opposite direction, sprinting into a side alley. My eyes darted left and right, searching for a reprieve. To my left, the back door of the nearest skyscraper was left ajar. I ran in, Liv at my heels, and shut the door behind us.

After several seconds, my eyes adjusted to the dim light: we were standing in a dingy gray stairwell. The only light came in through the narrow window above the door, its glass opaque with dirt and grime. I scrunched up my nose against the potent smell of mold wafting through the air. We were in a fire escape.

I let out a deep breath, momentarily relaxing the tension in my shoulders. It didn't occur to me before just how much danger we were in, exposed on the street like that, until we reached the relative safety of the stairwell. A stray bullet could have hit me, or worse… I swallowed, the dryness in my mouth scratching my throat. It could have hit Liv.

"Are you all right?" My eyes flitted to hers. Her face was pale even in the meager glow of the daylight seeping in from the alley.

Liv nodded, but her hand shook in mine, and her lower lip trembled.

"Hey, it's okay…" I enveloped her in a hug, feeling her slender but strong body beneath my arms.

"I'm okay…" She buried her face in my jacket. "But that boy, that little boy…"

As gently as I could, I shifted her so that I could look her in her eyes. They were glazed over and glassy. "Liv, listen to me. You couldn't have done anything."

"I could have. I could have—"

"No, you couldn't have." My voice was firm, more so than I intended. "I've seen that look in Johnson's eyes before. I know what he's capable of."

A shudder ran down my spine and the tips of my fingers grew cold. I didn't even want to think about what would have happened if that second bomb hadn't gone off and Johnson's gun wasn't knocked out of his grasp…

I brushed a finger along Liv's cheek, down to her lips. I took her face in my hands and kissed her slowly, feeling my mouth tingle and the now familiar electricity course through my body.

"And you're too important to me," I whispered in her ear. "I can't bear to lose you. Not now… Not ever."

THE CHAOS outside reigned for several hours. Liv crouched against the wall, her head tilted back and her eyes closed. Her breaths were ragged and uneven. I sat on the floor next to her, clutching her hand. She stirred and checked her comp with shaking fingers, before replacing it in her bag. The wall was cool beneath my jacket. I willed its icy chill to siphon the agonizing throbs in my arm, wrist and foot away. If I tried hard enough, I could almost pretend it was working.

A scream just outside the door jolted me out of my reverie. It belonged to a girl — a young girl, judging by its high pitch. I exchanged a nervous glance with Liv. Her face was pale, and her wide eyes flitted to the door, toward the scream. Nodding, I slid across the tiny space and lowered myself to the floor, positioning my eyes level with the crack under the door.

What I saw next made my stomach churn.

A girl — not much younger than Liv and I, was doubled over, clutching her side, mere steps away from our hiding place. Her straight, jet black hair fell in a short curtain to her heart-shaped chin. She pushed it out of her eyes, revealing a black eye and a bloody lip. An older boy, wearing a black long-sleeved shirt with cropped hair the same shade as the girl's, was supporting her. Neither were wearing jackets.

"Alma, shhh, it's okay."

The girl replied with a coughing fit.

"Hold on, it's just another few blocks to Uncle's."

The girl nodded, but then winced immediately as she tried to stand. The boy offered her his hand. She accepted gingerly, pulling her fingers away from her side. They were stained dark crimson.

"What's going on?" Liv whispered behind me.

"She's hurt…"

"Who is?"

A sharp intake of breath sounded from the alley, followed by a small cry of pain.

"Alma, shhh." The boy's voice was pleading. "I just need you to be quiet. We're almost there, I promise."

"No, we're not."

"I'll carry you."

"No. Go tell Uncle I'm here. I'll wait." She winced again.

"It's too dangerous."

"I'll be fine."

"I won't leave you. Alma…"

Another round of gunshots sounded in the distance.

Without thinking, I threw the fire escape door open. "Hey, in here!"

The boy and the girl named Alma snapped their heads in my direction. Their eyes were an identical shade of black. Hers were wide, while his were narrowed. The boy's lips settled into a thin line.

"Who are you?" The boy spoke first.

"There's no time, get in here." I stood aside to let them pass. Liv got to her feet next to me. She laced her fingers in mine.

The boy hesitated for a fraction of a second, but after a moment, he bent down, put his arm around Alma and lowered his voice. "Come on, let's get inside."

The girl didn't protest. They hobbled past me and I shut the door securely behind them.

"Who are you?" The boy asked again.

"I'm Theo, and this is Liv."

Liv nodded next to me, her eyes scanning the newcomers.

"I'm Everett, and this is my little sister Alma. We got caught in the crossfire."

"As did we."

Everett knelt beside his sister. "We're safe for now, Al, but you need to let me see your injury."

Alma shook her head. "No way, you're not a doctor."

"Neither is Uncle, but you'd let him see it."

"Uncle knows what he's doing."

"I won't screw up again, I promise—"

"No!"

Everett looked at Liv and me, his expression pleading.

Images of me cleaning Ian's bloodied wrist flooded my mind. "I can—"

But Liv cut me off. "No, Theo. You've lost too much blood yourself. I'll handle it." She stepped toward Alma and put a gentle hand on her arm. "Hey Alma, I'm Liv. Want to tell me where it hurts?"

Alma hesitated, her black eyes studying Liv's green ones.

"I won't screw up like your brother." Liv winked.

That seemed to win the little girl over. She tentatively lifted her hand from her left side, exposing her wound.

"What happened?" Liv asked Everett.

"She got hit with shrapnel from one of the bombs."

Liv nodded. "I see…" She tore off a piece of her shirt, dampened it with water from a small metal container she kept in her cloth bag, and wordlessly began cleaning Alma's injury. Alma flinched, but didn't pull away.

Everett bit his lower lip and watched the girls.

"Thankfully, it's not too deep," Liv said after a moment. "The shrapnel cut through her side, but it didn't sever any major veins or organs, as far as I can tell."

I raised my eyebrows at Liv. She was good at this, and

it was *my* Mom who was the nurse.

She blushed. "I actually pay attention in science class, Theodore." She paused. "And I've had a lot of experience lately… with Mom."

Before I got a chance to respond, Liv cleared her throat and busied herself with wrapping a makeshift bandage, fashioned from a fragment of her shirt, around Alma's torso. I watched her as she worked, and for the first time today saw what I'd noticed the other day at school. The dark circles under her eyes were even more pronounced than before, and her scarf, usually smooth and even, was now rumpled and disheveled.

A sudden thought struck me. I dug into my jacket pocket and pulled out a small vial of clear liquid, handing it to Alma. "Here, drink this."

"What is it?" Everett surveyed the vial, his eyes narrowed.

"Painkiller. My mom's a nurse."

"But you're hurt too." Everett's gaze traveled to my arm — I'd taken my jacket off, and blood was seeping through the bandages.

I shook my head. "She needs it more."

Alma accepted the vial and swallowed the liquid, making a face. "Bleurgh."

I smiled. "Not very tasty, but it'll make you feel better."

Liv took the girl's hand and led her over to the corner where she'd laid out her jacket and propped her metal water container against the wall. "Have a drink, then lie down here and try to rest, okay?" Alma did as she was told, sipping from the container, then wincing as she lowered herself onto the jacket and shut her eyes. After several minutes, her breathing slowed and evened out.

"She'll be okay," Liv said. "Just make sure your Uncle sees her when you get back, all right?"

Everett nodded. "Thank you."

"What happened out there?" I asked.

"We were attacked. The Safety Patrols sure do know how to escalate things," Everett said. "One minute it's a peaceful protest — against the electricity cuts, I think — and the next it's a full-blown fray. Our friend Em is still out there. I couldn't get a hold of her on my comp… All lines are down." Everett fixed his gaze in the direction of the avenue, his brow creased with worry.

"She'll be okay," I said, though I had nothing to back it up.

Everett smiled. "Yeah, she will. She's probably causing all sorts of trouble, as usual."

I glanced at Everett. "You said this started as a peaceful protest?"

"Yeah. Alma, Em and I saw it, right before the Patrols fired the first shots. Not sure against what, though — but it was clear the people weren't happy. We were on our way back home to Uncle's."

The Safety Patrols fired the first shots. Of course they did. "I'm not surprised about the Patrols."

"You're not? I am. I thought they're supposed to be keeping us safe."

I smiled bitterly. "One of them tried to kill me and my dog the other day." I paused. The image of Johnson and his gun pointed straight at me swam to the forefront of my mind. "And today too, now that I think about it."

"In which Sector?"

"Loop."

"We're from River." Everett said.

River… that's Ian's old sector. I wondered if he'd met the siblings, maybe even gone to school with them. It was too dangerous to ask, though. I pushed my hair out of my eyes, listening to the incessant stream of gunshots rippling through the avenue. When would this end?

I noticed Everett staring at my wrist, where my sleeve had ridden up, revealing my deathday. It was as vivid green as ever, even in the dim light.

"How long?"

I shifted my weight. "Two days."

"I'm sorry, man."

I grunted and fought off the wave of fire that surged in my wrist. It seemed to amplify every time I thought about my deathday. I lowered myself to the ground, my back pressing against the wall. Liv sensed my unease. She joined me, grabbed my hand and squeezed tight.

Everett crouched next to us and lowered his voice. "Listen… thanks. For letting us hide in here with you. And for—" he gestured to Alma.

"Sure." A beat passed. "Why did you help us? Why did you decide to trust us?"

I shot him a sidelong smile, tinged with sadness. "I know what it's like when someone you love is hurting. I could see it on your face, and on Alma's."

Everett nodded. "Well, thanks. Someday, somehow, I'll return the favor."

I thought about telling him that with my two days, it seemed unlikely. But I decided against it — it wasn't his fault that my deathday was approaching with lighting speed. "Don't mention it. You seem like a good guy. You would have done the same for me."

The corners of Everett's mouth tugged upward. That was the first time I'd seen him smile — it brought light and life into his gaunt face. "Yeah, I would have."

Everett closed his eyes and sighed. I followed suit. Until the shots ceased, there was nothing we could do but wait.

THE HOURS PASSED, and the overcast sky gave way to patches of brilliant blue. As the sun began its slow descent into the west, the shouts and gunshots from the street finally died down. Alma was still asleep in the corner, her breathing even. Liv had joined her. Everett sat upright against the cold stone wall, his jaw set and his teeth clenched. With trembling hands, I opened the door to the fire escape a fraction and peered outside.

The air smelled of burnt rubber and metal. Wisps of smoke wound their way upward between the buildings and dilapidated lampposts. I inched around the corner. Glass and debris were strewn along the length of the avenue. Several people were tending to the wounded, their hands and threadbare clothes stained dark red.

My stomach turned as I saw something else. People lying on the street, with no one tending to them. But they weren't people. Not anymore. They were bodies, lifeless and unmoving.

"Are they gone?" Liv's voice sounded behind me.

I grit my teeth and faced her, nodding. "Yeah. It's over now. But let's go that way." I pointed northwest, toward the residential area, and shot a meaningful glance at Everett, whose face had appeared in the doorway. "We all should." I didn't want Liv or Alma to see what I saw. It was bad enough that the image of the ravaged avenue was imprinted in my mind like cattle branding. I blinked repeatedly, trying, to no avail, to banish the vision.

Everett picked up on my cue immediately. He went back inside, grabbed Alma's hand and swiveled her around, turning her back to the avenue. "Come on, let's get to Uncle's. We need to get that wound of yours checked out."

Alma winced. "I — I don't think I can walk very fast."

"I'll carry you." Everett picked his sister up with ease, his muscles moving beneath his black shirt.

I took Liv's hand in mine and the four of us half walked, half jogged back across one of the red iron bridges dotting the river, toward the residential area of the City.

Everett slowed after several minutes. "River Sector is just north of here."

I nodded. "Get to your Uncle's safely."

Everett clasped my hand and nodded once at Liv. "We will meet again. I know we will."

I decided not to remind him that my deathday was in two days. Instead, I clapped him on back and offered him a small smile. "Till we meet again."

Liv approached Alma and squeezed her hand. "Heal quickly and stay safe."

The girl smiled. "You too."

MY PLACE WAS ONLY a few blocks from where we stood, so we navigated the streets until we reached my apartment block. I made a point of pausing at every corner to peer down the next street. Here and there I held up a hand to stop Liv, allowing stragglers from the protests to pass us undisturbed on their way home.

When we reached my apartment, the sun was hanging low over the western horizon. I pushed the door open and we stumbled inside.

Mom greeted us from the couch in the living room, her voice carrying over the clicking of her knitting needles. "Hey kids, how was school? Did you have a nice day?"

Liv and I piled into the living room — Mom's face turned ashen when she saw us. I looked down, and was surprised to see that both my jacket and Liv's were splattered in blood, our boots trailing in the red, sticky substance.

"Theo! Liv! What happened? Are you all right?" Mom dropped her needles; her half-finished sweater fell, abandoned, to the floor. She looked like she'd just seen a ghost as she hugged us both tightly. Laika got up from her usual spot on the threadbare rug and greeted us, her tail wagging.

"We're okay. There was just…" Liv began, but paused. She shot me a furtive glance.

"Unrest. In the City." I finished for her. It was best to be honest with Mom — she had an uncanny knack for sensing if something was off.

Liv swallowed and nodded. "The Safety Patrols, and the people…"

Mom blanched. "This is what Reg was talking about…"

"Dad knew about this?"

Mom eyed me up and down. "Yes, he did. Remember he works for the GA after all." She lowered her voice. "Even if at times he wished he didn't."

My mouth fell open. "Dad what—"

As if thinking better of what she said, Mom ignored me, rushed over to the cupboards and pulled out her medical kit.

I turned over what Mom had said in my mind. I bit my lip and chanced a glance over at Liv. Her expression was stony, but she said nothing. Our families had been friends for as long as I could remember, and I knew I could trust Liv with my life. And my family's life.

Mom unwrapped the bandages on my arm as Liv set the water to boil for mint tea. "Some stitches have come loose… oh Theo, what did you do…"

As she worked, Mom asked me to recount what

happened in the City in a hushed voice.

I told her, careful to mention Johnson only in passing. Mom was sharp though — she didn't miss a beat.

"Johnson? Not the awful Patrol who gave you the hole in your arm?" She frowned, and the crease between her eyebrows deepened.

"That's the one…"

Mom shook her head, muttering something that I didn't quite catch. Liv came in from the kitchen with a tray filled with three steaming mugs of tea and a small pile of biscuits on a chipped plate.

"Thank you, dear." Mom smiled at Liv, the warmth in her eyes unmistakable.

We sipped our tea in silence as Mom put the finishing touches on my wound dressing.

"There you go, that's better." She set her supplies down and motioned for Liv and I to sit on the couch.

Nibbling on a fresh mint leaf I fished out of my tea, I sat down, my mind still wandering back to what Mom said about Dad and his job…

"Liv, dear, will you stay for dinner?"

Liv shuddered, as if letting go of everything that happened today, then nodded. "All right, thanks Lisa. I can't stay long though, Mom will be waiting…"

"Send her our best, will you?" Mom drained her mug and took the dishes to the kitchen. The clink of crockery and the smell of baked potato wafting through the apartment made my mouth water.

The creak of the front door and Laika's loud barks announced Dad's arrival. I jumped up, wanting to ask him about what Mom had said, about what was going on in the GA, and about his conversation with Mom the other night. Not to mention that I wanted him to tell me something — anything — more about deathdays. But I was stopped short in my tracks. Mom got there first.

"Reg, thank goodness you're home, you won't believe what happened to the kids today…"

Every time I opened my mouth to ask Dad about what was going on, where all this unrest was coming from, I was cut short. I exchanged a knowing glance with Liv. I could tell she wanted answers just as much as I did. Dad was too busy worrying about what happened to us, especially as Johnson was involved. I reminded him that Liv and I had managed to escape unscathed.

"Thank goodness for that," Mom said, ushering us to the dinner table.

"The City isn't as safe as it used to be anymore." Dad chewed on a forkful of potatoes, his expression thoughtful. "If things continue this way, the Government will put up extra security measures."

"Extra security measures?" Liv swallowed a mouthful of potato. "What are those?"

"Stricter curfews, stringent electricity rations, Safety Patrols prowling the streets… The Grand Alliance had implemented them once before, some thirty years ago, before you were born."

Mom shuddered. "We were just children then…"

I glanced up at Dad. "But the Patrols still roam the streets like they own them. Just look at Johnson."

Dad exchanged a covert glance with Mom. "Johnson is an outlier, and outliers like him are dangerous, and not to be trusted."

Liv's lower lip trembled, her shoulders tight. "But what will happen if outliers like him become the norm? If violence, the kind Johnson displayed toward Theo and Laika, and today with that poor little boy… become the norm?"

"Let's hope they don't," Dad said quietly. "And trust me on this one — you don't want the Grand Alliance to reinstate the extra security measures."

"Why not?" I looked between my parents. "Maybe it would prevent people dying on the streets, like they did today."

Mom shook her head. "They were dark times, Theo. The measures were put in place to keep the City's citizens safe, but I'm afraid just the opposite happened."

"Many were killed, either because they refused to obey the curfew, or even for looking at a Safety Patrol the wrong way." Dad took another bite of his potato, this time mixed with peas. He then set his fork down. "No, you don't want the measures to be reinstated. None of us do."

"Is that how it started last time too? With the... unrest?"

Dad nodded, but didn't offer any more information. I didn't press him.

We finished the rest of the meal in silence.

LATER THAT EVENING, after dinner, Laika trekked after Liv and me to my room. She hopped on the bed and curled up at its foot, yawning. Liv perched next to her, stroking her behind the ear.

I didn't want to think about it, but this was probably the last night I was alone with Liv. The last night we could pretend that everything was all right. Normal. This time tomorrow, my whole being would be filled to the brim with thoughts about my impending deathday: as certain and absolute as the sun rising and setting every day. I balled my hands into fists in an attempt to keep them from trembling. My fingers were cold against my skin, and my breaths came in sharp gasps. My digits on my wrist blazed beneath my sleeve. The entire world seemed to be crushing down on me; the weight in my chest and shoulders nothing like what I've felt before.

As if sensing my unease, Liv titled her head toward me, her green eyes stark against the dying light. She straightened the fingers on my right hand and intertwined them with hers, giving me a reassuring squeeze. We lay back on my bed, hand in hand, for what felt like hours. My lips brushed her mouth, then her cheek, her forehead, all of her. I got lost in her scent — that fresh smell of a spring meadow — lost in a daydream of a future with Liv that was all but stolen from me.

With her presence alone, Liv had just now managed to lift the growing dread off my shoulders. Despite what was coming, I felt strangely peaceful. A sense of serenity washed over me every time my skin brushed against Liv's. It was as if, through her very touch, she could quiet my fears and disperse my demons.

Liv drew me in, closing the distance between our lips. She breathed in deeply and then giggled, shooting me a quizzical look.

"What is it?"

"Nothing." She flashed her brilliant smile. "It's just that you always smell like mint."

I laughed and pulled her close. "The stuff is good for you, you know." I kissed her, mirroring her smile.

After a moment, I leaned over and whispered, "I wish

we could stay here forever…"

"Me too." Her voice was soft and warm. Heat washed over me as her lips kissed my cheek. "It's cruel."

"It is. I wish I had more time with you… even forever isn't long enough."

Liv faced me, suddenly serious. "I mean the concept of deathdays. Why do humans have them, while other animals don't?" She kept her gaze trained on me, a fierce intensity painted in her features. "Why are we the only species alive with these awful digits on our wrists?"

I bit my lower lip and pushed my hair out of my eyes. Wasn't that exactly what Ian had said? That even though all species had the natural deathday biomarker, according to him, humans had managed to tag it somehow? Liv's words echoed his. Not for the first time today, I had a sudden urge to tell her everything: about Ian, about him surviving past his deathday, and how it *was* possible, somehow, although neither of us had the faintest clue how…

Liv didn't take her eyes off me for a second. She was clearly waiting for an answer.

I sighed. "That's a good question." That was all I could muster. I had to ask her something else though; I had to find out if she truly thought like Ian… and like I did now too… I shifted on the bed. "What if there was a way to survive past them?"

Liv's mouth fell open. "That's impossible."

"Is it?"

"Of course. I'd never heard of anyone surviving past their deathday."

I swallowed, but my throat was as dry as sandpaper. It wasn't my secret to tell. It was Ian's. And I promised to keep it safe. I hated this — sometimes it felt like I was leading a double life. I was caught between my two best friends — keeping one's secret to protect another. Or to protect them both. My stomach churned at the thought of betraying either of them. But it wasn't too late to convince Ian that Liv could be trusted with the truth…

I pushed my hair out of my eyes. "What if it was possible?"

"It's a moot question. It's not, and you know it."

"But what if?"

"What's with all these hypothetical questions, Theodore?"

I dug my fingers into my patchwork quilt, weighing my words carefully. I wanted to tell her it's not hypothetical, that I knew someone who'd survived past his deathday, and that it was possible, somehow…

Clearing my throat, I finally brought my gaze up to meet Liv's. I had to change tack. "Do you think the GA knows something about deathdays?"

Liv's eyes widened, then narrowed quickly again. She

chewed the inside of her cheek, the way she always did in class when contemplating a particularly tough question asked by Ms. Holloway. Finally, she shook her head. "They probably know as much as we do. Or they're trying to find out what they can through the Deathday Research Fund. Those constant comp broadcasts are getting annoying..." Liv paused. "No, they're doing what they can to keep everyone safe from... whatever's out there. And from other international threats. They're doing what they can to protect us, aren't they?"

"To protect us? Liv, did what the Safety Patrols did today look like 'protecting us' to you? You saw Alma and Everett, and that little blond boy... They were innocent." I glanced to the door and lowered my voice. "And you heard what Mom and Dad said about the extra security measures..."

Liv shook her head again. "No, not the Patrols. They must have had orders to keep the peace today, but..." She paused. "The Grand Alliance itself wouldn't give orders to the Patrols to kill anyone... would they?"

"Killing for the sake of killing, maybe not. But what about killing to keep the peace? Killing to keep control?"

"I just don't understand why the Grand Alliance would do something like this." Liv laced her fingers together. "They swore to protect us. All of us: everyone here in the Second City, and all the citizens in the other

Cities. In the Peace Pact, after the War. Do you remember that history class?"

"The Peace Pact? That shaky agreement?"

"That 'shaky agreement' saved many innocent lives, Theodore. The Asian Superpower might well still have been here on GA soil if they hadn't called a truce. They *promised* to protect us."

"Promises can be broken," I said in a low voice, just loud enough for Liv to hear. I thought again of the promise I'd made to Ian.

Once again, a wave of helplessness washed over me. I bit my tongue hard — to keep myself from voicing the one thought that threatened to consume me. I wished more than anything that I could tell her about Ian, about what he's been trying to do for the past five years… I knew she would understand, if she only had all the facts. Then she could help him when I no longer could.

But I knew I couldn't. That promise was one that couldn't be broken, no matter how much I wanted to bring Liv on board. I just hoped that someday, somehow, Liv's and Ian's paths would cross… and that Liv would understand. That she would forgive me for keeping this from her. I took Liv's hands in mine and pressed them to my lips.

The large clock in Eagle Square struck midnight. It only sounded once a day, to mark the end of one day and the arrival of another. Even from this distance, its unmistakable clang was clearly audible in the silence of the night.

"Happy deathday to me," I whispered into Liv's fingers. "Now, where's my cake?"

Liv laughed, and I could tell by her expression it was despite herself. She rearranged her features and cleared her throat. "Not yet!" But her smile faltered after a moment. "It's not your deathday yet."

"No, but after midnight tomorrow it will be."

She took my face in her hands and pressed her lips to mine, gently at first, but then her kisses became more and more desperate. I rushed to keep up with her. It felt like we were racing toward a mysterious destination, but were running out of time.

But I *was* running out of time.

The realization hit me as if I had run headfirst into a brick wall. I couldn't believe how mere moments ago I was joking about it. But it was true, it was happening. Within a maximum of forty-eight hours, I'd be dead.

I grit my teeth, pushing the thought out of my mind and pulling Liv close. Laika stirred next to us, her pet tag jingling in the otherwise silent room.

A sudden thought struck me. I gently released Liv's hands and shifted over to Laika. She lifted one tired eye and thumped her tail against the bed. I offered her a small smile — she was always so happy to see me.

Fumbling with Laika's collar, I detached the smooth silver medallion dangling from it. I brushed my hand against the cool metal, my fingers finding the small grooves engraved on its surface: Laika's name, my name, and my address. It caught the moonlight spilling in from the cityscape beyond my narrow bedroom window — the City had shut off the electricity several hours ago.

I extended the hand with the pet tag toward Liv. "I want you to have this."

Liv's eyes widened and flickered from me to the medallion. "Theo, I can't—"

"Yes, you can. It won't even be accurate after tomorrow…"

"She needs one though. You saw yourself what happened with Johnson…"

"My parents will get her a new one." I waited a beat. "But this one, it's yours now. I want you to remember me when you look at it, when you hold it." I lifted Liv's hand from her lap and closed her warm fingers around the medallion.

Tears welled in her eyes. "I'll miss you," she whispered, kissing me gently.

"I will too." My eyes stung. I blinked several times to get the moisture out of them.

She threw her arms around me and held me close. I wished, more than anything, that this moment would last forever.

But I knew what it was.

Fantasy.

At this time tomorrow, Ian and I would either be breaking into the White Tower, or we'd already be inside. I knew I should be spending tonight preparing for our mission — we'd only get one shot, after all. Ian would want me to focus, to get everything in order before the chaos of the morning. But Ian didn't understand… The allure of spending just one more night alone with Liv was too strong. If these were my last moments with her one-on-one, then I'd make sure they were good ones. That way, I'd at least have something to hold on to right before the green digits consumed me.

But Ian's voice, going over the plan, tugged at the back of my mind. Images of Everett and Alma's scared faces, the little girl's bloodstained clothes, the small blond boy on his knees, and all those bodies, lying lifeless on the cracked concrete of the wide avenue swam into my mind, unbidden. The people weren't happy. They were protesting, growing restless. The citizens of the Second City had coaxed the ember into a tiny flame. How long would it be before the GA extinguished it, together with all hope, once and for all?

Still, despite the gnawing feeling in my stomach, I wanted to spend as much time with Liv and my parents as possible… I closed my eyes, stroking Liv's soft chestnut waves, breathing her in. They all hated the Celebrations. I wasn't a fan myself, but asking them to come with me was the only way I'd be able to salvage a few extra hours with the ones I loved. Then, I'd have to say goodbye and find Ian. My mouth went dry at the thought.

But I gritted my teeth and made my decision. I had to do something. I had to carry through with the plan, even if it meant saying goodbye to my family, to Liv, prematurely. An entire afternoon and evening would be stolen from us. But this was the right way. The only way.

I took a deep breath and pulled out of the embrace. Liv's delicate features were creased with concern.

"Pix, will you come with me to this week's Celebrations?"

Liv stared at me, taken aback. "What? But why? Theo, those Celebrations are awful—"

"Please, pix." I kissed her forehead. "For me?"

She bit her lip, hesitating. Finally, she nodded. "Anything for you."

I smiled and kissed her again. "Bring Vi and Ralph too."

ONE DAY

THAT MORNING, I spent a long time with Laika in my room. We played a favorite game of ours: I threw an old ball, yellowed by age, across the room, and she'd scramble to bring it back to me. It took everything in me to be present with her, to not let my thoughts wander to what lay ahead. I watched the perkiness of her ears, her attentive gaze, her wagging tail.

Leaning backward, I sent the ball flying across the room again. When Laika brought it back, I threw arms around her and hugged her tight, taking in the warmth of her body and the softness of her fur on my skin.

"I'm going to miss you, girl."

Laika barked, her tail thumping against the floor.

A soft knock sounded on my door, making me jump.

After a moment, Mom entered, dressed in a plain navy dress. "Ready to go?"

I nodded. "Be right there."

Mom offered me a smile, but I knew there was an immense pain hiding behind her warm brown eyes.

With a heavy heart, I gave Laika one last hug and got off the floor.

The heat sensor rested on the dresser next to my old mirror. I cupped my hand around it and closed my eyes, allowing its cool, smooth surface to permeate through my entire being. I squeezed it and dropped it in my jacket pocket, next to a small knife I'd grabbed from the cupboard earlier this morning. I knew it would be dangerous to go to the Celebrations without my comp… but it was a risk I was willing to take. The Safety Patrols couldn't possibly do an identity check of everyone, so I hoped to slip through the checkpoint unnoticed.

As I moved to turn away, my eyes caught something in the mirror. My reflection stared back at me. I looked paler than I'd remembered — it must have been all the blood I'd lost from my wound, which, although it still throbbed, had lost some of its intensity. My hair stuck out at weird angles; I tried to flatten it, with limited success. I shook it out and pushed it out of my eyes.

I considered myself again. This was probably the last time I would see my reflection… I willed my frenzied heart to still its incessant thumping and pushed the thought out of my mind. Then I turned on my heel and left my little room behind.

Mom and Dad waited by the door, while Laika clutched her red leash in her muzzle, her expression hopeful, in anticipation of a walk that would never happen.

"Not this time, girl." I scratched her behind the ears. "Not where we're headed."

"Come, son." Dad held the door open for us.

I kissed Laika on the head one last time and stepped through the open door, unable to bear one last look back. Laika's whines filled my ears as she scratched the surface of the door with her paws. I blinked hard to get the moisture out of my eyes and let out a deep breath. With a considerable effort, I steadied myself and trudged down the stairs.

We walked side by side through the City streets, keeping close to one another. I wrapped my jacket tighter around myself, shielding my body from the bite of the wind. As we neared Eagle Square in Millennium Sector, a throng of families joined us. We were all headed in the same direction — to watch the Celebrations of those whose deathdays had passed recently.

But today, the City announced a special Celebration — Chancellor Graves himself would be addressing the crowds. Today, we would be celebrating Timothy Sinclair, a boy from our Sector School. He was in the year below me, and although I didn't know him very well, I needed to witness today's ceremony... I needed to see what it was like.

Liv said that before the War, the Celebrations were called funerals, and they were somber events. In the GA, those who reached their deathdays were celebrated and revered. It was a way for the Government to thank its citizens for their service, in an addition to their Ten Day Object. Not every family chose to allow the GA to hold Celebrations for them, but I'd been told it was a great honor for those that did. At least that's what they said. I wrinkled my nose — I suspected there was some sort of monetary incentive involved.

Chancing a sidelong glance at Mom and Dad, I noticed that both their lips were pressed into matching thin lines. They were only attending the Celebrations today because I'd asked them to. They would never have gone of their own accord — they'd much rather spend the time with me at home. But as I was a minor, I wasn't allowed to attend the Celebrations unaccompanied. And after the recent mess with Johnson, they weren't willing to let me get into any more trouble where there were Safety Patrols involved. They also agreed to supervise Liv, Violet and Ralph, which would be in line with the rules — two minors to an adult.

We continued our trek downtown in silence. My parents would also never allow the GA to hold a Celebration for me. They valued their privacy — and mine — too much, despite Dad's high-ranking job at the heart of the Government.

After a few blocks, I caught a glimpse of rich, wavy brown hair, catching and reflecting the afternoon light. Liv. All the tension left my body at the sight of her. A blonde girl in braids stood beside her, chatting to a stout, dark-haired boy in a maroon sweater. Vi and Ralph.

My lips widened into a smile as I threw up my good arm and waved. "Over here!"

Liv turned around, wiping her hand on her cheek. When she saw me, she replaced her downcast expression with a smile and came thundering toward me. "Theo!" She flung her arms around me, and I kissed her on the cheek. "There you are. Come on, the Celebrations are about to start."

But I wasn't fooled. I knew she'd been wiping away tears… tears for me. A pang of guilt shot through me. I couldn't bear to be the one causing her all this pain. But it wasn't up to me. It was my deathday.

I followed Liv through the thickening crowds, with Vi, Ralph and my parents close behind. Luckily, the Safety Patrols were conducting their routine ID checks on the other side of the Square. I breathed a sigh of relief.

Liv halted next to a large gray and white statue of an eagle situated near the middle of Eagle Square. The Eagle Statue — the official emblem of the GA, erected as a reminder of the nation's sovereignty and power. It was modeled after the bald eagle, which Liv said used to be the emblem of the old United States. The White Tower loomed above us, casting an imposing shadow on one side of the Square.

After a few moments, the first notes of the GA's anthem sounded, and the chatter of the crowd died down and gave way to a uniform hush that permeated through the gathered citizens.

As the final notes rang out, the ornate white double doors of the White Tower burst open. A small procession of Patrols piled out in a semicircle. Their guns, usually slung around their shoulders, pointed out at the crowd.

In their midst stood Chancellor Graves himself — tall and lean, his dark hair heavily streaked with gray and silver. A rich salt and pepper beard framed his tough, wrinkled face. Although I couldn't see them from this distance, I knew from mandatory comp viewings that he had a pair of deep-set, steel-gray eyes. Two thick white stripes cut through the wide sleeves of his otherwise black cloak, which billowed in the breeze behind him. His dark ensemble stood in stark contrast to the gleaming white of the Tower and of the stage that had been erected specifically for the Celebrations. Banners bearing a striking black eagle on a stark red background draped the side of the Tower — the same as I'd seen inside the Tower during my Ten Day Ceremony.

Graves wasn't often seen in public, and he rarely addressed the citizens in the open. He preferred the confines of his secure, secluded Tower, no doubt. Each year, he chose a few Celebrations to attend, and of course the annual Victory Day Celebrations, which marked the Grand Alliance's triumph over the Asian Superpower in the War. I'd only seen him once before, when Liv's dad took us to a special Victory Day Celebration many years ago.

But today, Graves was here in the Square, among us. "Welcome, citizens of the Second City, citizens of the Grand Alliance of American States." Graves extended his arms in a hollow attempt at being warm and welcoming. "We are gathered here today for a very special Celebration." He beamed, and I tasted something acrid in my mouth. A boy had just *died*.

On cue, another unit of Safety Patrols marched out onto the stage, carrying something long, polished and white. My stomach sank. A coffin.

Inside lay Timothy — the small, mousy-haired boy who had always sat by himself in the school cafeteria, who always did his homework on time, and who never got in trouble. Poor Timothy. He was a quiet boy, so unlike the other Fleeters in our school. Holding such lavish Celebrations for him in front of the whole Second City just didn't feel right. His parents surely knew that he wouldn't have wanted this… I shook my head. But maybe they didn't have a choice. Maybe his family needed the money, the extra rations, or whatever the GA had offered in return. At least Timothy's last act would be to help his family lead a better life.

The blinding white of Scott's coffin stung my eyes — it was far too large for his slight frame. But I couldn't tear my eyes away, neither from the coffin nor from the pure white of the Tower dominating over each and every one of us in the Square. What kind of things went on in there? My mind whirred with a thousand possibilities.

I felt a hand in mine and looked down to see Liv clutching it. Our eyes met and I gave her a small smile, which she returned.

"Today, we celebrate the life of Timothy Sinclair, a boy of only fifteen, who served his City, and his country, valiantly." Graves' voice was as oily as his hair. I shuddered and zipped up my blue-green jacket despite the warmth of the mid-September sun beating down on the Square.

I'd spent my whole life believing everything the GA did was for the good of its people. But what did this man, who stood before us today in his dark clothes and slicked back hair, ever do to earn the citizens' trust? He was Chancellor like his father before him, and like his son surely will be after him. Their power had never been questioned, not since Graves' great grandfather, a war hero, came into power once the War ended.

I scanned the small crowd gathered on the podium behind Graves. Sure enough, a tall slender boy with dark hair, high cheekbones and a strong jawline stood in the shadow of the White Tower, holding the hand of a small blonde girl with her delicate hair woven into braids. The boy, who couldn't be more than a year or two older than I was, wore a black turtleneck, while the girl clutched her yellow dress nervously with her free hand. Graves' children.

Somehow, they reminded me of Everett and Alma, but one glance confirmed the two pairs couldn't be more different. By the looks of them, the boy and girl on the podium were surely Timeless, with deathdays spanning decades, while Everett and Alma were raised by their uncle in River, one of the City's poorer sectors. I hadn't asked, but something told me Everett and Alma were more Fleeters than Timeless.

I tore my eyes away from the stage and searched the outskirts of the crowd for Ian. I knew he'd be watching the Celebrations, I just wasn't sure from where. Squinting, I looked up into the Tower and the surrounding buildings. The autumn sunlight reflected off the windows and blinded me for a moment.

"Timothy's family, as well as all of you, are here to honor his noble life."

Timothy's family. With eyes narrowed against the beating sun, I scanned the crowds close to the stage. Sure enough, in the front row, a man and a little girl with Timothy's mousy hair hovered beside the coffin. The girl's eyes, red and puffy even from this distance, flickered between the coffin and the faces in the crowd at regular intervals. Timothy's father and little sister.

A shiver ran down my spine as an unwelcome thought settled in my mind. I let out a small sigh and leaned in toward Liv. "That'll be me soon…" I swallowed hard. "And that'll be my family." A burning sensation erupted behind my eyes, but I blinked furiously to dissipate it.

Liv squeezed my hand so hard it went numb. "Oh Theo, don't say that." Her glazed eyes mirrored mine. "Pretend it's not true, it's not true, it's not true…" She held on to me, steadying herself.

But I knew it *was* true.

What happened to Ian was an anomaly. He said so himself. I couldn't hope, in my wildest dreams, for the same thing to happen to me on my deathday.

So I didn't.

Instead, I ignored the incessant burning of the poison green digits on my left wrist. It wasn't my imagination — it had definitely intensified over the past few days.

The anthem rang out over the square again, its notes harsh and unforgiving, like deathdays themselves. When the tune ended, the crowds stood still and solemn in a symbolic moment of silence for Timothy. I focused my gaze on his family and the people in the front row. They were unmoving, paying their respects to the boy who died too soon. A few leaned against the short metal barrier separating them from the stage.

All was still and quiet.

Until the barrier exploded.

TIME STOOD STILL. An ear-splitting blast whipped through the air. I was blinded by an impossibly bright light, which, within seconds, gave way to thick black smoke.

Chaos ensued. Safety Patrols shot blindly into the crowd. The screams of men, women and children filled the air, shouting their loved ones' names, piling into the streets and alleys off the square for cover.

Graves and his security squadron retreated into the

White Tower, shutting the double doors firmly behind them. Two Safety Patrols positioned themselves directly in front of the doors, their guns at the ready. A large blunt object soared through the air and hit one of them in the head. He toppled to the ground and lay still. I couldn't tell from this distance what hit him.

Liv's urgent voice in my ear and her hand tugging on mine brought me out of my stupor. Vi, her face pale, stood close by, but Ralph was nowhere to be seen.

Neither were my parents.

I scanned the crowds frantically, crouching and shielding my body behind the Eagle Statue, beckoning for the girls to do the same. Grabbing their hands, I pulled them down next to me. Liv's touch sent a thrill through my body, but I willed myself to focus. "My parents — have you seen them?"

Liv shook her head, but Vi pointed behind me and shouted, "There!"

I turned just in time to see Mom's face, as white as a sheet, and the back of Dad's head several feet away. She leaned over and whispered in his ear. As he spun around, our eyes met.

Dad didn't hesitate. He grabbed Mom's hand and together they closed the distance between us, hunched over against the push and pull of the maddening crowds.

"Theo!" Mom pulled me into a tight hug, her soft

hands gripping my shoulders and back, although she was careful not to touch my injury. When she let go, she shook her head at Dad. "I knew this was a bad idea, Reg. We need to get the kids home." She turned toward us, her jaw set and her gaze unwavering. "Come with us."

Dad grunted and nodded. "Your mother's right. But we can't all go at once. Bigger groups are easier to target."

My mouth went dry. "Target?"

"We don't know who or what caused those bombs to go off. But there's no time to talk now; we need to get moving."

I looked at my parents, at their caring, slightly lined faces. I hoped more than anything that this wasn't the last time I saw them, and I fought hard to keep my voice level. "You two go ahead. We'll follow."

Mom scowled. "We can't just leave you—"

"We're not leaving them." Dad put a large hand on her shoulder. "They'll be right behind us."

I nodded, but chose my words carefully. "I'll make sure the girls make it back safely." I glanced around the statue — where in the world was Ralph? I needed him, I needed him to help get the girls home… because I knew deep down I couldn't do it myself. I avoided Liv's and Vi's gazes, so I glanced up at Dad instead.

His bright blue eyes — the same shade as mine — bore into me. It was like he was peeking into my soul. I stared, unblinking, back at him. He then gave me a small smile and nodded. "Be safe."

"I will."

Mom wrapped me into another tight hug, a pained smile overlaying her delicate features.

"We will meet again," I said, my jaw set. "This isn't goodbye."

My parents held my gaze for a split second longer, before turning on their heels and hurrying away, disappearing into the crowds. I stared after them until their silhouettes were indiscernible in the endless human sea, swelling and rolling like waves during high tide at the Lake.

Finally, I tore my eyes away from the masses and turned back to my friends. "Liv, take Vi and go back to my place. My parents will be waiting."

"What? What about you? Aren't you coming with us?"

I shook my head and took Liv's hands in mine. The now familiar electric current coursed through me at Liv's touch, but this time, it was tinged with something empty and hollow. A sadness that stemmed from the realization that I had to split from Liv now, and that I wasn't sure if I would see her again. I let the words tumble out of me before I could change my mind. "I can't. There's something I need to do."

Another round of gunshots ripped through the air —
I clamped my hands over my ears to quell their deafening
cracks. They were close. Too close. It seemed that
someone with a loaded gun was firing it directly on the
other side of the statue.

"I'll come with you." Liv's expression was one of
stony determination.

"No, you need to get home, people are getting
shot—"

More gunshots. But they weren't coming from the
other side of the statue anymore. The gunman was
moving. Liv grabbed my arm and pulled me out from
under the statue, away from the gunshots. Violet stumbled behind us, her eyes wide with fear.

"Theo, I want to come with you. I want to help, I
want to—"

Vi's scream filled the air. I watched, in slow motion,
as Liv toppled to the ground.

My world slowed. I threw myself beneath her, hoping
I would be fast enough to break her fall. My hands
caught her just before she hit the concrete, sending a stab
of pain through my injured left arm, which I ignored. I
gently lowered Liv the last few inches and knelt next to
her, Vi at my side.

"Liv, Liv…"

Liv's wide eyes and ragged breaths reassured me she

was still alive, but her expression said it all. My stomach dropped to my knees. I shifted my trembling arm from underneath her — it came away stained a deep crimson. Vi stroked her arm, repeating Liv's name over and over.

"Liv, can you hear me?" I put my mouth close to her ear and felt for a pulse. It was weak — she was losing a lot of blood — but it was there.

Liv made a noise that was halfway between an acknowledgment and a grunt. She winced as I shifted her onto her side so that I could examine the wound.

Liv's blood trailed down her back, a stark red river against her pale skin. I had to do something to stem the initial onslaught of blood. I tore off a part of my shirt and tied it tightly around Liv's arm and shoulder, like Mom had once showed me. My white shirt turned red immediately. My heart pounded in my throat; I could hardly think straight or hear anything over the ringing in my ears.

Despite the pandemonium that reigned on the Square and in my heart, one thought rose up clearly above the rest: it was all my fault. After yesterday's near miss in the avenue, how could I have thought that bringing Liv here was a good idea? And Vi, Ralph and my parents? I balled my hands into fists under Liv's trembling body to prevent them from shaking and grit my teeth. Now was not the time to blame myself.

Now was the time to help Liv.

"Ralph." I turned to Vi, who stood numb and wide-eyed, her cheeks streaked with silent tears. "Where's Ralph?"

As if on cue, Ralph stumbled out from behind the Eagle Statue. His face was as pale as the rest of his body, and his clothes, face and dark hair were smeared with red. My blood ran cold. "Are you hurt?"

Ralph shook his head, but his mouth dropped at the sight of Liv in my arms. "Is she—?"

I lowered my voice. "She's alive. Can you help Vi carry her back to my house? Mom will tend to her there." I paused, willing for my racing heart to slow. "If all goes well, they should be home first." I didn't want to think about the alternative.

"What about you?" Ralph asked.

I shook my head, and our eyes locked for an instant.

"I'm coming with… you." Liv's voice was a hoarse whisper, but the determination in her tone was unmistakable.

"You have to get home. Mom will help stem—"

"I'm not leaving you." Her sharp intake of breath was audible even above the commotion raging around us. "Not… today."

"You're not leaving me. I just need you to go home with Vi and Ralph, and stay safe." *I'll be right there* — I wanted to add, but I couldn't bring myself to… It would be misleading, a harsh half-truth uttered to soften the shock of a bullet wound.

"No way in hell, Theodore. I'm… not… leaving you!"

"Liv, you have to, it's not safe here—"

"I'll go with him, Liv," Ralph said.

"No. I need you to look after her. Promise me you'll take care of her!"

After a moment's hesitation, Ralph nodded once, his hands trembling as he moved around Liv to hoist her up.

"Whatever you're doing, I'm… coming with you. Remember our list?"

"This isn't on our list."

"Then… add it." She took a shaky breath. "Whatever we do, we do together."

A hollowness filled my chest; a pang of emptiness so heavy it weighed on me like a boulder — impossible to move or shrug off. Taking Liv into the White Tower was out of the question. She was hurt and needed urgent medical attention. But I allowed myself to indulge in the fantasy, just for a moment… Liv and I, in the White Tower together, evading Safety Patrols and finding out what the GA knew about deathdays… She'd make a great ally, as she'd proven during our stint in the old abandoned skyscraper.

But it could never happen. Our plan was way too dangerous — it wasn't just one of the adventures on our list. This was real, and it could be deadly. For me, it almost certainly would be… Not only that, Liv was in danger of bleeding out. She needed to get to safety — now.

"I can't, pix," I finally managed to say. "You need to go. Vi, Ralph, can you carry her?"

"No! Theodore, no—"

But I interrupted her protests by lowering my mouth to hers and kissing her deeply. She responded with the same fervor, despite the amount of blood she was losing and the bright sheen of sweat on her brow. Adrenaline coursed through my veins as I kissed her, electricity tingling through every nerve ending in my body. She would never stop having this effect on me.

I knew that we were exposed, that gunshots whipped and cracked around us, that Safety Patrols mercilessly asserted their power by attacking the faceless crowds… and that the faceless crowds were fighting back.

But I couldn't let her go, not just yet… I savored our kiss and held her in my arms, for a moment not caring about the shower of bullets, not caring about the puddle of crimson pooling on my arm and jacket where I held Liv, not caring that both Vi and Ralph were staring at us, mouths open and eyes wide…

Finally, after one last kiss, I pulled away. Liv's eyes were closed and her shallow breaths were warm against my skin.

"I'm still coming," she whispered. It wasn't a question.

I shook my head. Liv never gave up easily, that was for sure. I thought back to Ian, and how I'd promised never to reveal his secret. A wave of powerlessness washed over me, momentarily paralyzing me. Here Liv was, bleeding in my arms, and I couldn't even give her something to hold on to, not even a shrapnel of hope to light her way in the darkness. It was an ache so tangible I felt it in my very marrow.

I couldn't tell her Ian's secret… but Ian could.

"Find Ian," I breathed into her ear. "If you want answers, find Ian."

Liv's eyes shot open. "What? Who?"

"Find Ian and believe in the impossible when it comes to deathdays."

"Who's Ian?"

"You have to go now."

"Who's Ian?" Liv repeated, a note of urgency in her voice.

"A friend. Find him. And go, now!"

"No—"

Vi appeared at our side, doing her best to mask that

her cheeks had taken on a distinct pink shade. "Liv, we need to go right now, the Patrols are marching this way—"

Sure enough, a squadron of Patrols had entered the Square from the east side. Home was west. There was no time to lose.

Ralph took Liv under his arm and Vi grabbed her feet. They started carrying her back to Loop. Back home.

Liv thrashed in Ralph's grasp and twisted onto her uninjured side, facing me. "No, I need this, I need this! Theodore!" Liv screamed and kicked out at her friends, tears streaming down her cheeks.

"I need this! I need to come with you! Let me go, let me go!"

But I shook my head silently, and with an ache that threatened to split my heart in two, I turned away from the one I loved, and ran. I ran past the Eagle Statue, Liv's screams and protests still echoing around the Square. Even through the commotion of the unrest, I could make out her voice clearly above the noise. I pictured Liv's face in my mind, memorizing every detail as I ran: her brilliant green eyes, the shine of her long brown hair, the curve of her pink lips.

As I ran, one thought rose up above the rest: It was more important for me to save Liv than to stay with her.

I now knew what I had to do; I could see it with

more clarity than ever before. I had to find Ian and to carry out our plan. I couldn't let Liv suffer the same terrible fate that awaited me... She deserved to live, and I would do everything in my power to make it happen. A quiet determination to do whatever I could settled in my heart.

And in that moment, I knew there was nothing better I could do with my last day than to save Liv.

I CIRCLED BACK through the chaotic crowds and crouched beneath the Eagle Statue, once again using it as a shield. I scanned the perimeter of the Square for a glimpse of Ian, looking for a hint of his tan skin or a glint of his keen, hazel eyes in the afternoon light.

Nothing.

A stray bullet hit the statue dangerously close to where I was hiding, ricocheting off its metal facade and darting back into the crowd. I couldn't stay here. It wasn't safe anymore.

Several Safety Patrols jogged by me — they didn't seem to notice the bloodied up kid hiding beneath the statue. "This way!" One of them shouted in a coarse voice, motioning for the others to follow. I let out a breath. When they passed, I jumped out from under the statue and sprinted in the opposite direction.

In the open air of the Square, I was exposed. There was nothing to shield me from a potential onslaught of bullets. It was just me, the looming White Tower to my left, and the Square.

I tore my eyes away from the Tower just in time to see a man running straight toward me, a blunt rod in his hand and a frenzy in his eyes. He wasn't a Safety Patrol, but I skid out of his way, tumbling to the ground, preventing a nasty collision between us at the last second. He didn't stop — his shock of dark hair billowed behind him as he headed for the nearest Patrol.

I clambered back to my feet and glanced down at my hands. Shards of glass intermixed with blood were wedged into the fleshy part of my palms. They burned, but I ignored the sensation. Just as I'd learned to ignore the burning of my deathday digits.

Glancing around me once more in the hope that I would catch sight of Ian, I took in the carnage before me for the first time. Men, women and even children lay sprawled on the ground, some unmoving, some stirring, others groaning in pain. Several women tended to the injured. On the far side of the Square, gunshots and shouts still rang out in the early evening air. The battle was still going strong there.

My heart ached for Timothy. An attack, death and destruction during his Celebrations was the last thing a quiet boy like him would have wanted. And what about his father and sister? Where were they now? I swallowed. Were they still alive, or were their lives claimed by the initial explosion?

And, more alarmingly still, who set off that bomb near the front of the Celebrations? The GA? But for what purpose? To assert their dominance and quell dissent? An inkling in my stomach told me that no, the GA had other means to control its citizens. Was it set off by the people then? The Fleeters? Or a calculated attack, targeting Graves? Was it a sign of the people's discontent with the electricity cuts, the food shortages, or something else? I thought with a pang of Dad's warning. He would know more.

But so would Ian. I had to find him.

Shaking myself off, I looked over my shoulder, made sure the coast was clear and kept running.

I side-stepped the body of a young man dressed in a tattered gray coat, wishing that I could help him. One side of his head was covered in a thick, dark, oozing liquid. He wasn't moving. At this point, there was nothing I could do for him.

I stared at the scene before me, stunned at how much damage humans could do to one another. The digits on my wrist stung, as did the wound in my arm, but it dulled in the wake of the carnage in the Square. My heart thudded in my chest, and I tasted something warm in my mouth. Blood. I must have bitten the inside of my cheek harder than I'd intended.

Despite everything, I felt numb. I fumbled in my pocket for the knife I picked up this morning. Its metal blade jingled against the glass of the heat sensor, but the sound was muted, muffled by the roaring of blood in my ears.

I dodged another pair of Safety Patrols speeding past me in the opposite direction. Lucky for me, they didn't pay attention to a pale kid with unkempt hair who was running into the chaos rather than away from it.

My thoughts turned back, as they so often did these days, to Liv. To her warm lips, her solid embrace, the steady feel of her slender body against mine. I wondered where she was now… Did Vi and Ralph manage to get her back to my parents? Did Mom treat her injury? Part of me resented leaving her. Especially now, when she needed me most, when my whole family would be gathered at her bedside and tending to her wounds. And me? I was nowhere to be seen. My throat constricted at the thought.

I knew, deep down, that what I was doing was right. Finding Ian, carrying out the plan, all of it. But no matter how I tried, I couldn't suppress the tiny voice that crept into the back of my mind, little by little, whispering that this was in vain — all of it — this whole excursion to the Celebrations, the plan, everything. I exposed Liv, my parents, Vi and Ralph to serious danger by asking them to join me in the Square today. I put not only my own life on the line, but theirs too — and for what?

An icy chill coursed through my body, initiating in my head and making its way down to my extremities. I was willing to risk the lives of the ones I loved for a desperate attempt at finding something — anything — about deathdays that could help Ian and I understand them better. Selfishly, I had wanted to spend as much time with my friends and family as possible before my own time ran out and my deathday hit. But at what cost? Liv was hurt — the vision of her bloodstained shoulder imprinted in my mind — and I'd left my parents with a hasty goodbye in the midst of gunshots and chaos. Not exactly how I imagined our last conversation. And Laika… I blinked back the moisture from my eyes. It was too much.

Gritting my teeth, I set off through the faceless crowds again. But with each step, my resolve weakened. I'd been running in circles for at least half an hour now, without so much as a glimpse of Ian. What if something had happened to him?

This was it.

I wasn't going to find him, I wasn't going to carry out the plan with him, I was going to die right here, in the middle of the Square, surrounded by bodies, cracked concrete, debris, gunfire and smoke. The Eagle Statue Liv and I had taken refuge behind now had a huge chunk of its side missing. The GA's red and black banners hung loose and lifeless from the side of the Tower, torn and smoldering.

The burning on my wrist, which had faded to a persistent tinkle as the turmoil in the Square ramped up, now increased again and pulsated under the dirty sleeve of my jacket.

A warning. It was coming.

I might as well just sit down here, in the middle of it all, and wait for it to take me. My eyes prickled, and I didn't have to wonder why — I wouldn't get to spend my last moments with my family. Why did Ian and I come up with this stupid plan, anyway? It was never going to work. Maybe I should go back home, see them one last time and make sure Liv was all right…

I wandered aimlessly through the Square, suddenly not caring if I got caught in the crossfire. My fight was done. The sunlight reflecting off the glass panels of the White Tower blinded me momentarily. I squinted, raising my hand to shield my eyes, and winced as a piercing pain

shot through my shoulder. Gingerly, I lowered it again —
I needed to remember to use my other arm. I looked
down and noticed it was caked with a layer of brown and
red. My chest tightened as the realization set in: it was
dried blood. Liv's blood.

Taking a deep breath, I tore my eyes away from my
palm and begged my imagination to stop flashing images
of Liv's bloody body in my mind. Instead, I lifted my
gaze to the mass towering above me. The glow of the
dying day bathed sections of the White Tower in its
warm, orange aura. Dark shadows claimed the recesses of
the Tower that the sunset's rays failed to lick, turning its
facade an ugly, unwelcoming gray. My gaze flitted back to
the sun. It was sinking fast, disappearing behind the dark
silhouettes of the neighboring buildings.

For a moment, I was glued to the spot, marveling at
the beauty of nature, at its power. When one day ends,
another inevitably begins, just beyond the bend, just out
of reach. Perhaps that's what will happen to me. Maybe
tomorrow, after my deathday, I'll wake up somewhere
new. In a world without pain, without suffering, and
without green digits burning into my wrist.

But tonight, I wanted to soak in as many of the sun's
rays as I could. The realization that this was the last
sunset I'll ever see hit me like a brick wall. I wished, more
than anything, that Liv were here, or my parents, basking

in the warm glow of the rays with me, their faces catching and reflecting its heat.

The sun had now turned from the soft, bright orange intermixed with yellow that I so loved to harsh reds and purples. The reds reminded me with a jolt of the substance caking my hands and clothes.

A blood red sun.

I sighed, willing the thought to leave my mind, just as a hand grabbed my arm and pulled hard.

I CRASHED TO THE GROUND, and multicolored spots sprang up and danced at the periphery of my vision. Fortunately, I broke the fall on my good arm, which tingled with the shock of the impact. I raised my head slowly and shook the matted strands of hair out of my eyes. I couldn't be sure, but I had an inkling it was matted with blood.

Standing before me, with an outstretched hand and a wide grin plastered on his face, was a familiar figure. Ian. The remnants of a summer tan gave his already tan skin a golden bronze glow. He winked at me and pocketed his knife inside one of the numerous compartments of his ragged brown jacket — the same one I'd given to him last year, during a particularly cold winter.

I'd told my parents I lost it. They weren't too happy, but I brushed them off. For Ian, I'd do it again in a heartbeat.

My lips curled into a small smile before giving way to a full-blown grin of my own as I grasped Ian's hand. He pulled me upright and held me for a moment in a tight, brotherly embrace.

A heavy weight fell from my chest. Ian was here, and he was safe.

"You look rough." There was a slight edge in Ian's voice.

"I got a little caught up in the Celebrations." I gave him a wry smile. "Where have you been?"

"In the cracked building behind the Tower." He raised an eyebrow. "Like we'd planned?"

"Oh," was all I could say. Of course. Amid all the chaos, commotion and destruction surrounding the Celebrations, not to mention Liv getting hurt and the final look on my parents' faces, I had completely forgotten that Ian and I had agreed to meet in one of our hiding places in the City.

"Are you hurt?"

I shook my head.

"Good. Come on, let's go there anyway, we have to discuss our plan."

My heart leapt. Who was I kidding? Sitting idly and

dying here in the Square was never a viable option, anyway.

I followed Ian as he slipped through the side streets around the Tower and disappeared into a crack in a squat, crumbling gray building at its rear.

"Hiding in plain sight," Ian said, his face glowing, as I ducked and climbed inside behind him. He liked to say that about this particular hiding place. He had a point though — no one in their right mind would go into a building in this state. The run down walls threatened to cave in at any moment, and old electrical wires stuck out at strange angles — I dodged one on the way in. A bomb had probably gone off not far from here, creating the deep crack in the building's facade and reducing most of it into uninhabitable rubble.

We had a few hiding places like this one in the City. Ian preferred not to draw attention to himself inside the City's borders, in case he was stopped by a Safety Patrol who demanded to verify his identity through his comp or his deathday, like Johnson had done with me. But Ian had gotten rid of his comp years ago — it was too dangerous for him to keep using it after his deathday.

I slumped against the wall — it slanted above me, forming a makeshift ceiling where the real one had fallen in. I let out a deep breath and closed my eyes for a moment, willing my heart rate to slow and my mind to quiet, attempting — fruitlessly — to shut out my raging thoughts of the events of the past few hours.

"Are you all right?" Ian's voice floated across the narrow space.

My eyes flew open. I nodded. "Yeah. Let's go over the plan again?" I dug into my jacket pocket. For a second, my fingertips collided with the cool blade of the knife. Then, they brushed against the heat sensor, its glass smooth against my skin. I closed my palm around it and handed it to Ian. "I brought this."

"Great. We'll need it to get into the Tower, and again once we're inside. Here, check this out." Ian smoothed a cloth on the floor with a hand-drawn map of the White Tower and its surroundings. I could make out the Square, the Tower itself and several entrances and exits clearly labeled in Ian's shaky scrawl.

"Took me three days to map this out," Ian said. "Initially I tried swiping actual blueprints of the Tower from Security Compound 3, but I didn't manage."

"You *what?*"

Ian shrugged. "That's where the Safety Patrols are trained, aren't they? I figured I could slip through a bunch of rookie Patrols and get the blueprints from their back office, but I almost got caught." Ian tapped the map with this forefinger. "So I had to map it out myself."

I gawked at the map, studying the marked air vents.

"Hang on… where did you learn to write?" They didn't teach handwriting at school, not since it became illegal to cut down the trees in the forest beyond the Edge due to the pollution in the City. Now, paper was scarcer than gold. Everything had been digitized, and the GA believed there was no use for such archaic communication methods. But I stared at the letters in awe.

"My mom secretly tried to teach me penmanship when I was younger, seeing as the schools wouldn't." Ian considered his handwriting, cocking his head to one side. "It's not the prettiest, but you get the idea…"

We spent the next ten minutes going over the plan. We would wait for another diversion from the still rioting crowd and enter the Tower together through an air vent Ian found. With a little luck, it would lead us into the basement. From there, we'd travel to the seventeenth floor and try to find the Deathday Department that Dad had mentioned. Although we had no exact blueprints of the Tower, we had our intuition, and we had our knives. They were no match against the Safety Patrols' guns, but they were all we had.

I smoothed down my blue-green jacket and glanced up at Ian. "Assuming we do get into the Tower—"

"We will."

"—how will we get out afterward? What if they lock all the doors, blocking our escape? I remember a lot of high-sec doors when I went in there with Dad…" Deep down, I didn't expect to get out, but I had to ask all the same.

"Don't worry, leave that to me. That's where my cool gadget comes in."

I raised my eyebrows. "Your cool gadget?"

Ian winked. "You're not the only one who got a useful Ten Day Object, Theo."

I wracked my brain but couldn't recall Ian ever speaking about his Object. "What is—"

"You'll see. Wouldn't want to spoil the surprise."

"Now's not really the time for surprises."

"It is for this. Besides, you've seen it before."

"But—"

"Do you trust me?"

"Of course."

"Good. Then help me with these maps, will you?"

We gathered up Ian's maps and made our final preparations for tonight. As we were getting ready to leave the safety of our hiding spot, I paused. There was one more thought swirling in my mind, bubbling just beneath the surface. I had to come clean to Ian about what I'd done. I took a deep breath.

"Ian?"

"Mhm?" Ian was once again examining the heat sensor, his fingers deft on its smooth surface.

"I told her to find you. That if she wants answers, she should find you."

Ian looked up sharply, placing the heat sensor on the flat stone in front of him, which we often used as a makeshift table. "Liv?"

I nodded slowly. "I couldn't leave her with nothing, I had to give her something to go on, so she could figure this out for herself."

Ian shook his head. "We've been through this, buddy — it's too dangerous."

"It's not! She deserves to know."

"It's not your secret to tell."

"I know. That's why I didn't say anything about your deathday. Only about you." I chewed on the inside of my cheek. Why was it so hard to bring my two best friends together? I tried again. "But Ian, promise me — promise me, that if Liv comes to you, if she finds you, that you'll tell her everything? You can trust her."

"Can I?" Ian raised his eyebrows, considering me. "But the real question is… would she trust me? If I showed up out of nowhere, telling her that it's possible to survive past our deathdays? Or at least with me it was. And what if I told her we think the GA is hiding something?"

At those words, as if on cue, my own numbers blazed. I was able to keep the pain at bay when I didn't actively think about it, so I forced it out of my mind. The burning sensation dulled a fraction. "She would. And it wouldn't be out of nowhere — I told her to find you, and she trusts me, just like I trust her." I paused. "I trust her with my life."

"I told you — what happened to me was an anomaly. For all we know, it's only happened once."

"But isn't that why we're here? To find something — anything — to prove that it wasn't a one-time thing?"

Ian nodded. "You're right. That is why we're here."

I laid my palm on my friend's arm, keeping my eyes locked on his. "Ian. Promise me."

Ian hesitated, then nodded slowly. "All right. But only if she finds me first. I'll tell her then. But I won't seek her out."

"But you'll protect her?"

"I'll do what I can, from a distance. I'll distract the Patrols so they miss their house inspection, I'll swipe and slip her and her mom some medicine and food… That I can do. But no more."

"Ian, please. She needs to know the truth."

"You said she's smart. If she is, she'll find me."

I set my jaw. "She is. And she will."

Ian offered me a few nuts and a gulp of water from his metal container. I splashed some on my face and wet my hair, trying to loosen a few strands tangled with blood, while Ian took off his jacket and put on a harness — the same one he'd shown me back at the Hideout a few days ago.

"Ready?" Ian finished strapping in the harness and adjusted a grappling hook hanging from his belt. He stood poised by the entrance to our temporary hiding place, his hand resting on the wall.

I filled my lungs with the musty air of the confined space and nodded. Together, we left the crumbling building.

The day steadily bled into darkness; the dying sun cast long and ominous shadows on the Tower and surrounding skyscrapers. We crept silently through the alleys separating us from the Tower. Ian covered me as I took the lead.

We were almost at the chubby base of the Tower when I rounded a corner and crashed headlong into a Safety Patrol. My heart jumped into my throat and the hairs on the back of my neck stood on end.

It was Johnson.

JOHNSON'S FACE contorted into a grimace. Then, his eyes lit up in recognition and his lips curled into a leery smile that chilled my blood.

"Well, well, well… back again, are we?" Johnson's tone was mocking, but there was a bite in it that rooted me to the spot. "The wittle bitty boy with the doggy?"

I swallowed hard, my eyes searching for a way to signal to Ian to stay behind without giving him away.

"Where's the doggy now?" Johnson cocked his gun, and his small beady eyes shifted from side to side, as if expecting Laika to turn the corner at any moment. "And where's your lady friend?"

"She's—" My voice cracked. Not only was he bringing Laika into this, he was also threatening Liv. I cleared my throat, pushed down the rising dread gripping my chest, and tried again. "She's not here," I said as loud as I could without shouting, hoping against hope that Ian would hear me above the din of the crowd in the Square.

The malicious gleam left Johnson's eyes. As it did, the pressure in my chest eased a little. He could hurt me, but at least he couldn't hurt Liv or Laika.

"That's a shame now, isn't it? I would have liked to finish what I started."

At this, my blood boiled and white hot anger surged through my body. Next thing I knew, my hands were balled into fists at my sides. I tensed my muscles to prevent them from shaking. I wouldn't let him threaten Laika like that. "She's more noble than you could ever hope to be."

"So defensive, are we? What's that you're hiding behind you? Could it be the filthy mutt?" Johnson took a step toward me and smiled broadly, revealing a set of yellowing teeth. His breath was foul on my face.

"She's not here," I repeated, louder this time, hoping that Ian would hear me and take cover in the shadows of an adjacent building. I chanced a glance around the corner behind me, and the weight in my chest lifted a little more. Ian was nowhere to be seen.

Now all I had to do was figure out how to get the hell out of here — alive.

As I turned back to Johnson, a deafening roar sounded in my ears, immediately followed by a powerful whooshing sound. It felt like a deep vacuum had sucked the air right out of my lungs. An explosion rocked the street a few dozen feet away, cracking the pavement beneath our boots. A shower of glass rained down over us as black smoke billowed and rose in plumes in the cool evening air.

My feet shook from the impact, and I threw myself to the ground, ignoring the pressure and ringing in my ears. I shielded my head and prayed that the explosion would provide enough of a diversion that I could slip away from Johnson unscathed.

A rough hand grabbed the hem of my pants. Guess I

wasn't so lucky. "Where do you think you're going?" Johnson snarled.

I grabbed the tiny blade from my pocket and sunk it into Johnson's hand. He screamed and let go, as bright red blood gushed from where the knife punctured his skin. I must have injured his shooting arm; he fumbled for the gun with his other hand, but couldn't hold it up straight. His teeth were bared as he fired blindly in my general direction, the bullets sinking into the crevices in the pavement or ricocheting off the long-defunct lampposts.

The gun was too heavy for Johnson's untrained arm, but I wasn't about to stick around to find out if he could still use his injured one well enough to aim and fire. I scrambled to my feet and sprinted toward the Tower, away from Johnson, away from his screams of rage that pierced the night like blazing arrows.

Swinging around the corner, I surveyed the horizon for a familiar brown coat or stealthy gait. If I knew Ian well, he would have circled around the back of the Tower and met me here.

But there was still no sign of him.

I wracked my brain, trying to think like Ian. Calm, cool and collected Ian. Last time, he was waiting for me in the cracked building, like we'd planned. So this time, he would also be where we planned... by the Tower's air vent!

Lunging forward, I raced toward the far side of the Tower, where I knew an air vent was hidden behind a hinged cover.

Instead, I was launched backward as another deafening roar sounded in my ears, and my vision was obscured by darkness and debris.

DEATHDAY

WHEN I FINALLY CAME TO, apart from the ringing in my ears, the air was still and silent. Night had fallen. I tasted metal in my mouth, and the odor of burnt rubber hung thick in the air.

After a moment, I realized what had woken me: the shrill chime of the clock at the top of the Tower.

How long was I out for? I pushed myself into a sitting position on the cracked pavement with quivering hands. They stung. Upon further inspection, I noticed they were bleeding, and their surface was covered with myriad cuts and scrapes. Fresh glass and stone shards wedged themselves deep inside my palms. I took out a particularly nasty one and tried to stem the steady flow of blood oozing out.

Legs shaking, I pulled myself to my feet, using the

nearest building for support. I glanced around the corner behind me and heaved a sigh of relief — at least Johnson was nowhere to be seen.

But neither was Ian.

My chest tightened — where was he now?

Carefully, I tread forward, hoping I wouldn't trigger any further explosions. I'd had enough of them in the past couple days.

I pushed forward, the pounding in my chest growing with every step. Dust and debris littered the street. That was a close one. Although I didn't realize just how close, till I saw what was in front of me. I swallowed, but my mouth was so dry the movement burned my throat.

The most recent blast had blown a hole in the street the size of a small crater — it dug deep into the earth and was as wide as the street itself.

And it stood between me and the air vent of the White Tower.

I EDGED BACK the way I came, veiled in the shadow of the Tower. The streetlights were all out by now, and I was grateful for the cover of darkness. Inching forward, I stepped over jagged rocks, pieces of pavement and other debris that were now the only souvenirs of the earlier explosions.

The marching of boots and the crunching of rocks and glass beneath them put me on high alert. A couple of Safety Patrols were making their rounds. I slunk into the shadows and held my breath as they passed.

Wiping the sweat from my forehead, I started forward again, my heartbeat keeping time with my steps. I caught sight of the hidden air vent, and my stomach plummeted to the ground. The panic gnawing inside me had now morphed into a frantic frenzy.

Ian wasn't here.

Where could he be? Had he gone back to the Hideout? Was he hurt? Or... I swallowed hard. Worse? I couldn't bear the thought, so I pushed it away with every fiber of resolve I could muster.

I reached the vent and pulled back the latch on its cover. It gave way easily. As I lifted my hand to remove the cover, a blinding, burning pain shot through my wrist. It converged there, then expelled in every direction with the force of a geyser. Every nerve in my body was on fire.

My knees buckled under me and I dropped to the ground, unable to bear my own weight any longer. Multi-colored stars and spots danced in front of my eyes. I pressed my wrist to my chest, willing the burn to stop, the pain to subside.

But it didn't.

The seconds dragged on, and the agony along with them. The blaze increased in intensity until it bordered on unbearable.

And that's when I remembered.

It was my deathday.

I SLUMPED against the wall of the Tower, panting heavily. After several agonizing minutes, the brunt of the excruciating pain had subsided, but my vision was still blurry and blood rushed to my brain. I blinked several times and closed my eyes in a futile attempt to regain composure.

It was coming. I knew it now. There was no denying it.

One question floated to the forefront of my mind and settled there, like an itch I couldn't quite scratch. How much time did I have left? Would I be quick enough, and conscious enough, to get into the Tower, find something — anything — and pass that on to Ian before I succumbed to total oblivion?

Ian. Where was he? Could he already be inside the Tower?

I pulled myself to my feet. My knees threatened to give way, but I grit my teeth and tensed my muscles. With shaking hands, I lifted the air vent cover and peered inside.

Darkness.

With another colossal effort, I hauled myself into the narrow opening and kicked the vent cover until I heard it clatter shut behind me.

I was engulfed in a darkness so complete I couldn't even see the tips of my fingers. My heart raced, and my breathing was fast and shallow. I closed my eyes and willed my heart to calm and my breathing to slow. This was the only way in.

The cramped walls lining the vent seemed to shrink with every breath I took. They pressed in on me, threatening to crush me in their powerful jaws. For a split second, I considered sliding back through the vent and into the open air of the street. I imagined the breath of fresh air that would fill my lungs the moment I crawled out.

But Ian could already be inside. He could be waiting for me.

Or he could be in danger.

No, I had to keep going. I refused to give up now. If I

never drew in another breath of fresh air, so be it. I was doing this for Ian. And for Liv. I had to remember that.

After a moment, my breaths, although still shallow, slowed and evened out. I inched forward through the vent on my elbows. The sweat gathering on my forehead trickled down my temple.

After what felt like an eternity, I saw a tiny light in front of me, beckoning me on, calling my name. *Theo, I'm waiting.*

"I'm coming for you," I breathed, and pushed myself forward another few inches.

The light was not at eye level; it was slightly below. It was easier to move through the vent from here — I was now traveling downward, into the basement.

There was no turning back now.

The tunnels veered off left and right, but I kept my eyes trained on the light up ahead. When I finally reached it, I was drenched in sweat. My body shaking, I glanced through the air vent grille into the chamber beyond. It was bathed in a pale red glow. In its center, two large gray machines emitted a soft whirring sound. Apart from the machines, the room seemed to be empty.

To make sure, I quickly pulled the heat sensor free from my pocket and activated it. The holo confirmed that no one else was down here. Beyond the single door leading from the basement, a set of stairs spiraled upward. Those too were deserted.

I thrust the heat sensor back in my pocket and pushed hard at the grille with my uninjured arm, my body screaming for air, desperate to leave this narrow tunnel behind.

There was only one problem.

The grille was locked.

I was trapped.

MY HEART WAS BEATING SO HARD I thought it was going to jump out of my throat. I swallowed air in deep gulps, but my lungs refused to accept it. They felt constricted, as if an invisible rubber band had wrapped itself tightly around them, causing deep, stabbing pains in my chest. I grasped at the air, gasping and struggling to fill my lungs, but it was no use. I was suffocating.

Sweat beads dripped down my forehead and into my eyes. My palms, already bruised and bloody, were now clammy; they clawed at the grille while my lungs screamed for air.

The walls of the vent were closing in on me again. The space between them narrowed at a steady, determined pace. Before long, they would squeeze the life out of me. I couldn't think straight. My mind was one big, hazy fog, and I was swimming in its ocean, spinning round in circles. I didn't know which way was up. I was drowning.

The harder I tried to calm down, to breathe, the more difficult it became, and the less air I seemed to be taking in.

I closed my eyes. The spinning subsided slightly.

I did what I had been doing my entire life when stuck in cramped spaces. I focused on my breathing. It was the only way.

Inhale.

Exhale.

Inhale.

Exhale.

It took all the willpower I could muster to keep going.

Inhale.

Exhale.

After what felt like an eon, but what in reality was probably only a few minutes, my breathing slowed and my heart fell into an almost even rhythm. My tense muscles ached from the pressure I'd put on them. I moved my stiff neck gingerly.

Exhaling once more, I risked opening my eyes. The world had stopped spinning. I smiled to myself. Progress.

But I knew one thing. I had to get out of here. Immediately.

The tunnel was narrow, so there was no way I could bend my body and position my head in the opposite direction. Instead, I began sliding backward, inch by inch. The space between me and the grille grew with each passing second, and I was finally able to take a breath that seemed to deliver a small dose of oxygen into my bloodstream.

After another few feet, the tunnel began to slope upward. I muttered a curse under my breath. I forgot about that.

Carefully, I pushed myself backward, using my aching arms for support as I slid up the shaft. I managed a few feet, but then the tunnel curved upward at a steep angle, like some sort of twisted slide. I lost my grip on the wall and skid forward violently, nearly colliding with the closed grille that I had just tried to so desperately escape.

My heart raced in my chest again, and I couldn't hear anything above the blood pumping in my ears. If I didn't get out of here soon, I was going to die in this tunnel. If not because of my deathday, it would be because of hunger, thirst, and — I was sure of it — panic.

Closing my eyes, I focused on my breathing again.

Inhale.

Exhale.

I was stuck here, in this godforsaken tunnel, deep in the bowels of the White Tower.

There were only two ways out of this predicament. I'd already tried going back — to no avail — so the only way I could go was forward. If only I had something to get the grille off… I didn't have much. I had a few uneaten nuts in my pocket, the heat sensor, and… my eyes widened.

The knife.

I thrust my hand into my jacket pocket and groped around its contents, my palm closing over the sharp blade. I felt the familiar twinge of pain that accompanies cutting flesh on the edge of a knife, but I ignored it. The cramped space prevented me from grasping the knife in another way. I tugged at it till it came free from my pocket and gently pulled it up.

After some uncomfortable shifting, I was able to stretch my arm out in front of me, knife in hand. Positioning myself as close to the grille as possible, I slipped my blade into the small gap underneath the grille, and pulled upward.

It didn't budge.

I tried again, this time applying additional pressure.

Nothing.

Panic crept up my spine, but using all the willpower I could muster, I forced it to stay down. Swallowing the bile building up in my mouth, I focused on my breathing again.

Inhale.

Exhale.

In that moment, a glint of silver near the corner of the grille caught my eye: tiny nails that kept it in place. A burst of adrenaline coursed through my veins. Could this be my way out? I wedged my knife into one of the nails, turning it counterclockwise.

Nothing happened.

I kept turning. Finally, it started to give way.

Little by little, I worked through the nails, droplets of sweat clouding my vision. I blinked them away furiously. I was so close to getting out of here. I twisted the knife and the last nail fell to the floor with a clatter, taking the grille with it. I heaved a sigh of relief. With one last push, I stumbled out of the vent and toppled to the floor.

Breathing deeply, I lay where I landed, allowing the relatively cool air of the basement to wash over me and fill my lungs.

I was in. I could breathe again.

Now I just needed to find Ian.

The sound of marching boots on metal clanked through the basement.

"Who's there?"

The blood drained from my face. I was not alone.

HOLDING MY BREATH, I lay completely still, as if glued to the floor. Frozen. Paralyzed.

I hoped that the Safety Patrol couldn't hear my heart pounding in my chest. That was all I seemed to hear, even over the ringing in my ears.

"Show yourself!"

The Patrol's boots banged against the smooth, dark gray floor to my left. I studied the two machines in the center of the room: the pale red glow I had spotted through the grille earlier emanated from them. The Patrol was hidden from view behind the farther machine.

As soundlessly as I could, I lifted myself a fraction off the ground and crawled toward the nearest machine. Its metal surface was strewn with pipes and its soft hum grew louder as I approached. I hoped it would muffle the sound of my footsteps as I edged ever closer to its broad side.

My palms were slippery with sweat. Small half-moon marks punctuated the surface of my skin where I'd dug my nails in. The hand I had cut on the knife was stained with fresh blood; it now trickled over the layer of reddish brown that caked my palms.

The knife. I frantically scoured the ground for it — I

couldn't leave it behind. They would trace the DNA back to me, and it would lead them straight to my parents. Besides, it was my only weapon. Spotting it next to the grille and the nails strewn along the back wall, I slid an outstretched hand along the floor, my fingertips inches away from the blade.

The thud of the Patrol's boots pierced through the basement like a whip in the night. His footsteps grew louder.

By now, the Patrol had circled around the first of the machines. He was now going to check this machine — *my* machine — and see me sprawled on the ground, dirty and bloody, grasping for a knife. Although it was no match for his gun, a knife was still a weapon, and he would not be questioned in the slightest for killing an armed intruder. 'Kill first, think later' was the unofficial motto of the Safety Patrols for a reason. My head throbbed. If I didn't act fast, I would be caught, and that would be the end of my grand plan.

Without thinking, I propelled myself forward and grabbed the knife off the floor, scooping it up with one hand along with a few of the fallen nails. I jumped to my feet, crept back toward the nearest machine and slid around it, sensing the Safety Patrol directly on the other side.

The nails sent a sharp stab of pain into my palm as I

clenched my fist tightly around them. Their cool, metallic, twisted edges brushed against my fingers.

And in that instant, I knew what I had to do.

Peeking out from behind the temporary refuge of the machine, I thrust the nails into the air with all the strength I had in me. They ricocheted around the second machine, emitted a loud jangling noise, and fell to the ground with a clatter.

The Safety Patrol's boots retreated immediately, and I heard the unmistakable click of his gun's safety.

Without a backward glance, I threw myself toward the door of the basement. Luckily, the Patrol had left it ajar. I slammed it shut behind me, bolted it, and sprinted up the stairs to the upper floors of the White Tower.

THE MUSCLES in my legs burned as I took the stairs two at a time. But I hardly noticed; I had to get as far away from the basement and the Patrol as possible. And the only way to do that was to disappear in the endless corridors of the White Tower.

I trudged on until I heard muffled voices just around the next bend. Slowing, I glanced around the narrow stairwell. I had to assess my options if the voices —

which surely belonged to Safety Patrols — decided to wander down the stairs.

I tugged the heat sensor free from my pocket and activated it. Sure enough, a pair of Patrols hovered around the turn of the spiral staircase. I slunk back into the shadows, but remained within earshot. Pressing myself against the cool metal wall, I strained my ears, struggling to pick up what they said.

"Copy that."

A few beeps sounded. "This is Lieutenant Rogers, we've got intruders in the building. Over."

My body grew cold. Intruders? Had the Patrol from the basement managed to communicate with his comrades upstairs?

"—the basement."

That answered my question. Beads of sweat formed on the back of my neck, and my palms grew warm and slippery. I wiped them on my pants, further sullying the taupe fabric, and groped around my pocket for my trusty knife.

This was all I could hope for right now.

"Copy."

As the sound of boots filled my ears, I gripped the knife so tightly that my knuckles turned white. My heart threatened to beat out of my chest, but I willed it to slow. I held the blade out in front of me, ready to strike at the first sight of Lieutenant Rogers or his Patrol partner. I hoped they wouldn't see just how much my hand was shaking.

Instead, the sound of their boots receded into the depths of the Tower.

Until there was only silence.

I stood stock still, my knife still outstretched before me, in case it was a trap, in case they had paused just around the bend, waiting for me to fall straight into their iron clutches. But the only sound came from the pounding of my own heart.

I couldn't risk using the heat sensor — pulling it out and activating it would make too much noise. I had no choice but to go on. So I set my jaw and plunged forward around the corner, my eyes darting from wall to wall, knife at the ready.

After a momentary reprieve, what I saw next made my breath catch and my heart sink to my stomach.

THERE WERE NO SAFETY PATROLS, but the door at the top of the staircase was slammed shut. I knew it before I even approached it. It didn't even have a handle. That was a problem.

My heart had picked up its rhythmic pounding again.

I now had two options. I could either go back down the stairs, into the basement, face the Patrol that I'd locked in there, and try to get back out of the Tower through the vent. That obviously wouldn't work, even if I did manage to take the Patrol out with just my knife. I'd tried that. I'd just slide right back down that awful tunnel. Besides, I could do without more cramped spaces this evening… Not to mention taking that route wouldn't yield any information about deathdays, either. And I've come this far…

My only other option was to keep going. I'd have to force the door open and then continue deeper and deeper into the Tower.

I ran my hand along the door's surface. It was perfectly smooth, with no grooves and no visible hinges. It was probably one of those doors that slid into the wall if triggered. But how would I trigger it? Placing my palms flat against the door, I pressed the weight of my body into them, heaving at the effort.

As expected, it didn't budge.

Even in this poor lighting, I could see the layers of dirt, grime and blood that coated my hands. I brushed them along the metal surface again, looking for a trigger, or maybe a safety mechanism that would prevent Patrols and GA officials from getting stuck down here.

I slunk to the floor and rested my head against the

metal door. My left wrist still throbbed from my death-day's latest attempt at killing me.

Think, Theo. What had Dad said about the way the GA's security systems worked?

I balled my hands into fists and slammed my head backward into the door. I hardly noticed the jolt of pain that coursed through my body at the impact. Why couldn't I remember?

But I'd come this far, and I'd be damned if I let some stupid door stop me.

With a renewed energy, I jumped to my feet and scanned the door again. The light in the stairwell seemed to be dwindling. Or I was just getting tired. It was well past midnight by now. I blinked several times and focused on the door, poring over it inch by inch.

I was still clutching my trusty knife tightly. Turning it over in my hand, I examined it, the pale light reflecting off its surface. The handle was dark brown, almost black, and made of a durable metal. The sharp blade, about four inches long, curved near the top. My lips curled into a small smile. It had already served me well today.

I glanced between the knife and the door.

What had Dad said again?

I wracked my brain, trying desperately to recall the conversation we'd had a few weeks ago, when he told me he couldn't get into his office.

Why couldn't he get into his office?

I closed my eyes and took several deep breaths, beckoning the image of Dad to the forefront of my mind.

He did say that all the doors in the upper levels of the Tower used the same security mechanisms. And something about a power cut... yes. The nightly power cut at curfew had somehow spread to the White Tower — the Chancellor was furious, apparently — and that's why the office doors wouldn't open the next morning.

What had he said? He said... he had to use a small metal pin to pry the door open. That's it! The doors were all powered by electricity, but a backup mechanism had to be installed to ensure they open in an emergency.

And this was how. If Dad had been looking for a metal pin, then there must have been a narrow groove designed for that pin somewhere around the door.

I strained my eyes against the dying light, which seemed to fade with every passing minute. It wasn't my imagination then. The light *was* dimming. Maybe it was an energy conservation tool?

I didn't have much time. In a few minutes, I'd be plunged into complete darkness. *Good luck getting out then, Theo.* My heart was pounding again, and my adrenaline shot through the roof.

I examined the door again with shaking hands. Inch by inch, I drove my fingertips over its surface. Nothing. It was completely smooth. Not a single bump or imperfection tarnished its uniform exterior.

The light was almost gone now.

I focused on the edges. The mechanism had to be readily available to anyone who wanted to open the doors manually. GA officials would rely on it when there was no electricity — and therefore no light.

So it must have be somewhere easy to access. And it must be obvious. Why couldn't I find it then?

By now, I strained my eyes to see anything. Although a hint of light remained in the stairwell, its only true source was the tiny sliver between the metal door and the floor. The ringing in my ears had returned, competing for attention with the thumping of my heart and the throbbing in my wrist.

This was my last chance.

I crouched down and groped the frame along the left side of the door, where the hinges would usually be. Still nothing.

I ran my fingertips over the area again, slower this time. My heart skipped a beat as I felt a tiny groove *next to* the door, not *on* the door.

The stairwell was now plunged into complete darkness.

Fumbling with my knife, I marked the groove with a finger and jammed the tip of the blade into the hole.

With a click, the door opened, revealing a corridor bathed in a blinding white light.

STUMBLING OUT, I blinked several times before the stark white hallway came into focus after the darkness of the spiraling stairwell. The door slid shut behind me with a low thunk.

I glanced around; the corridor seemed deserted. I did a quick check on my heat sensor, positioning it on the floor and lowering my palms onto it. Immediately, red and orange waves danced around its surface. I moved my fingertips over the black glass and slowly raised them. The holo sprung to life, presenting me with a detailed map of the adjacent floors of the Tower. Tiny dots on its surface revealed a pair of Safety Patrols standing motionless at the end of the corridor one floor down. On the floor above, a lone Patrol marched back and forth along the hallway to my right.

My floor was deserted. As the realization washed over me, I let out a breath I didn't know I was holding. A sudden surge of warmth erupted inside me. Is this what Dad meant when he said to "use it well"? I would never know for certain, but right now, the sheer possibility was good enough for me.

As I was at the very end of a long corridor, there was only one way to go. I shut the holo off and proceeded cautiously, conscious of what a palpable difference there was between the eerie cleanliness and brightness of the Tower's halls and my own appearance. I was covered head to toe in grime, debris and blood. Lots of blood. Most of it had dried by now, but patches of bright red remained here and there. They were especially prominent on my taupe trousers.

I trailed dirt on the pristine tiles, which seemed to reflect the blaring lights overhead. An occasional floor-to-ceiling window interrupted the immaculate white walls. I couldn't see outside though — all was dark in the City. It was long past curfew, after all, and the harsh lights overhead made it difficult to see anything at all beyond the glass. I squinted, but it didn't help.

As I continued, the corridor branched off. I took several turns and soon found myself unable to tell where I was, or where I had come from. This place was a maze. I made my way methodically through the Tower, climbing sets of spiraling stairs and checking my heat sensor along the way up to the seventeenth floor. To Dad's office. To the Deathday Department.

I wondered why it was so empty. Shouldn't there have been more Safety Patrols wandering around, especially after the unrest at the Celebrations, or after that com-link transmission about intruders in the basement? That is, that transmission about me. I'm the intruder. I pushed the thought away and trekked onward, pausing only occasionally to check the sensor, peer around a corner or to press myself against a closed door to see if it would budge and reveal yet another staircase.

It was late now — the GA officials working in the Tower must have been home by now, spending time with their families or fast asleep. My thoughts wandered to my parents. What were they doing now? And Liv? Were they all still awake, sitting at the dinner table, clutching mugs of freshly brewed mint tea? Or were they in bed, thrashing around, willing the vines of sleep to bring them under, despite knowing that I wasn't coming home again? I swallowed, but the lump in my throat made it difficult to do so.

Shaking my head, I tried to coax the image of my parents and Liv out of my mind as I reached the seventeenth floor landing. Taking a deep breath, I made sure the coast was clear — the entire floor was empty — and turned right down the next corridor. I had to focus on my mission. And my family, even though my heart ached for them, was only distracting me from it.

As I turned the corner into yet another identical hallway, my eye caught a glint of black on the otherwise uniform white surface of the wall. My curiosity piqued, I approached it with trepidation.

A bright blue light emanated from behind a flat rectangular device resembling a keypad, only without the keys. It hung on the wall next to a sturdy black metal door. Markings forming an intricate pattern I didn't recognize were etched into the door's surface: vines twisting and threading, then converging in its center.

Instead of carrying on down the endless corridors, a sudden, inexplicable compulsion to open the strange door took hold of me. It was so unlike anything I'd seen in the Tower — or in the entire City, for that matter. The GA was all about harsh, clean lines, not intricate patterns.

I pushed myself against the door, but it didn't give way — I didn't think it would. I pulled the knife out of my jacket pocket and grazed my fingertips along the walls on either side of the door.

Nothing.

Straightening back up again, my gaze flitted along the length of the door. My eyes landed on the small black rectangle hanging on the wall that I was first drawn to. Squinting, I scrutinized it. Thin gray lines branched out on its surface. I blinked and moved closer, still clutching the knife, and considered the tiny threads that spread like a spider's web through the rectangle. They reminded me with a pang of the cracks on my floorboards in my bedroom back home. A tiny circular imperfection sullied the side of the keypad on the otherwise pristine wall.

Except it wasn't an imperfection at all.

It was an engraving. An engraving of a tiny fanged snake eating its own tail. I ran my fingers over the marking — its texture grated against my skin, and I couldn't suppress a shudder as the prickle of gooseflesh erupted on my arms. Something was off about the self-eating snake. I'd seen this symbol before…

My heart wouldn't get a break from me today; it was pounding again. Holding my breath, I pressed my palm into the rectangle.

I half-expected an alarm to blare in my ears, announcing my presence next to a high-sec door to everyone in the Tower. But no such thing happened.

In fact, nothing happened.

I pushed my weight against the door again, but it held fast. Sighing, I replaced the blade in my pocket. As I did, my fingers brushed against a smooth, half-dome object.

The heat sensor.

I pulled it out eagerly. I'd already used it to check for Patrols before leaving the relative safety of the stairwell. Apart from me, there wasn't a soul on the seventeenth floor of the White Tower. That meant there was no one in the room on the other side of the door with the mysterious snake symbol next to it.

And that snake… *where* had I seen it before?

The heat sensor felt heavy in my palm. I had to think fast — just because the floor was deserted now didn't mean it would stay that way for long. I glanced down at the sensor again, playing back what Dad had said that night. *Pay special attention to the grooves and markings. They're often more than just a design feature.* My eyes widened, and suddenly, despite the late hour, I was very alert.

I fumbled through my pockets for the knife again and jammed it into the small groove on the side of the dome, next to the base. Immediately, the sensor clicked and opened on its hinges. With trembling hands, I examined the inside of the hollow dome, near the crown. Sure enough, there it was. Another tiny snake eating its own tail.

I moved toward the black rectangle, lifting the heat sensor to compare the snakes. They were nearly identical. I then placed the dome against the surface of the rectangle.

In that moment, the blue light surrounding the rectangular device turned green. I nearly crashed to the ground as the heavy door slid open before me, splitting the intricate vines in two.

I DRAGGED myself to my feet and staggered into the room, squinting against the blue light emanating from within and leaning against the wall for support. The door slid shut behind me with a low thud.

My heart pounded rhythmically in my chest. I clutched the open heat sensor in my hand, staring at the fanged snake inside, my mind racing. The tiny snake symbol next to the door was easy to miss if you weren't looking for it, but now, it all made sense. Dad wanted me to have the heat sensor as my Ten Day Object for a reason. And this — I glanced around the room — was why.

As my eyes adjusted to the eerie blue glow, I took in the scene before me.

The room was circular and spacious. Four bright spotlights beamed down from the would-be corners toward a large rectangular glass tank, illuminating the objects within.

My mouth fell open as I registered what was in the glass tank. I moved closer. I'd never seen one before — they were incredibly rare — but I knew the second I laid eyes on them what they were.

Thin sheets of paper, stacked one on top of the other and bound together on one side.

Books.

I leaned over the tank, my nose and palms flat against the glass, and stared at them in wonder. There were maybe fifty books in there. My mouth was still open, and I didn't bother closing it. Nowadays, we used the e-books and e-textbooks on our comps for everything. Paper was both rare and invaluable, especially after the ordinance prohibiting cutting down trees due to pollution came into force. That's why the GA didn't bother teaching us penmanship.

But that still didn't explain why all these books were here. Were they part of the Chancellor's private collection? Had Dad wanted me to find them? Their timeworn yellowing pages looked ancient against the backdrop of the sterile chambers of the White Tower. Several looked close to falling apart, but the lettering was still legible. I studied the nearest one.

Homo Sapiens, Historia Vitae.

I had no idea what that meant. Some ancient language. Were these history books? *Historia* certainly suggested so.

One of the books inside the tank seemed to have been closed haphazardly — I could just make out the words on the corner of one of its pages. Tilting my head, I began to read aloud, "...the origin of the human race…" I narrowed my eyes, then shook my head. That was all I could make out.

What about the origin of the human race? Did this book detail the history of how humans came to be? At school, we were never taught anything going back farther than the War. The GA believed it was of paramount importance for us to study the country's relatively recent history. But I'd never really considered what happened before the War… just that they were dark and devastating times, apparently.

Peering around the tank, I combed its underbelly for an opening or a latch. My hands trembled at the thought of holding a real book in my hands, and maybe even reading a bit more from its age-worn pages. They were the stuff of legends.

I snapped my head up, suddenly alert. Adrenaline rushed through my veins as I remembered my mission. My heart hammered in my chest as I moved my hands along the glass with an increased urgency. Maybe I could find a scrap of information in these volumes about deathdays.

But the tank was perfectly smooth and seemed to have been assembled around the books themselves. There was simply no way of opening the tank without breaking the glass.

I glanced around for an object that could get the job

done. It had to be quick and clean. But the room was empty save for the tank. My gaze flitted to a nondescript door directly opposite the one I had entered through. I hadn't noticed it before.

I examined the contents of my pockets again. My knife, a few nuts and the heat sensor. I thrust the nuts in my mouth and considered the knife. Maybe I could smash it against the tank? It was worth a try.

I gripped my knife tightly, preparing to run toward the glass. How many steps could I manage? Two? Three? I backed up to the far wall, leaning against the door for support.

It slid open, and I fell through it, tumbling to the ground, just as the cryptic snake door on the opposite end of the chamber opened with a low hiss. For a fraction of a second, I caught a glimpse of the legs of two men striding in, just as the door slid shut before my eyes and I was plunged into darkness.

I RAISED my hand to my forehead. It was drenched in sweat, and my heart was pounding so loudly I was sure the two men could hear it.

That was close.

Too close.

They would have executed me on the spot if they caught me trying to break the glass tank filled with books.

"…here they are," one of the men said. I couldn't tell which at this point.

Holding my breath, I dropped to the ground in the tiny closet, which appeared to be empty save for a switchboard with blue and green blinking lights, and squinted through the crack underneath the door. The tiled floor was cold beneath my cheek. One of the men wore dark gray robes, with a high collar and wide sleeves that fell along his body as he walked. The other wore a Safety Patrol uniform.

The man in dark gray robes circled around the tank of books, tapping a long, thin finger on the glass. "…books from the Chancellor's private stores." His voice was nasal and pinched. He spun around, and I saw his face. It was General Horatio, who'd overseen my Ten Day Ceremony. Even though it was just over a week ago, it felt like a lot longer. His face was contorted into a grimace, as if a permanent foul smell lingered under his nose.

Now that I thought about it, I couldn't recall seeing him at the Celebrations earlier… what was he up to? And what did he want with all those books? I was so curious about Horatio's suspicious behavior that I momentarily forgot about my precarious predicament. My heart had slowed, my hands were less clammy, and the muscles on my back relaxed somewhat. I strained my ears, hoping to catch snippets of the conversation between Horatio and the other man.

Horatio droned on, in the same monotone voice. "… scanned and encoded on the chip. Then, the chip is to be hand-delivered to the Chancellor, who will choose a location for its safekeeping in due course."

On the chip? What chip? My heart raced again as adrenaline shot through my blood. Could this chip be the key to finding out what the GA knew about deathdays?

The man in the Safety Patrol uniform nodded and murmured his assent. I still couldn't see his face — his back was turned toward me.

"The Chancellor will then determine what to do with these." Horatio waved a bony hand over the tank. "He will see whether it's best to transfer them to a high-sec site, or to destroy them, as per the High Government's orders. For now, they are to be left untouched."

"Yes, sir. When should their contents be transferred?"

"Immediately, Lieutenant Johnson, is that clear?"

I froze. Johnson? That was Johnson? He must have gotten out of the blasts unscathed. I peered at him through the slit. Sure enough, when he shifted slightly, I caught a glimpse of his unmistakable yellowing teeth and ragged black stubble. Dried blood lingered on his temple, and a clean white bandage was wrapped tightly around his right hand. I smiled under my breath at my handiwork.

"Absolutely, sir. I'll get my men up here and we'll get started right away."

How friendly was Johnson with Horatio? Or Graves? Did Dad know about this?

"Good." Horatio paused. "Oh and Johnson?"

"Sir?"

"Keep it discreet, will you?"

"Yes, sir."

Horatio nodded, folded his hands behind his back and stepped out through the metal door, which slid open at his approach.

Johnson remained behind. For a few seconds, he stood still. He then ran his fingers over the top of the glass tank and studied one of the books. I followed his gaze. Judging by where he stood, I guessed it was the same volume of *Historia* that I had examined just minutes before.

My blood ran cold at the sight of his face. A flashback of him aiming his gun at Laika, his rotting teeth barred, washed over me. Holding my breath, I squeezed my eyes shut, willing the image to dissipate, but the harder I tried to push it away, the more it loomed in my mind's eye, as vivid as ever.

After what felt like an eternity, Johnson spun around on his heel and left the circular room full of mysterious books, leaving me alone in the darkness.

I LAY motionless for a few seconds, my cheek still pressed to the cool floor. Now that Johnson had left, I had a moment of respite to process what I had just witnessed. I looked, unseeing, at the book-filled tank in the center of the room, but my thoughts were elsewhere.

I couldn't help thinking about what Horatio had said.

The GA instructed Johnson to transfer the contents of the books in the tank onto some sort of chip and then deliver it to the Chancellor himself. What could these books contain that was valuable enough for Graves to request their electronic safekeeping? And didn't Horatio say something about destroying the books afterwards?

I hauled myself to my feet and pressed against the door separating me from the books. It parted at once. I inched toward the tank again, staring at the books in wonder once more. Could they be the key to figuring out the origin of deathdays?

That's when I knew what I had to do. I had to steal at least one of these books and get it to Ian.

Johnson said that his men would start the job immediately — soon this place would be swarming with Safety Patrols. If I didn't break the tank now, I wouldn't get another shot. I'd be a goner before I could even tell Ian what I'd heard.

This was my only chance.

With sweaty palms, I pulled the knife out of my pocket again and prepared to carry out my initial plan. With enough force, I could conceivably break the glass that stood between me and the books.

I backed up to the wall, careful not to trigger the sliding door again, and took a deep breath. I broke into a run, covering the short distance to the tank in a few strides. Pulling my arm down as hard and fast as I could, I thrust the knife into the glass.

A sharp pain flared up in my arm, sending shock waves through my entire body. My arm grew numb, and I dropped to my knees, blinking away the colorful green and pink spots that materialized before my eyes.

The glass, however, was still intact — the cracks on its surface were almost imperceptible. Thin, lighting shaped fissures branched out from where my knife had collided with the glass. But it wasn't nearly enough to break it.

I scrambled to my feet and raised the knife high above my head, preparing to deal another blow.

In that moment, a deafening alarm blared in my ears. I winced from the pressure in my eardrums. If the Safety Patrols hadn't been on their way to the circular book room before, they sure as hell were now.

I dropped my knife to my side and considered my options. Try to break the glass again and grab a book that could possibly answer our questions about deathdays… or get the hell out of here, find Ian, and tell him what I knew before I got caught or the pain in my wrist intensified again. It seemed to come in waves, and so far, I had just about managed to keep it at bay.

After a split second's hesitation, I skidded around the glass tank and threw myself against the metal door, which thankfully slid open before me. Swerving right, I sprinted down the hallway. The sound of boots marching reverberated in my ears. Or was that just my imagination?

I turned right again at the first turn at random, and then left. My heart was in my throat. I swallowed air in huge gulps, but the stuffy Tower air made it hard to breathe. I careened around the next corner and immediately crashed backward to the ground as I collided with a sturdy figure.

Hot panic washed over me as I lay on the ground. Stars erupted in the corners of my eyes and my head was spinning. The world had transformed into a white blur, distant and out of focus. The alarm that had moments ago threatened to deafen me now sounded like it had been submerged underwater, remote and immaterial.

If this was Johnson, advancing toward the book room with his men, I was as good as dead. If the agonizing jolts of pain springing out of my wrist didn't kill me, Johnson surely would. And if I was executed on the spot, no one, not even my parents, would question my death — today *was* my deathday after all, and the digits on my wrist matched today's date. I swallowed, but my throat was as dry as sandpaper.

Blinking furiously through the blurry veil that had settled over my vision, I squinted at the figure who was still standing before me. While I had tumbled to the ground, he hadn't so much as flinched at the impact.

When my eyes readjusted to the brightness of the corridor, the first thing I noticed was that he wasn't wearing the signature white of Safety Patrol uniforms. The pressure in my chest eased a fraction, although my muscles still ached from the tension. It could be Horatio. Or worse. It could be Graves.

The figure extended a hand to me, which was wrapped in a thick, bloody bandage that disappeared underneath his brown sleeve. It was Johnson, showing me the wound I inflicted, taunting me before he killed me, I was sure of it…

After a moment, my head and vision stabilized. Taking a deep breath, I summoned the courage to look up into the figure's face. As our eyes locked, my mouth fell open. The person standing before me wasn't Johnson at all.

It was Ian.

"Ian…" I breathed, but my voice came out coarse and cracked.

"Are you all right, buddy?" A grin spread across his face.

I nodded and let him help me to my feet. "Where have you been, all this time? Where did you go after Johnson ambushed us?"

"I could ask you the same question." Ian shot me a quizzical look. "Come on, let's walk, and I'll fill you in. We shouldn't stay in the same place for too long."

"Let's use the heat sensor to check where the Patrols are." I'd been too wrapped up in getting as far away from the circular book room as possible to conduct my usual check.

"Good idea. Let's do that when we reach a safe area."

We started down the bright hallway, my spirits

considerably higher than I would have ever thought possible on my deathday.

"After Johnson blocked our path, I snuck back toward the other side of the building," Ian said. "I took a circular detour around the Tower and ended up finding another air vent."

"Where did that one lead?"

"Not into the basement, like the one we planned to use. It branched out dozens of times, but I followed the tunnel straight ahead, taking as few turns as possible. It came out on the ground floor, right next to the giant Atrium. Have you seen the size of that thing? Everything is white, and it goes up ridiculously high. Just as big as I remembered it being on my Ceremony Day."

I thought back to my own Ceremony Day. It was hard to believe that I was in the White Tower again, just as I had been ten days prior. Horatio handing over the little black box containing the heat sensor felt like an eternity ago.

Ian held up a hand, bringing me back to the present. He peered around the corner, checking for any stray Safety Patrols. "Coast is clear."

We walked a few yards in silence before Ian spoke again. "I spent my time following a few Patrols." Ian shook his head. "They're about as clueless as they look."

"Minions of the Head Safety Patrol?" I paused,

thinking of Johnson and Horatio. "Or the Commander of the Patrol Forces?"

"Probably. I didn't find anything useful, except for maybe where the best bathroom in the Tower is."

I raised an eyebrow and glanced sideways at Ian.

"On the seventh floor." He smirked. "What about you, where have you been all this time? And why are you so grimy? What happened to you?"

I recounted what had happened since Ian and I split. I told him about the explosion, the encounter in the basement, the locked stairway door, and how the heat sensor was actually a key that opened the double doors with the strange vines. I told him about the twin fanged snakes and how I'd thought Dad meant for me to find the circular room. Finally, I told him about the books in the glass tank and what Horatio had said to Johnson about the chip.

Ian's eyes widened. "There's a chip?" His voice was low.

I lowered mine to match his. "That's the thing. Even though I didn't manage to get any of the books out of the tank, this chip could be everything we've been hoping for, and more."

Ian nodded, and I continued, my words tumbling out in a rush. "If Graves himself wants the contents of the books on the chip, who knows what other valuable information could be on there… not just about the books, but maybe about deathdays themselves!"

"Theo, you did it." Ian's eyes glowed bright, even in the harsh artificial light of the Tower. "This is it… this chip is the key to finding out what the GA knows. This chip could help me get back to my family… and to save Liv's life."

My lips curled into a wide, genuine smile, revealing my teeth. "You can definitely use this as a starting point, when I'm… you know." My smile faded as quickly as it appeared.

Ian looked at me from behind the collar of his coat. "I can't believe it…" His voice faltered. "That it's…"

"I know. Me neither." I cleared my throat. "For now, we save who we can save. And that means, whatever happens, Ian, you save yourself."

"I'm not leaving you."

"Trust me… I want to live, more than anything in the world right now." I waved my left wrist, thinking about Liv. "Just these digits seem to think otherwise. So you have to go on."

"Theo, I—"

"You have to. Because you have the knowledge about the chip now. And with knowledge comes the power to save the people we love. Your family… my family… Liv." My voice cracked. "It's the only way."

After a moment, Ian nodded.

"And you'll protect her, all right?"

Ian nodded again. "Promise." Deep lines creased his features. "You're my best friend, Theo."

"And you're mine." I turned away, unable to bear the truth that this might be the last time I see my best friend. He stood before me, tall and vulnerable, his emotions bare. I clasped his hand and wrapped my arm tightly around him.

"I'll miss you," I blinked back the moisture threatening to spill over onto my cheeks.

"So will I."

Taking a deep breath, I held on to my friend, steadying myself, and prepared to utter the words I'd dreaded for months. "Well, I guess this is goodbye. In case we don't get another chance."

"Goodbye, Theo." Ian's voice cracked.

I'm not sure how long we stood like that, holding onto one another, my mind playing back dozens of happy memories. Images flashed before my eyes of all the walks with Laika, the long lazy summer afternoons in the Hideout or on the Pier... Even slicing Ian's wrist open just the other day carried an air of nostalgia that crushed my heart and threatened to rip it in two.

But a cold voice in my ear jolted me out of my reverie.

"I thought I'd see you here, Theo."

THE HAIRS on the back of my neck stood on end, and I froze, my muscles tense. I released Ian; his expression mirrored mine. My heartbeat thrashed in my ears and I could hear nothing but the roar of blood in my brain.

As one, Ian and I turned toward the voice.

Standing before us, his wide sleeves billowing after him, was Horatio. He was flanked by two Safety Patrols on either side, their guns trained on us. One of them was Johnson.

Ian blanched, and my chest tightened. This was it.

I opened my mouth, but no words came out — my lower lip trembled so violently that I had no choice but to close it again. Ian shifted beside me. I felt, rather than saw, his questioning glance in my direction. But I didn't dare look at him now. I was too transfixed with Horatio, whose sneer and stony demeanor rooted me to the spot.

Horatio's lips curled into a wicked smile. "Surprised?" His tone sent an icy shiver straight down my spine.

I seemed to finally regain control of my voice. "How did you—?"

"Know?" Horatio let out a cold mirthless laugh that caused gooseflesh to erupt on my arms. "Silly boy. My men were monitoring you the entire time — sneaking up deserted buildings, skipping school and loitering close to the Edge, engaging in seditious activities…"

My breath caught in my chest and a piercing cold rippled through me. Horatio had been watching me? I stole a quick glance at Ian. He looked like he'd just seen a ghost. I knew what he was thinking — had Horatio and his men followed us to the Hideout? Was that sound that we'd heard in the woods a Safety Patrol after all?

Horatio continued, seeming not to notice the look I'd shared with Ian. "…typical Fleeter behavior, that is true. But we'd observed strange errors in the system for you and a few others that we couldn't explain. Surely you noticed that the system didn't recognize you on your Ceremony Day?"

I thought with a pang back to my Ceremony, and the numbness I felt staring into the barrels of four Safety Patrol guns. It was lucky that Patrol with the blood scan had intervened…

"But the error we observed for you, Theo, was the first of its kind that we'd seen in a very long time. I came to your Ceremony so I could meet you in person. To see if you posed a threat… because your father is already on our watch list."

My mouth went dry. Horatio had already been watching Dad? So Dad wasn't only being cryptic because he was following orders… He was being cryptic to protect not only himself, but all of us.

Horatio crossed his arms. "A skinny boy, trembling with the fear of death, I thought you wouldn't do much harm. But we kept an eye on you all the same. The Board was foolish and sentimental to allow your father's gift as your Ten Day Object — I shall be having a word with them."

Horatio circled around us, like a predator circling its prey, a malicious gleam in his eye. He took my face in one of his cold, bony hands and turned my head upward so I would look him in the eye. While mine were bright blue and full of electric energy, as Liv had always said, his were dark and dull, devoid of all light and life. Two black, empty cavities embedded in his skull, devouring everything good in the world and withering it to darkness and decay with a mere glance.

His face inches from my own, Horatio studied me. I could see every wrinkle, every pore in his paper-thin, yellowing skin. "But no, you're just as meddlesome as your father, and now you'll meet the same sticky end as he will."

"Leave him out of it," I said through gritted teeth. Johnson leered behind Horatio.

The General rearranged his lips into a sneer, but he didn't answer. Instead, he swung around to face Ian and surveyed him with the same scrupulous detail. "And who are you…?"

I could tell by his clenched jaw and balled fists that Ian wanted nothing more than to punch Horatio in his flat face. And maybe he would have done it, had there not been two guns pointed at our heads. So, instead, Ian said nothing.

"This one's a quiet one," Horatio muttered under his breath, to no one in particular. Then, louder, "Present your comp for inspection."

Ian tensed, but didn't move a muscle. My stomach sank. Ian didn't have a comp. And neither did I. Bile rose to my throat as my gaze darted from Ian to Horatio.

"Did you hear me?" Horatio's voice was a whisper, but I could hear every word clearly. "I said—"

"Here's mine." I jumped between Ian and Horatio and thrust my hand into my pocket, knowing very well that my comp wasn't there. I hadn't seen it in days… But at least this would buy us some time.

Horatio waved me away with a claw-like hand. "I don't need yours. I know perfectly well who you are. But your friend…" His voice was unlike anything I'd heard before — quiet, menacing, and full of unspoken threats. I shuddered, despite myself. "Search him."

The second Patrol lowered his gun and patted Ian down roughly. "No comp, sir."

"I see," Horatio straightened and cleared his throat. "No matter. We'll find out who he was after he's dead. Let's start with this one, then." Turning to the Safety Patrols, he signaled toward Ian.

My mouth turned dry, and my lungs felt as if they were in a vacuum, empty of air, disconnected from the rest of my body. Ian. *No…* Beads of sweat broke out on my forehead as the gravity of what Horatio had said sunk in.

Ian was going to die. And I would follow shortly after. Right here, in this overly lit hallway of the White Tower. Streaks of our bright red, freshly spilled blood would be mopped up by a Patrol or an unfortunate janitor who happened to be on duty tonight.

My mouth was paper dry and my lungs heaved, but I tried to remain calm even as these thoughts threatened to swallow me whole. I glanced at Ian. His nostrils were flared, and his breaths came in sharp rasps. His clenched fists and white knuckles screamed that he wouldn't go down without a fight, but his trembling hands betrayed him and told a different story. He'd been through this once before, five years ago, thinking he was going to die at any second… but he survived. Now, there was no way out.

My feet were heavy, leaden. No matter how hard I

tried, I couldn't persuade them to yield to my mind: to move, to do something, anything…

By sheer force of will, I cleared my throat and took a step forward. "No. You're wrong. He's not dying here tonight, Horatio."

"Oh?" Horatio raised one eyebrow and considered me from behind the high collar of his robes. "Is that so? You're brave, Theo. Very brave."

The Patrol making his way toward Ian had stopped short, unsure of his orders. This was it. I had to keep Horatio talking, at least until Ian and I could find a way out of this mess.

"We know about the books." The words were out of my mouth before I had a chance to think them through.

A sharp intake of breath to my right signaled that Ian had not expected that. In truth, neither had I.

"You know about the—?"

"Yes."

"Those worthless ancient things?" Horatio sneered, but I swore I saw a flicker of worry crease his features for a split second.

I stood my ground. "And we know what you're going to do with them, too."

"How do you—"

"Never mind how. We can't let you do that."

Horatio laughed again. A cold, cruel laugh that

chilled me to the core. "Dear boy, did you really think we would let you leave this Tower alive?" He shook his head, as if pitying me.

My head spun, and I fumbled for words. I opened my mouth to speak, but nothing came out this time.

Thankfully, Ian came to my rescue. "We're not the only ones who know about the books."

I shot him a surreptitious glance, but played along. Ian was sharp. He'd taken my messy, blurted attempt at trying to buy us time and formulated a plan.

I nodded several times, my jaw tight. "There are others."

"Others? What others?" Horatio's gaze flitted from me to Ian, finally resting on me. "Does your Father have something to do with this, Theo? I can send a Patrol squadron there right now and find out."

I shook my head. I had to keep Dad out of this at all costs.

"Then who?"

Both Ian and I remained silent.

Horatio clicked his tongue. "We can either do this the easy way, or the hard way." He turned and called behind him. "Johnson."

Ian stiffened next to me. I chanced half a glance at him. When our eyes locked, I understood. I couldn't tell for certain, but I thought I saw Ian give an imperceptible nod.

At this point, we had nothing to lose. I sucked in a breath. "They know the contents of the books are to be transferred onto the chip, which will then be hand-delivered to the Chancellor himself."

Horatio narrowed his eyes. "I was wrong to underestimate you." Then he shook himself off, like an oversized bird ruffling his feathers, and spoke again, his voice low. "The information on that chip is the City's most prized commodity. How you two…" He paused, considering us for a moment.

My heartbeat quickened. The chip contained other valuable information? What else did it contain?

Horatio changed tack. "No matter. Let's get this over with." He signaled to Johnson. "Take care of it."

Johnson took a step forward, his boots closing the distance between us in an instant. He was going to shoot at point blank to make sure he didn't miss. My head spun, and my feet had glued themselves to the floor again. I couldn't move.

"Start with the quiet one."

My entire body tensed. Ian.

A piercing flash of pain soared through every inch of my skin, my wrist at its epicenter. I bit back a yelp and dropped to my knees. Instinctively, my hand flew to my wrist, pushing back my sleeve and revealing my deathday.

Against the white of the Tower, the vivid, poison-green digits were unmistakable.

A KALEIDOSCOPE of colors clouded my vision, creeping in from the periphery toward the center. The burning in my wrist increased in intensity, gathering momentum and threatening to spill over like a tidal wave. My breaths came in shallow gasps. With my right hand still clamped around my wrist, I writhed in agony as another shock wave seared through me. Was this it? Was it finally happening?

I let go of my wrist and thrust my hand in the air blindly, searching for Ian. His warm, strong hands found mine, and he gave me a reassuring squeeze. He was still here.

I opened my eyes a fraction and peered up at him. His expression was stony, determined, and silently urged me not to give up.

I wouldn't.

Horatio's malevolent cackle cracked the air like a whip a few feet away. "His deathday is here! What perfect timing!"

I yanked my sleeve down, trying to cover up those bright green digits, but it was no use.

Horatio beckoned to Johnson, but his gaze was still trained on me. "No need to take care of that one. His deathday will do that for us."

Johnson's face fell. He wasn't quick enough to hide the flicker of disappointment that flashed across his features. I'm sure he wanted to deliver the killing blow himself, but at least he wouldn't have that satisfaction.

Horatio placed a bony finger on Johnson's arm. "Don't worry, death by deathday will be much more excruciating, I assure you. It will crawl through him like a shadow, wrapping its lethal tendrils tightly around him until he is devoured by darkness."

At this, Johnson's twisted smile reappeared, his barred yellow teeth exposed. "Yes, sir."

My heart pounded in my chest, making me light-headed. Was that really what a deathday death was like? I grit my teeth, and using Ian's hand for support, pulled myself up to something that resembled an upright position. I leaned on his shoulder, panting.

"Even at death's door, you're still fighting." Horatio shook his head. "Why? Why not just join me?" Horatio extended his arms, his sleeves undulating at his sides. "Look at the order and protection the Grand Alliance has provided you with your entire life. Don't you want to die an honorable death on your deathday? Don't you want to ensure your family's heath and safety?" A glint shone in Horatio's dull eyes. "And don't you want to be revered at the next Celebrations?"

"You saw how those went yesterday," I spat, massaging my still burning wrist.

"Those who caused the unrest will be severely punished, I assure you," Horatio said. "I'm giving you one last chance. What do you say, Theo? Join us now, and be rewarded in death."

I lifted my chin and stared straight into his cold black eyes. My fists were clenched, my nails digging into the fleshy side of my palms. They were already split open by the shards of glass that I'd fallen on earlier. Releasing my hold slightly, I noticed I had opened up those wounds again. Spots of crimson dripped onto the pristine floor, but I didn't care.

"The people are finally waking up, aren't they? The Timeless don't have to suffer through food shortages like the Fleeters, do they? They get to live comfortable lives here in Millennium Sector while the rest of us starve. And the electricity cuts? You use that power to keep this damn Tower brightly lit throughout the night while people freeze to death in their homes." I paused, staring straight into Horatio's sunken face. "Tell me, General, the way you treat the Timeless and the

Fleeters… it's not all just one big game of chance, is it?"

"Enough." Horatio flared his nostrils. "Johnson."

Johnson clicked the safety off on his gun.

Ian stiffened beside me. "You can kill us, but rest assured, what we know will live on."

"The information you have is worthless," Horatio snapped. "Johnson, go ahead."

My head swam as the jolts from my wrist threatened to overpower me, triggering sharp flashes of pain in every crevice of my body. I gripped Ian's shoulder, resisting the burning aches that fought to pull me under. Out of sheer force of will, I collected every sliver of strength and fought to remain conscious.

Horatio's words echoed through my mind. *'Even at death's door, you're still fighting. Why?'*

A memory of Liv laughing as she kissed me lit up my mind. And then another one — Liv kicking and screaming as she fought to stay with me tonight. And then I knew. I was fighting for my loved ones. For Liv. I would give anything, anything at all, to live tonight, to see Liv one last time. To feel her warm embrace, to kiss her soft lips, and to get one last whiff of that spring meadow scent I loved so much.

But I saw it clearly now.

The only way I could give Liv hope to survive past *her*

deathday was by ensuring Ian got away. I couldn't protect her now, but Ian could. If Ian escaped tonight with the information about the books and the chip, then maybe one day Liv would be safe. Although my heart split cleanly in two at the thought I wouldn't be there to see it, I knew that, no matter what happened now, Ian had to get away. Because if Ian died, then the information that could save her would die with him. I was fighting so that Liv could live another day and be free of the green digits plaguing our wrists.

In the split second these thoughts rushed through my mind, Johnson raised his gun and pointed it directly at Ian's forehead.

"Any last words?" he growled.

"Yeah," I said. "'Not today'."

Instinctively, I threw myself at Johnson's gun, knocking him to the ground and sending a stream of bullets down the corridor behind us, ricocheting off the brilliant white walls. The Safety Patrol positioned behind Johnson cowered, shielding his head from the rogue bullets.

Johnson lay on the tiled floor for a moment, rubbing his bleeding jaw. He then jumped up and threw himself at me. I countered his weight as best as I could, struggling for control of his gun. My arm burned where Johnson had shot me the other day, but I ignored it. I focused all my strength on ensuring his gun pointed down at the floor.

I caught Ian's eye and yelled, "Go!"

He nodded once and charged at the other Safety Patrol. With a powerful swing of his arm, Ian dealt him a crushing blow. A crunching sound filled the air, and a wave of nausea hit me as I realized Ian's fist had connected squarely with the Patrol's nose. The Patrol's knees buckled beneath him and he stumbled to the floor, keeping a firm grip on his gun. His pristine white uniform immediately turned scarlet as it soaked up the blood spilling from his broken nose onto the floor.

"Theo, the window!"

Understanding dawned on me. I kicked Johnson's shins, pointed his gun at the window and fired.

The glass shattered around us, as if in slow motion.

The Safety Patrol with the broken nose seemed disoriented — he flattened himself to the ground and dropped his gun, shielding his head from the falling shards.

Ian aimed a kick at the Patrol's side and scooped up his fallen gun. He then checked his harness, loosened the grappling hook I'd seen him tether to his belt earlier and attached it to the ledge. For a split second, our gazes met. I then shook my head, almost imperceptibly — I was still locked in combat with Johnson, feeling the stench of his foul breath on my neck.

Ian nodded once, cast me one last look, and jumped.

I stared after him, momentarily loosening my grip on Johnson's gun. The Patrol twisted the gun out from under me and threw me against one of the still-standing windows. He pinned my arms behind me, dug the barrel of his gun into my back, grabbed my hair and pressed my cheek against the window. His face was inches from mine, and his eyes bulged with frenzy. "Look down, boy — there's your friend falling to his death!"

But Ian wasn't falling at all. He was scaling the side of the Tower, unraveling a cord on his winch — the same one I'd seen in the Hideout just the other day. Despite the mess I was in, I couldn't suppress a smile. Ian was getting away. He would make it.

The Safety Patrol that Ian had been fighting jerked out of his stupor and stared after Ian, realizing what he was doing.

Horatio, his face red, screamed, "Cut the rope!"

The Patrol fumbled with the grappling hook, trying to hold it steady with one hand while he sawed at the cord with a pocketknife. But his hand slipped and he dislodged the cord — hook and all — and sent it flying out the window.

My scream was drowned out by Johnson's cackle in my ear. "He got what he deserved!"

I couldn't bear to look — how far had Ian fallen? Had

he made it down, or was his body splattered on the concrete at the base of the Tower — lifeless and unmoving?

I took a deep breath and chanced a glance out the window I was still pinned against. A shadowy figure, lit up from the brightness of the White Tower's lights, picked himself up and ran into the darkness beyond the Tower's perimeter. The figure then disappeared into the safety of the shadows of the nearby buildings.

My breath escaped me in a low hiss. A new hope filled my heart. His run was unsteady — he was clearly beat up from the fall — but he was *alive*. Ian was alive.

Horatio cried for backup. I saw the other Patrol out of the corner of my eye disappearing down a long corridor and raising his com-link wrist communicator to his mouth.

Johnson let out a roar and knocked me backward. My head hit the wall with such force that my eyes filled with tears — or stars — I couldn't tell which. He straddled me, attempting to pin my arms under his knees.

With a sudden burst of adrenaline fueled by Ian's escape, I set my jaw, tilted my head to the side and thrust it forward, connecting with Johnson's forehead. He let out a shriek and his hands flew to his face. A purple bruise bloomed above his left eyebrow. He clasped it tightly, dropping his gun to the floor.

My head pounded as chaos and the fire in my wrist lit up my body. I grabbed the fallen gun and stood on shaky legs, pointing it at Horatio. It was just the two of us now.

Our eyes locked. His were wide, fearful. Mine narrowed, determined. I knew I could shoot him now. But if I did, I wouldn't be any better than he was. Than *they all* were. Instead, I broke our eye contact, turned on my heel and sprinted down the hallway.

AFTER SEVERAL MOMENTS, the sound of boots pounding on the white tiles filled my ears. I cursed under my breath. Horatio's backup had arrived. I ducked, running doubled over as the bullets ricocheted off the walls and followed in my wake.

A sudden deep, intense ache spread through my shoulder blade, setting my very skin on fire. Its sting was unlike the one sprouting from my wrist. I must have been hit, but I didn't dare stop to find out.

I raced down the pristine hallways, turning left and right at random. I fired backward blindly, my boots trailing streaks of red and black — blood intermixed with grime I'd carried in from the street.

Horatio's shouts were barely audible over the din of

the ricocheting bullets, the thundering in my ears and the pounding of my heart.

I made a right turn and sprinted toward the far wall, throwing all caution to the wind and taking my chances that this was another sliding door… it was. It slid aside on my approach, revealing another set of spiraling narrow stairs, just like the ones I made my way up earlier. Thrusting the door shut behind me, I bounded down the stairs, two at a time, my heart in my throat and my dejected muscles protesting with each step.

I ignored them, but my deathday had other plans. The pain in my wrist exploded in full force. Its jolts coursed through every nerve in my body, lethal and electric.

I smiled bitterly. *Happy deathday to me.*

My aching legs, despite their earlier protests, now carried me of their own accord. *Faster, faster.*

And suddenly, the realization of what had happened in the last ten days dawned on me. I had failed… failed to protect Liv before my deathday. That one thought hit me harder and burned stronger than the explosive pain in my wrist.

But all was not lost… Ian had escaped — I saw him with my own eyes. He had escaped, and with him, the knowledge of the mysterious books and the chip lived on. She may live yet.

I allowed that hope to fill me up as lightning shot through my body once again, piercing the very marrow of my bones. It ran up my spine and down my limbs. With every step, its severity increased. My eyes watered, but I blinked the moisture away. Pain was nothing now. It paled beside what truly mattered: that there was hope for the future. With the knowledge I learned and passed on to Ian tonight, freedom — genuine freedom — was now a real possibility.

As I ran, gunshots still ringing behind me, I imagined that freedom: a world without deathdays, where our wrists were clean and unencumbered. Those eight little digits, those little markings, shaped our lives more than we knew from the day we were born. Every step we took, every decision we made, it all led up to one moment.

To this.

And then, darkness.

EPILOGUE — IAN

I HURTLED toward the concrete at the base of the Tower, the cord and my grappling hook flying after me. I didn't have long to brace myself for the collision.

The second my feet touched the ground, I bent my knees and did a forward roll, which absorbed most of the impact. I stood on shaky legs, reeled in my cord and hook, and checked that the Safety Patrol's gun I'd stolen was intact.

Wiping sweat off my brow and massaging my legs, I hobbled into the shadows, away from the permitter of light cast by the brightly lit Tower. I glanced up to the seventeenth floor, where my best friend had sacrificed himself just so I could get away. He sacrificed himself, and I left him behind…

The wind howled through the broken windows, but

there was no sign of movement. I averted my gaze and willed the tightness in my chest to loosen. *Come on, Theo. Don't give up.*

I slipped through the buildings, passing in and out of darkness. The night was clear, and the crescent moon cast long shadows on the concrete. I traveled west, toward Loop Sector.

I must not have timed the impact with the ground quite right, because my left leg threatened to buckle beneath me with every step. Hoping it wasn't a sprained ankle, I grit my teeth and continued my trek through the deserted city, pausing at every corner to shift the weight from my ankle and check if the area was free from Patrols. But I didn't have to — my routes were foolproof. I'd spent enough time on these City streets to have memorized the nightly Patrol schedule.

As if on cue, a pair of Patrols greeted their replacement on the far corner of the avenue. I shrunk into the shadows, waiting. After several moments, the clank of their boots died down, and all was still again. Here, in the old downtown, the wind had quieted into an easy breeze, gently sweeping back my dark curls.

By now, the light of the White Tower was a mere speck in the distance: bright, yet still ominous. I finally stopped in front of an old apartment block in Loop, crouched behind a fallen container, and waited.

Time ticked away, a precious commodity my best friend had been robbed of prematurely. Where was Theo now? Was he still alive, or had his deathday claimed him? Or had a Patrol's bullet done the deed instead? I sighed, feeling the hollow weight of my friend's absence on my shoulders.

Part of me hoped they'd never show. That I'd be sitting here till daybreak, until the birds started singing and the shopkeepers opened up their wares. But I had to see it for myself, so I stayed put.

After nearly an hour, I heard a rustle of movement outside the block. Sure enough, two Safety Patrols marched through the deserted street, carrying something between them. My heart sank. It was a stretcher with a piece of cloth thrown over it.

No. *No.*

I dug my fingernails into my palms, blinking several times. My eyes were deceiving me. A pang of emptiness cut through the pit of my stomach. I clutched the stolen gun for support, my knuckles white against the barrel.

The chime of the intercom slashed through the silence. I winced. The sound was harsh in my ears, like a blade grating against a plexiscreen.

After several minutes, a figure appeared in the doorway. I squinted, and I could just make out a man running his hand through his chestnut hair — the same shade as

Theo's. A woman leaned on him, her face pressed against his shoulder. Reg and Lisa Vanderveen. My heart ached for them both. I wished I could run to them and tell them everything: that Theo was like a brother to me, and that I'd be forever indebted to him for what he did tonight.

But that would have been the most dangerous — and stupid — thing I could do. So I dropped back into the shadows behind the container, watching Theo's parents speak to the Patrols in low voices.

After a moment, the apartment door swung open and a girl ran out, her long brown hair flying behind her. A red stain bloomed from the bandage on her shoulder. My breath caught — this had to be Liv.

"No. No! *No!*" She screamed, dropping to her knees before the stretcher, her sobs filling the barren night air. The sight nearly shattered my resolve — I stood up behind the container and almost ran to her. But I tensed my muscles, set my jaw, and resisted. Blowing my cover right now was a surefire way to get us all killed.

Reg bent down and put an arm around Liv, steering her back inside. But she broke free from his grasp and collapsed in front of the stretcher again. I turned away, unable to watch.

"Liv, honey, come inside. You're hurt—"

"I don't care. He's... he's—" But she couldn't finish her sentence, succumbing to a renewed fit of sobs.

The Patrols approached Liv and said, "Get up girl—", but she lashed out at them with such vitriol that I couldn't suppress a sad smile.

"I can't do this." Liv shook her head at Theo's parents, turned on her heel and ran off into the night.

The Patrol nearest to me fiddled with his com-link communicator. "I'm afraid it's still curfew. We're going to have to send backup to track her down."

Reg grabbed the Patrol's hand and pulled him closer. "That won't be necessary." He lowered his voice, and I couldn't make out his next words.

The Patrols nodded at each other, shook Reg's hand, and melted back into the night, toward the Tower. Away from Liv.

A quiet determination settled in my heart, replacing the hollowness I felt seconds before.

In that moment, I knew one thing. Theo's sacrifice wasn't for nothing. I would avenge my best friend. I would save Liv. I would find the chip and finish what we started.

This wasn't over. Far from it.

This was only the beginning.

Thank you for reading *The Countdown*!

If you want more in *The Deathday Chronicles* universe, *The Hacker*, which takes place three months after the events of *The Countdown*, is available for free on Kasia's website!

Get your free copy of *The Hacker* now at:
kasialasinska.com/the-hacker-tc

You can also check out the cover and description of *The Hacker* below. You may need to turn the page to do so.

Everyone has secrets, but mine could get me killed.

I'm Em, and my deathday was yesterday.

At least, that's what the Government thinks.

The digits on my wrist may not have killed me, but they've put a target on my back.

Now, a fugitive in my own city, I need to figure out how I lived past my deathday. And why I was the only one…

It's not just about finding answers. It's about survival.

One thing is certain: I'm out of my depth. Even my hacking skills might not be enough to get me out of this one…

Full of action, intrigue, and a heroine who doesn't take 'no' for an answer, *The Hacker* is the addictive companion novella to *The Deathday Chronicles*, the young adult dystopian series that's perfect for fans of *The Hunger Games*, *Divergent* and *Legend*.

What are you waiting for? Grab your free copy of *The Hacker* now ➜ Visit:

kasialasinska.com/the-hacker-tc

Curious as to what happens next?

The Countdown is Theo's story. Book 1 in *The Deathday Chronicles* series follows Liv and takes place six months after the events of *The Countdown*, and three months after the events of *The Hacker*.

"My name is Liv, and my deathday was yesterday."

The Deathday Chronicles (Book 1) ➜ Coming 2022

If you'd like to get instant updates on when *The Deathday Chronicles* (Book 1) is available, subscribe to Kasia's newsletter. You'll also get free books and other exclusive content. Visit https://kasialasinska.com/newsletter-tc and subscribe now!

I hope you enjoyed *The Countdown*! If so, I'd love if you left a review. Reviews are very important to authors and help other readers find the book. I also read each and every one of them :)

A NOTE FROM THE AUTHOR

"Every writer begins as a reader." I distinctly remember reading those words in a book about myths, legends and magical worlds that I picked up from the neighborhood library when I was eight or nine. They rang true, even then.

I was an avid reader before I became an avid writer. Carrying my huge *Harry Potter* hardbacks from room to room (they were almost bigger than me!) and talking to anyone who would listen about my favorite characters and scenes. One time, my parents and I were going out. (I can't recall where, but it was surely to one of those mysterious places where parents take their children.) We'd already left the house, but Mom had forgotten something. When we stepped back inside, I ran into the kitchen, popped my book open and rejoiced that I could steal just one more minute reading.

But then, I started writing. In third grade, I won a creative writing competition with a story about a talking money tree (which also, curiously, grew oranges). I still consider it as one of my biggest accomplishments.

Then, when I was fifteen, I learned that Christopher Paolini wrote *Eragon* when *he* was fifteen. I thought, in my wide-eyed wonder, well, if he can do it, then so can I.

These were some of the little moments when I decided that yes, I wanted to write a novel *someday*.

That *someday* is today.

That little story about the money tree and my awe at completing a task as colossal and daunting as writing a book, today stepped aside and handed over their crowns to my first published novel.

While *The Countdown* is the first book I publish, it's not the first I've written. I actually wrote Book 1 in *The Deathday Chronicles* series first. (I'll share where I got the idea for the series in my author's note for Book 1!)

So chase your dreams, and under no circumstances give up on them, no matter how high the obstacles or how many bricks the nay-sayers throw at you in the process.

And although writing is a solitary exercise, behind

every writer there's an army of people who helped make it happen.

I spent the majority of 2020 hunkered down in the editing cave, writing and rewriting to make *The Countdown* the best book it could be. I had the most amazing help, encouragement and support from my tribe.

Thank you to Emilia, who provided excellent developmental feedback. Emilia took my story, brought out the best in it, elevated it and made it shine. She wasn't afraid to ask the hard questions and force me to look at my work objectively. *The Countdown* wouldn't be what it is today without her.

Huge thank you to Derek Murphy for the gorgeous cover! It fits my story perfectly, and the typography is jaw-dropping.

Love, hugs and hand hearts to the Coronitas, who sprinted with me every day since March. Thank you to Robyn, Merri, Susan, Alice, Las, Fatima and all the Coronitas for the daily encouragement, butt-kicking and jumping on sprints with me at random times (*read*: late at night, inevitably before a deadline). Big thanks to Marion for the cover expertise and photoshop tips. Huge thank you to Erika for brainstorming in Edinburgh with me at that fateful fairy tale retelling dinner (Erika influenced *The Deathday Chronicles* more than she knows!) And a massive thank you to Chelle and Elaine, who held my hand every step of the way (literally), right up to and over the finish line. I'm not exaggerating when I say I couldn't have done it without them.

Thank you to my parents, who bought me my very first book and sparked all this madness. Thank you for never complaining when I asked for the next book in a series.

Big love, hugs and thank you to Domi, who celebrated with me, cried with me and supported me through thick and thin. Love you! A huge thank you to Carolyn for her medical expertise and research – the book is so much better for it. Big thank you to Kasia, who showed me unconditional love and support from the very beginning. Thanks to Olga and Vicky for spending our years in law school asking me if I've written a book yet. Thank you to Tessa asking me the same, just this past year. Well ladies, I have now!

Thank you to caffeine, in its many forms – you get a shout-out too. I couldn't have done this without you.

And to you, dear reader, thank you for sticking with me this far and for reading Theo's story. I hope you'll join me for Liv's adventures in Book 1, and beyond!

Kasia Lasinska
October 2020

ABOUT THE AUTHOR

Kasia Lasinska writes series of fast-paced young adult fantasy and dystopian novels filled with daring quests, action, adventure, magic hidden in unexpected places and a splash of romance that will keep you reading late into the night.

Kasia likes to tell people she's actually a vampire, given she's a night owl, is usually quite pale and can't eat garlic. She loves books, travel, a good cup of coffee and dogs.

Visit author.to/KasiaLasinska to view a full list of Kasia's novels on Amazon. To get free books and be the first to hear about news and updates from Kasia's life, giveaways and new releases, visit https://kasialasinska.com/newsletter-tc and subscribe to her newsletter now!

You can also connect with Kasia by joining her exclusive Facebook reader group, Kasia's Kingdom of Books ➜ https://facebook.com/groups/KasiasKingdom

Printed in Great Britain
by Amazon

83544516R00205